LONG W͟ ͟

A Wild Ones Novel

RACHEL EMBER

ISBN (ebook): 9781735443072
ISBN (print): 9781735443089

Cover Design by Cate Ashwood Designs
Beta Reading by Blue Beta Reading
Editing by Jennifer Collins
Proofreading by Jennifer Griffin

Chestnut Press

CONTENTS

CHAPTER ONE

Lance

Fourteen years ago.

It's the first day of school, and Lance can't find his new shoes.

He tries not to panic, but his mind is spinning. *How could this have happened?* He'd put them under the floorboards by his bed, the only place in the house where his father couldn't find anything. He'd been determined that, when the time came to get on the school bus, for once he'd be wearing decent shoes. Not his worn-out boots, with their soles gaping apart from the toes like ragged tongues.

It's not like the other kids don't already have enough to make fun of him for. He doesn't want to add his old boots to the list.

Lance fits the floorboards carefully back into place and stands up. The lace curtains, once white and now dingy gray, hang perfectly still over his bedroom window even though he pushed the bottom sash all the way up last night when it was so hot that he couldn't sleep. There isn't a breeze to be found on this sticky August morning. His throat is dry, too. He forgot to bring a glass of water in with him last night, and once his father had been home by the television, draining one can of beer after another, Lance had known better than to risk coming out of his room.

He doesn't have time to keep looking for the shoes, and it would be pointless anyway. If they aren't in the hiding place, then he knows where they are, and he won't be getting them back.

Lance leaves his room cautiously, the way a cowboy on the black-and-white shows his dad likes would leave a saloon when shots have already been fired in the street. The house is small—a single-story box with a triangular roof, the way a child would draw one. That means Lance's father is never far away.

From the narrow hallway outside his door, Lance immediately looks to the sofa in the living room. His father sleeps there in the summer, in front of the window-unit air conditioner, which is the only thing in the house that can banish the summer heat. A couple of wadded-up pillows are the only sign his father was there. He must already be in the kitchen.

Lance only goes into the kitchen because he's too thirsty to wait until he gets to school for a drink of water. The old, orange-ish carpet in the living room ends in one step, and the cracked linoleum of the kitchen and covered porch begins in the next. As Lance knew he would, he finds his father in a chair at the round table in the middle of the room, slumped on his elbows. The small fan on the countertop is plugged in and whirring, but the room still smells wet and dank. Nothing can beat the steamy heat of an August morning stuck between hundred-degree days.

Lance's boots are set by the back door, next to the washing machine. The sight of them makes him miserable all over again, but he shoves his knuckles against his right eye before a tear can fall. He's eight—almost nine. Almost nine is way too old for crying.

His father looks up at him. "The fuck are you still doing here? You miss that bus and you can walk into town. I ain't driving you."

Hating his father is a familiar feeling. But right now, it's got substance and weight, his hate. It feels like an animal that's barely contained by the cage of his body. He can practically feel it clawing at his chest from the inside, determined to get out.

But when he speaks, his voice is weak, almost a whisper. "Can't find my shoes."

He hates how soft the words sound—how *scared*. It's nothing like the roar that angry animal in his chest would make if it got free, but although his body is a feeble container, somehow the hate doesn't escape him. None of Lance's feelings ever do.

He's watching his father closely. Closely enough that he notices his father flinch faintly at the word "*shoes*." But that reaction is as good as a confession. He'd already been fairly sure his dad had swiped his school shoes, but now he's certain. He wonders where he sold them, and for how much. Hopefully, it was close to what they'd cost new, at least; they'd still been in their box, with those wads of paper stuffed inside them to protect their shape. As soon as he'd tried them on, Lance had immediately packed them back up exactly the way they'd come, paper and all, and put them carefully under the floorboards.

His aunt had sent them. She sent him what she could— and what she assumed his father wouldn't steal. Her gifts were never cash, which Lance suspected she knew would wind up in his father's pocket. Apparently, she didn't realize that a brand-new pair of Nikes was just as irresistible to Paul Taylor.

"Waste of money, that fancy shit," says his father, standing up to rummage in the fridge. "Sending that stuff—does she think you're ashamed of who you are? Nothing wrong with those boots we got from Bill's kids."

Bill is someone who goes to the bar almost as much as Lance's dad, and he has triplets. They're two years older than Lance, but they were bigger kids even when they were Lance's age, so all of their old things fit him funny. Bill sends everything they outgrow home with Lance's dad in black trash bags.

"They're kinda getting worn," Lance can't help muttering, even though he knows it's useless to argue. But he's so angry —at his father for taking the shoes and at himself for not hiding them better. Or at least, he should have been careful to check that they were still under the floorboards before that morning. Now, he doesn't even have time to try to tape the boots together.

So, worn-out boots with split soles, it is. He slips into them and flees the house as his dad delivers his parting shot in a low growl.

"We'll talk later about what else I found."

Lance had forgotten that if his father found the shoes, he also found the little odds and ends that always made their way into Lance's pockets. Things that were bright or strange and that he thought no one would see him reach for—it was almost impossible for him to resist. Shiny beads; buttons; lost earrings; and once, in a moment that was one of the most thrilling in Lance's memory but that also made him burn with shame, a page of glossy stickers from the display by the drugstore checkout.

Eager to reach the bus and the escape of a day at school, Lance runs harder. He hopes the shadow of worrying what his dad will do when Lance gets home won't follow him all day.

The bus doesn't come down driveways, not even the ones

as long as theirs, so every school day, Lance has to make a quarter-mile trek to meet it at the road. He doesn't mind. The steps put his dad and the too-small house behind him and let him be someone else for a while. Someone who doesn't have to be as careful; someone who doesn't have to hide.

The bus is already waiting for him, but the driver, Mr. Dale, sees him coming and doesn't pull away. He's an older man with a bald head beneath a flat-billed mesh ballcap, and his smile is always kind.

"Hey, sport," he says cheerfully as Lance climbs up the big steps into the bus. As soon as Lance clears the accordion door, Mr. Dale pulls the lever so it whooshes closed.

"Hi, Mr. Dale," Lance replies politely, and then he takes a deep breath and stares down the aisle at the seats, which are already more than half-full.

He does spy one empty seat and makes a beeline for it like it could disappear. When he slides across the hot, sticky vinyl, a rush of air escapes him. The bus jerks as Mr. Dale puts it in gear, and off they go.

Lance rests his forehead against the window, staring out at the grass meadow bordering the gravel road, the blades beginning to burn red at the tips to signal fall. The bus sways as Mr. Dale takes the sharp turn just before the one-lane bridge. As they cross it, Lance holds his breath like always, sure the ancient boards and crossbeams will split under the strain of the bus's weight. The river bridge looks like something built for horses and carriages, not heavy vehicles.

But like always, they make it. In reality, nothing is quite as fragile as it feels in Lance's imagination.

As the bus rumbles over the gravel on the far side of the bridge, Lance sits up in his seat, anxiousness forgotten in favor of eagerness to see the Chases. Their driveway is winding and gravel-surfaced like Lance's, but it's also much better groomed—a level stretch of fresh white rock curving to disappear toward a house not visible from the road.

The Chases don't walk out to meet the bus. Their older brother, Robbie, drives them. They're waiting in the bed of an old truck, its pale blue paint making it stand out like a robin's egg on the backdrop of verdant oak trees that hedge the Chases' long driveway. As the boys see the bus pulling around, they spill out of the back of the truck one at a time.

First is Danny, who's Lance's age, sliding off the tailgate. Robbie hovers beside him, his hands outstretched but not quite touching, like he's worried Danny will fall. But Danny lands on his feet and bats his brother's hands away.

Then, there's Johnny, who's four years older than Lance. He clambers out after Danny and tousles his hair, which makes Danny scowl.

Unlike his golden-haired brothers, Robbie, the eldest Chase, has black hair and a black, untidy beard. He pushes his hands into his jeans pockets while Danny and Johnny rush up the bus steps.

Lance doesn't know why he's so fascinated by the Chases. Maybe because he's heard his father grumble about them since before Lance could talk. Maybe because, in class, Danny knows every answer and quickly becomes every teacher's favorite. Which, incidentally, makes him most of the other kids' least favorite. Maybe it's because Johnny is so popular that even kids in grade school know who he is. He's a football quarterback and plays some of the leads in the school plays. He can even sing.

But the main reason that Lance watches the Chases is for glimpses of their quiet older brother, Robbie; Robbie, who always seems a little sad and a little tired, but watches the younger boys with warm protectiveness. It's an expression Lance has never seen anyone turn in his own direction. He watches Robbie Chase so that he knows exactly what to picture when he closes his eyes and imagines mattering enough to someone that they look at him that way.

The younger Chase brothers pile onto the bus and Johnny heads straight toward the back, where a couple of boys are calling to him. Danny pauses at the top of the steps, his hands wrapped tightly around the straps of his backpack and his expression uncertain as he looks down the aisle.

Lance understands that look. It's like he's seeing himself —well, a shorter, blond version of himself, with freckles and really nice shoes—when he got on the bus one stop before.

The other kids don't like Lance, and they don't like Danny, either. That fact makes Lance lonely. Maybe Danny's lonely, too.

"You can sit by me," Lance says, before he can overthink it. Danny's head jerks in his direction, and a pink blush flares behind his freckles.

"Okay. Thanks." Danny ambles forward and drops onto the seat next to Lance. Their elbows touch when Danny leans forward and slides off his backpack. "Sorry," he says, shooting Lance a look out of the corner of his eye.

"S'okay," says Lance. He feels hot and itchy all over, the way he always does when he has to talk to someone who isn't Mr. Dale or a teacher. He sees a pin on the pocket of Danny's backpack, though, and blurts out, "You like *The Team*?" Their librarian, a young woman with purple hair, got the first set of the comics. Lance has had to read them in small doses, keeping them in his cubby in the classroom because he's afraid to take them home.

Danny looks up, something sharp in his eyes. "Well, yeah," he says, like it's a stupid question, and then his voice softens and his eyelashes fall down to his cheeks. They're dark gold, like autumn leaves turning.

"I got the new issue. Y'wanna see?" He pinches the zipper on the front pocket of his bag and looks at Lance again.

"Yeah!" Lance exclaims, wiping his sweaty hands on his knees. "Yeah, I want to see."

The bus starts to pull away and Lance happens to glance up—a conditioned habit. He's just in time to see Robbie Chase put on a battered straw cowboy hat and climb back into the truck.

Today.

"You got somebody you want to call?"

Lance looks up at the question, wondering how long he's been staring at his shoes, far away in memory.

He's sitting on a bench that's bolted to the wall inside an otherwise empty cell on the third floor of the courthouse in Trace County—the same building that's probably storing his original birth certificate, first driver's license application, and who knows what else. When he left Nebraska at sixteen, he never intended to come back...but if he had, he would've pictured himself spending the night in the Moonlight Motel, not the jail.

The attendant, or whatever his title is, is probably ten years older than Lance. His hair is just beginning to thin at the temples and his uniform is too tight in the stomach and the arms.

"I get one phone call? Just like the movies?" Lance loops an arm around his knee.

"You can have more than one if you want," says the guy, "but each one has to be fifteen minutes or less."

"Really?" Lance frowns. "I thought that 'one phone call' thing was like...official."

Now, the attendant looks a little nervous. "Uh, I don't know? But I've worked here for eleven years and we always let people make calls if they want to. But each one has to be—"

"Fifteen minutes or less," Lance finishes for him. The attendant nods. Lance sighs and admits, "I don't have anyone to call."

"Is it because you don't have any phone numbers memorized? Because I can give you your own phone."

"*Really?*" Despite having had the three longest and worst days of his life in rapid succession, Lance is incredulous. Maybe he's just seizing on any distraction from the prospect of spending the night in jail, and the surrealism of being under arrest in the first place. He offers the attendant a lopsided smile. "They'd never allow that on TV."

The attendant just shrugs. Lance lets his head fall back, all of the energy leaving him with the full weight of his next words even before he speaks them. "I still don't have anyone to call."

There *are* a few people he's fairly sure would answer, but he rules them out one by one. His aunt would help him however she could, but he does his level best never to ask her for anything. He can't bear to call her from a jail cell.

Maisie would hitchhike halfway across the country if he called her, ditching classes without a second thought even after busting her ass to get into her grad school program. But he's not clear on what she'd be likely to accomplish if she were there, except yelling at a lot of people—Lance included —and possibly protesting his arrest on the courthouse lawn.

He thinks about calling Niall and demanding, *What the fuck?* He knew Niall was mad at him, but this? Seriously? If Niall had just called and asked for the car back, Lance would have returned it.

Probably. Eventually. He isn't sure he actually checked his phone during the whole drive from Chicago to the Nebraska state line.

If Lance calls Niall, though, he'll be giving Niall the ultimate satisfaction. It wouldn't surprise Lance if that's all this was to Niall: a ploy meant not to punish Lance, but to make Lance need him. Depend on him. That would be just like Niall.

Once, knowing how Niall craved specific things from him had been useful—information that informed Lance's approach to their two-year relationship. Now, thinking of trying to pull Niall's strings makes Lance's skin crawl. It wouldn't be worth it if Niall took the opportunity to get his hooks back in.

Honestly, Lance would rather stay in jail. Even if the idea of being locked up in here for much longer is making his heart race. As the light has been fading outside the window, he's begun feeling worse and worse.

And...there is one other person he could call.

"Actually," he tells the attendant, "maybe I do."

CHAPTER TWO

Robbie

Thirty years ago.

Even at six years old, Robbie's always been a light sleeper who wakes when he hears the first person stirring in the house. That person is usually his dad—making coffee, tugging on his boots, and heading outside before the sun rises.

This morning, Robbie pads downstairs to see the warm glow of light spilling through the kitchen door and snow piling up in every window. His dad is poised by the back door, halfway into his winter gear.

"Dad," Robbie whispers. "I wanna come help you do chores."

His dad grins. "You sure, buddy? It's cold out there."

Robbie nods solemnly, so his dad bundles him into his snow pants and boots, his heaviest coat, and his hat. Then, he finishes his own preparations, wrapping a silk scarf twice around his neck. He seems to sense Robbie watching him, and hesitates, but then he bends down in front of him and folds another scarf carefully, doubling it down until it's a third of its original size.

"You know the secret of silk, buddy?" The rag is one his father wears often, pale sky blue and dusted with a subtle floral pattern. Robbie shakes his head. "It's cool in the summer and warm in the winter," his dad confides. He wraps the scarf around Robbie's neck and knots the ends together, just like Robbie has seen him do a hundred times for himself. "There you go. Now, you really look like a Chase." He winks, his eyelashes golden and bronze in the lamplight. "What do you think about that?"

Robbie grins. "Cool," he says, and his father laughs.

They step outside into a snow-blurred sunrise, and Robbie squeals when his dad grabs him around the waist with one arm and swings him over the banked snow on the steps, landing him safely in the fluffy drifts on the ground.

"You know the secret of snow?" his dad asks.

Robbie shakes his head vigorously, feeling the silk move against his throat, soft and warm against his skin.

"Three months after a heavy fog, you'll get rain or snow. So, in the fall, you can start marking your calendar for the snowy mornings. What do you think about that?"

"Cool," Robbie says, and his father laughs again.

Today.

Robbie didn't jot down the dates of every foggy morning last November, but he remembers a string of days where it was so dense that he could barely see. He smiles at the realization that this January morning falls ninety days later, and then touches his neck, where a plain charcoal scarf is knotted around his throat. It's not the blue one his dad gave him; he carried that with him almost daily after his dad died, until it went missing one day. The loss still stings. Even now, he can easily picture the faded roses in its pattern and feel the glide of the fine old silk between his thumb and forefinger, and smell the hint of coffee on his father's breath when he knelt in front of Robbie and tied it around his neck the first time.

Standing in the renovated hayloft on the ranch where his dad, grandfather, and *great*-grandfather worked all their lives, Robbie watches snow tumble down through the large window on the south wall. "You were right this time, Dad."

The sky is so cloud-dense, it looks like a single roll of cotton, promising knee-deep snow by sunset. Robbie finishes washing his hands and turns off the tap, casting an automatic frown down into the sink, where he still needs to install a drain. Anywhere he looks in the apartment, he sees something on his to-do list—caulking the countertop, installing the drawer-pulls, grouting the tile around the wood stove. He keeps the list even though he hasn't checked anything off of it since Johnny moved out.

He looks out the window again. So far, the snow is just a picturesque dusting on the stone buildings and row of evergreens north of the barnyard, but by tomorrow afternoon, the whole ranch will be buried.

Robbie finishes his coffee and tosses the dregs in the sink. By the door, he shrugs into his heavy duster coat and winter boots, takes a black felt hat from its peg, and heads out. This might be his last chance to get anything done for a few days, and there's always plenty that needs doing. In particular, he has to make sure the horses have enough feed if he isn't able to get to them for a while.

He still keeps four saddle horses, which is two too many, but he has yet to fully accept that Johnny is gone and shows no signs of ever coming back. Instead, Robbie throws twice as much hay and shovels twice as much crap as he should so that Johnny's two bay geldings, who Robbie has always just called "the clones," can stand around and look good. With them in the pipe corral is Dusty, Robbie's old palomino mare, who's enjoying semi-retirement. And then there's Poco, the big black gelding who Robbie rides almost every day.

The other horses are standing in the shed, not a single snowflake clinging to them, but Poco is camped out by the hay feeder, coated in snow and completely unbothered by it. He turns his white-blazed face toward Robbie when he hears him come outside, then nickers a greeting. When he sees that Robbie is headed toward the gate, he hurries to meet him. His hooves crunch through snow and freezing mud on his way.

"You're a workaholic," Robbie observes, adjusting his hat on his head and grabbing the halter off the gate.

Riverside Ranch has been in Robbie's family for six generations. Until the fire last year, the sprawling white farmhouse his ancestors built stood at the center of the outbuildings. Robbie tries not to look at the empty place in the scene where it used to be. The limestone barns, sheds, and the old chicken coop are all that's left of the original farmstead now. To the northeast are two more modern structures for equipment and feed—an old silver-metal Quonset and the newer, hulking rectangle of the tractor shed, both erected in the 1980s by Robbie's dad.

He takes Poco into what they've always called the saddle barn. It's a small building originally built as a corn crib, but Robbie's grandfather converted it for use for horses. It has two old wooden stalls that now contain scrap lumber and the riding and push mowers, but Robbie still uses the ties and tack room.

The five barn cats saunter out after Robbie has the horse tied, all of them stretching and rubbing against his legs. He staggers to avoid stepping on them, spreading some cat food from a bin into their tin bowls before he retrieves Poco's blanket, saddle, and bridle. While Robbie settles the saddle blanket over his withers, Poco stares out at the piling snow with his ears forward, like he can't wait to get back out into it.

"Like I said, he's a workaholic," Robbie tells one of the cats—an orange and white female called Lemon who never eats until the other cats have cleared away from the dishes. Lemon yawns and meows, and Robbie can't help pausing to scratch down her back. Sometimes he feels self-conscious, talking to his animals like they're people, but then he remembers no one is around to notice.

When Poco is saddled, Robbie slips off his halter to bridle him, then mounts in the barn aisle, ducking his head as he rides out so that he doesn't hit the beam over the doorway.

Poco can be hard to handle at the beginning of a ride, so Robbie just gives him his head and lets him spring straight into a canter, barely having to guide him toward the north trail. There's a break in the trees just on the edge of the farmyard, which Robbie maintains with a chainsaw and brush mower once every couple of years. It quickly narrows as it dives toward the first of several creek crossings.

From there, the path is just a horse trail, wide enough at times to ride two abreast, but mostly forcing a nose-to-tail orientation. It's winding and sloping and snow-spattered, but Poco knows every inch even better than Robbie does, and he navigates it at high speed without a stumble or hesitant step.

It's still reckless, letting Poco charge through the bends and leap the creeks instead of navigating at a conservative walk or trot. Robbie should probably be more careful. If he fell and hurt himself out here, no one would know.

Still, he ignores the fleeting thought and grins as Poco bounds over the fourth creek crossing, then surges up the steep embankment on the other side. Robbie grasps the saddle horn to help hold himself over the horse's shoulders, his center of gravity, with his other hand resting on his hat so that he doesn't lose it.

When Poco crests the incline, he slows of his own volition and Robbie gives his neck a pat. Residual adrenaline keeps his heart pounding even at the slower pace. There's no sound except their combined breaths—horse and rider, briefly one—and the whisper of snow settling on the dense branches overhead.

Over the years, especially the last few, Robbie has felt like there's no lonelier person than him, on horseback at what can feel like the ends of the Earth. But even though he sometimes hates this place and the unbreakable hold it seems to have on him, he desperately loves it, too. Especially in moments like this.

If he has to be trapped, at least he loves his cage.

Poco senses the horses before Robbie can see them. One moment, he's ambling along with his head low and his neck outstretched, reaching for the few low branches that still have some stubborn-clinging yellow leaves, then bobbing his head and spitting them back out when they prove bitter to the taste. In the next moment, the gelding raises his head and quickens his steps, staring out amongst the trees with interest. He doesn't break into a trot, but there's a definite spring in his steps as he walks faster.

The horses range all over the property, hemmed in only by the perimeter fencing. Occasionally, they used to drift past the house and barns, though that hasn't happened for a couple of years, not since the neighboring property to the west changed hands again and the new owner started keeping cattle in the meadow close to the property line. Apparently, the wild ones don't like cattle. Robbie knows their habits like they're a gang of teenaged troublemakers and he's the beat cop in their neighborhood. Based on the time of year, the weather, and the time of day, nine times out of ten, he can find at least one of the bands in the first place he looks.

Today, he's expecting them to be in the trees, anticipating the winter storm more keenly than any radiologist, and spread out into the four bands that have stayed more or less consistent since their first year here. They aren't proper bands, Danny would be quick to remind him. They don't behave like they would if they'd been left truly wild because the males are all geldings now and the mares aren't busy minding foals. The closest thing they have to a juvenile are the few that were yearlings when they came, and they're now seven years old.

Nonetheless, Robbie thinks of them as bands, the family units that wild horses naturally form. There's Millie's band, which is strictly female and consists of Millie and the other three oldest mares, the greys—Pewter, Silver, and Dot—and with them is Sage, Millie's daughter, who was a yearling at her side when the horses were brought here that first summer.

Then there's Kyle's band, or "the bachelors" as Johnny affectionately refers to them. They're the closest thing to friendly of all the horses, even though Robbie tries not to encourage them.

The third group is the wiliest, and sometimes weeks go by without Robbie getting a good look at them. He calls the sly black mare who heads up their ranks Bandit.

Finally, there's Lucky's band, the largest of the four bands at nearly two dozen strong, and they're the ones that he and Poco have stumbled across, it seems. They don't startle and run from the approaching horse and rider the way Bandit and her renegades would, or venture close to touch noses with Poco like the bachelors sometimes do. Lucky has one remaining eye after a close call during his first week on the ranch, which won him his name. He holds his head at an angle to get a good look at them. He's a reddish palomino, with a coat the color of a burnished penny and a silvery-white forelock that falls over the blemished side of his face.

"Hey, handsome," Robbie calls softly, nudging Poco onward with his calves while his eyes skate over the horses visible through the trees, their group standing close together, chins resting on one another's snow-damp backs. When he has a good count, and sees that they're all bright-eyed and seem to be in one piece, he starts scanning the trees for the next band.

He sees Millie's band next. Or, at least, he gets a quick glimpse of Sage. The other mares must be tucked down along the creek bank where the wind can't reach them, but Sage's dark head pops up above the brush that hedges the embankment, standing out against the snowfall. He rides Poco in that direction, ducking the grasping tree branches that glance off the waterproofed canvas and leather of his duster, but snag on his jeans and Poco's mane and tail. When he's close enough to peer over the edge, the mares have already moved downstream. They're drifting away—except for Millie, who stands facing Poco and him like she's guarding their retreat. Robbie gives her a respectful little nod, and she chooses that moment to pivot and charge after the others, her hooves crunching in the shallow ice.

Robbie guides Poco back to the trail and they follow it along as it continues to weave north. Predictably, Bandit is nowhere in sight, but Robbie does hear crashing brush and hoofbeats further up the trail. He assumes Bandit heard them coming and scattered her band somewhere out of his line of vision. Poco jerks his head in the direction of the noise and lets out a long, rumbling snort that vibrates in his whole body and makes Robbie grin, cautiously.

"Easy, son. Now's not the time to rediscover your wild side." It takes a certain kind of horse to be the only domesticated one in sight or smelling distance and not cotton on to the wild ones' energy. He reaches behind the saddle and gives Poco's rump a gentle pat. Poco snorts again, then puts his head forward and trudges on, back to business.

The path forks out, breaking into a few narrow trails that the wild ones have cut, and the broader, main trail opens into the hay meadow. That summer, Robbie had swathed and baled the grass on these fifteen gently sloping, relatively clear acres, then rowed up the tightly rolled bales and put a few strands of electric wire around the perimeter to keep the horses out of them. This way, he can feed them without getting a tractor up here or forcing them into corrals by the house for the winter. They're only halfway through the available bales. Kyle's band is gathered around the mound of dried grass, eating contentedly, when Robbie and Poco break out of the trees.

Kyle is a dark bay, and he looks nearly all black in his full winter coat. He calls out a sharp whinny to Poco in greeting. Poco answers, which Robbie should probably discipline him for, but Robbie and Poco don't really have that kind of relationship, so he lets it slide. He's been riding Poco almost every day for the past ten years, and if the horse hasn't decided to rebel, unload Robbie, and join the wild ones in their wild ways yet, he probably won't start now.

The bachelors are a small band; it's just Kyle, another three bays, three dun-colored seven-year-olds, and two lanky sorrels that look like siblings. The sorrels are starting to show their age. According to their paperwork, they're sixteen. Robbie reminds himself to ask Megan if there's another kind of mineral supplement that might help them keep their weight on. He gives them each a critical once-over, but he can see they still have healthy, round barrels, apparent even through their plush winter coats. Still, they're leaner than the rest of the group, despite constant access to hay.

"Clear out, gentlemen," Robbie says, waving his arms, and

when that doesn't faze them, whistling and cracking the ends of his reins against the leather saddle. It makes a sharp noise that finally scatters the bachelors, but they're more grudging than afraid as they trudge off toward the trees.

Robbie wraps the reins around the saddle horn and dismounts, leaving Poco ground-tied. He turns off the solar charger that's feeding a pulsing electrical charge into the wire that he can hear like a tick. When it's safe, he adjusts the fiberglass posts and the wire strung through them so that the horses can reach a fresh bale. He's using his pocket knife to cut loose the twine bundling the bale together when his phone rings.

Hearing his phone while he's up in the meadow is always a little surreal, like he imagines it would be to get a call from home while visiting the moon. He has a sense of being a world apart and out of reach, and yet he can hear the tinny voice of someone in his ear when he takes the call.

It's Danny calling, which leaves Robbie instantly worried. Even though he wishes that Danny would call him from school on the east coast every few days, like a dutiful younger brother might, he doesn't. So, Robbie's first thought is that Danny is in the middle of some emergency.

And as it turns out, he's not exactly wrong. It's just not Danny's emergency.

"Danny?"

"Robbie? Hey...can barely hear you."

"I'm up in the hay meadow. What's wrong?"

"Nothing. Or I mean, nothing with me. Listen, I need you to do me a big favor, okay? Lance called me. He's in jail, and I need you to go bail him out."

CHAPTER THREE

Lance

"Hey, man," says the jail attendant, who Lance now knows is named Tim. Hard to pass a night with a guy who talks you down from a panic attack and not emerge on a first-name basis. "I've got really good news. Robbie Chase just posted your bail."

Robbie Chase.

Just his name manages to penetrate the ugly haze Lance has been swimming in since sometime around eight last night. It's better now, with a little bit of sunshine coming through the high, small window opposite the cell, but not by much. He still feels sick, like a fever rages in his body, building toward a breaking point that won't come.

"Okay," he mutters, lurching to his feet, palms slick. He picks up the crumpled piece of paper with his charges on it— the citation, Tim called it. It's been sitting on the bench beside him because it doesn't seem like the sort of thing he should shove in his pocket, and it's been his only reading material.

"So, you're letting me out?" He takes a half-step toward the door, daring to hope, even though if he lets himself imagine the door opening and himself stepping out, he'll be doubly crushed if it doesn't happen. Tim has explained that if no one answers his calls, he'll be out no earlier than Monday, when the judge will be in and can consider waiving his bail.

"Yeah, man. Come on." Tim unlocks the door, and Lance feels a rush of relief so powerful that he almost sobs.

Instead, he takes hurried, shuffling steps to mask how unsteady he feels, and slips through the door the moment Tim opens it and steps back. He hadn't realized his ears were ringing until now, when the sensation abates.

"Come on," Tim says quietly, guiding him by the arm out of the jail vestibule and into the adjoining office. "Just need to sign you out."

Tim's office is basically a carbon copy of the room with the cell, except without the bars. The desk is heaped with stacks of files and reams upon reams worth of paperwork. Floor-to-ceiling shelves take up most of the wall-space, stuffed with more files, some of them in binders, and banker's boxes with their lids askew, revealing yet more files and loose paper.

"You wouldn't want to light a match in here," Lance murmurs.

Tim laughs. "Hadn't thought of that." He hands Lance a pen.

Tim explains each form in the monotone of someone who's repeated his lines so many times that he knows them by heart. Lance barely catches a word, but scrawls his signature on each one nonetheless. Tim feeds each signed page into a noisy desktop copier, then stacks the copies in Lance's hands on top of his crumpled citation.

And then they go out into the hallway, and just like that, Lance is looking at Robbie Chase.

Robbie's hands are tucked in the pockets of a pair of battered, dark-wash Wranglers. He's wearing a coat that's a little too puffy to be fashionable, or to flatter anyone else, but Robbie always looks good, no matter what ridiculous crap he wears. His hair got long at some point. He always used to keep it carefully trimmed above his collar, but now the strands are long enough to cling to his throat at the ends—vividly black, like they're wet. The black cowboy hat on his head is damp, too. It must be snowing outside. The window was too small and the glass too opaque for Lance to have realized it.

The sight of him is a slap to Lance's already abused senses.

It's a slap he isn't braced for, either. Lance's world takes a hard lurch, his vision narrowing to a pinpoint, and his knees fail.

When he's aware of anything again, it's of strong, warm arms around him and a familiar scent he's tried so hard to forget. Pine needles, leather, and the clean salt smell of horses. That old, burning sensation of longing and shame in equal, agonizing parts fills his chest.

Lance is more or less sprawled on the floor. Robbie is kneeling beside him, supporting his upper body, and the sleeves of Robbie's coat are damp. He has the untidy beard he always used to sport in the winter, dark and looking softly touchable, although Lance has never actually touched it. His eyes are warm and worried, and moving fast over Lance's face like he's looking for something.

"Jesus," he says at last. Their faces are close enough that Lance can feel the warmth of his breath as he speaks. "Are you okay? Do we need to call a doctor?"

He sounds the same, too. The rush of memories and feelings his closeness triggers makes Lance dizzy again. Ignoring the way his surroundings continue to tilt and sway, Lance grits his teeth and pulls away, sitting up on his own.

He hates being helpless. He hates being transparent. He hates the ghost of his last encounter with this man, which has haunted him into manhood. The anger and frustration filling him are familiar, too. He knows how to use them, to patch the dark feelings together into a kind of flimsy raft he can use to navigate the rapids. Not ideal, but better than trying to swim.

"I'm fine," he says, his voice coming in a rasp, hardly convincing. Swallowing, he goes on with more energy. "It's just...I was—"

"Locked in," says Robbie with quiet emphasis. He's still kneeling, but he's leaned back a bit to allow Lance some space to sit up, and now they're not quite touching, with Robbie's knees a hair's breadth from Lance's hip.

Lance, surprised, shoots him a glance. "Yeah," he says quietly. *You remembered*, he adds, only in his head. He marvels at that fact in silence, and it's a little flame of brightness and warmth he can tuck next to his heart.

"Danny didn't get your message until this morning, and I came as soon as he called me." Robbie's voice is suffused with so much regret that Lance's ears burn. "I'm so sorry you had to be in here all night."

Lance swallows and starts to get up. Not because he trusts his body any more than he did a minute ago, but because he *has* to put some distance between them.

"It's okay. I mean, thank you. For coming at all. I—owe you," he says, tripping over the last few words as he slowly clambers to a standing position. Because it isn't just an expression. Robbie literally spent money to post Lance's bail. One thousand dollars, according to Tim, which may as well have been one hundred thousand for Lance, who has access to exactly sixty-three dollars.

Robbie rises gracefully along with him, his brow still furrowed with concern.

Without looking at him, Lance presses on doggedly. "Unfortunately, I can't pay you back right now," he manages in an almost-normal voice. All of his money is in his accounts with Niall, or wherever else Niall put it. Maisie would tell him he's an idiot for running off without figuring out how to get at least some of it first.

Robbie isn't saying anything. Lance dares a look.

They're almost the same height, which is a realization that appears to be striking Robbie, too. His eyes widen when Lance meets them without having to look up more than an inch. Sure enough, Robbie says, "You really grew up."

Lance studies Robbie in earnest, even if it hurts to spend more than a moment seeing that face—one he couldn't forget if he tried, but hasn't seen in so long. Robbie *has* changed a little, Lance realizes with a start. It's not that he's aged, exactly—he looks tired, like he needs more than one good night's sleep. And the slight smile that tugs on the left side of his mouth when he catches Lance's eyes looks rusty, as though no one has coaxed it from him in a while. Lance feels a familiar spike of the old commingled jealousy and frustration toward Megan, apparently undiluted by the past several years and his supposed transformation from a child to an adult. *You're supposed to make him smile*, he thinks viciously at her, wherever she is.

To get out of his own head, Lance speaks with a shrug. "Well, I'm not sixteen anymore." So much for banishing intrusive thoughts. Lance immediately ducks his head. If *that* comment doesn't raise the specter of his sixteen-year-old self between them, and that final, desperate, pathetic stunt—

"No," Robbie agrees, his voice steady and without judgement. "I can see that."

Lance's eyes dart to Robbie's and their gazes lock again, this time for longer. A second, two, three. Lance feels something pass between them...something he can't quite articulate, but which startles him into the momentary belief that feelings beyond Robbie's general sainthood and faithfulness to Danny brought him here. But then Lance remembers the years through which Lance fed his own delusions—blinded by a destructive fantasy. He looks away sharply, pushing his hand up against the wall less to steady his body and more to anchor his mind to something real, even if it's just the texture of whitewashed cinderblock.

"Is there..." Robbie starts, and then trails off. Lance can't bear to look at him again except out of the corner of his eye, but he seems like he's biting his lip, showing a flash of perfect white teeth in the frame of his beard. "I want to ask if you have somewhere to go, but maybe it's not any of my business."

Robbie's speaking very softly, and Lance is suddenly too aware of Tim hovering awkwardly to his left.

He shoots Tim a strained smile. "So, is there anything else I need to do?" Tim has turned out to be a really decent guy. He could have just shut the lights off and left Lance to tolerate the night of locked-in darkness as best he could; he didn't have to bring all of his paperwork in and do it on a clipboard on his lap in the vestibule, leaving the lights on, or tell Lance a dozen long and wandering stories that ranged from his days in high school marching band to the difficulties of learning to two-step in time for his cousin's wedding.

"Nope. You're all set," Tim says with a guileless smile. But he's definitely looking between Robbie and Lance with a bewildered sort of curiosity that makes Lance itch again to get away.

Tim hands Lance a plastic baggie that contains everything Lance had in his pockets when they checked him into jail. Then, his eyes rest on the crumpled paperwork Lance has to pass to his other hand in order to take the baggie. Tim holds up a finger and disappears again into his office.

During the long few seconds Lance and Robbie are alone, Lance avoids Robbie's gaze by staring at the baggie. A cell phone with a dark screen. Sixty-three dollars and twelve cents. A stick of gum with some lint stuck to it. His slim wallet, with a couple of useless credit cards and his ID.

When Tim comes back, he has a manila folder, dogeared around the edges and with rectangles of blacked-out ink here and there on the front.

"Here, for your docs," Tim says with a half-smile.

Lance is so emotionally raw that his hand is shaking a little when he takes the folder. The gesture, no matter how small, hits him hard. He meets Tim's kind, close-set eyes with a sincere smile. "Thanks, man."

"You bet." After watching Lance tuck his wrinkled documents into the folder, Tim gives his shoulder an awkward pat in farewell.

Lance takes a deep breath and heads for the stairs. For the first two steps, Robbie is right behind him, and then he hurries past Lance, getting slightly ahead of him on the stairs as they descend, like he's prepared to catch Lance if he should pitch forward.

From two stairs below, Robbie has to look up at Lance from under the brim of his hat. "Do you have a coat? It's snowing, and the wind is starting to blow."

"I've pretty much got the clothes on my back and the contents of this Ziploc," Lance says, waving the bag demonstratively. So that he doesn't have to see Robbie's reaction, Lance looks down at the thin jacket he was lucky to keep when everything happened yesterday. It's a fitted fleece intended to be worn under a heavier coat, like the one he left in the back seat of the car that's now locked in an impound. "I'll be fine," he insists, and it's probably true. He's been cold before. And he has enough cash to get a night at the motel— maybe two, if they only want half up front.

Then again, how much does a motel cost these days? It's been a long time since he's stayed in one. Not since the weekend trips he went on with his aunt at the end of high school. He's thinking that over when they reach the first landing of the broad staircase and Robbie turns and steps in front of him, putting them chest-to-chest.

Lance is startled enough that he accidentally meets Robbie's eyes. Again, he notices the strangeness of their similar heights. For so long, Lance was always looking up at him. Usually from afar.

Now, it's no strain for him to see Robbie's crow's feet, and the inky darkness of his eyelashes, and the shorter, fine hairs as his beard feathers away to bare, smooth skin on his cheekbones.

"If you're in trouble," Robbie says firmly, his murmur low and distracting, "then I can help you."

Lance can't contain an incredulous laugh, but there's a tremor to it that makes Robbie's eyes grow steely, determined. He leans a fraction of an inch closer, but still they're not touching.

Even now, all these years later, he's so very careful not to touch Lance.

"I mean it, kid."

That word—*kid*—brings Lance back. He doesn't have to force the flint into his voice when he says, "I don't need your help."

He shoulders past Robbie, feeling a rush of adrenaline that carries him down the rest of the steps and out the heavy glass and oak doors onto the snow-covered steps, where a gust of wind penetrates his fleece jacket like a punch.

Lance stops there, frozen by that burst of wind. Like a character in *The Team*, struck by Mister Ice's storm gun, he thinks, with a bolt of longing for Danny. They've barely spoken in years, but he still knew when he called that Danny would do whatever he could for him. Lance feels guilty for manipulating that neglected, but still-strong bond. Then again, it isn't like he did it with cool calculation. Tears had streaked his cheeks for the entire forty-five second duration of listening to the phone ringing unanswered, and then leaving a clumsy voicemail.

Robbie is behind him. Lance knows it without seeing or hearing him. The wind twists around him, its icy fingers penetrating Lance's jacket and stinging him from head to toe, but some of it is blocked by Robbie's body, and it's not quite as bad as it was a moment ago.

"Lance," Robbie says in that soft voice Lance remembers him using around skittish horses. "If you haven't already made other arrangements," he continues, slow and measured—like they're meeting under pleasant circumstances, and not on the steps of the building where Lance just spent the night in jail, "I'd like it if you stayed with me at the ranch for a couple of days."

The courthouse square is spread out in front of Lance— lawn and flag poles and two oak trees. Beyond it is the facing row of downtown storefronts lining the block, all looking just as he remembers. He supposes six years isn't exactly a life-time. There's the corner pharmacy with the old-fashioned soda fountain in the back. There's the Wicked Cut, where he got every terrible haircut he received in the first eleven years of his life, before rebelling and growing his dark curls out into a ponytail. There's the hardware store where his dad once yelled at him so violently, right in the middle of the aisle beside the big bins of nails and screws, that Lance dug his hand into one of the bin's sharp contents and squeezed. He'd made his palm bleed in six places, but he didn't think his father had even noticed. He'd spent the next couple of weeks terrified he was going to get tetanus.

"Kid," Robbie says quietly, bringing him back to the present again. "Lance. You're family. Please."

Lance pretends for another second that he has a choice...

that spending the very last of his money at a motel is a viable option. Then, he swallows and nods. "Yeah. Okay." He's sure he does the least convincing impression of a casual shrug ever. His body is quaking, mostly from the cold, so all that really happens is that his right arm jerks. "Okay," he repeats. "Sure."

Robbie lets out a gusty sigh, so close all of a sudden that Lance can hear it even over the snow-laden wind, and then the heavy warmth of Robbie's coat lands on Lance's shoulders. The feel of it is almost overwhelming, like being wrapped in Robbie's arms for that moment after he collapsed back in the jail.

"I don't—" Lance starts to protest, but Robbie is already walking past him, down the handicapped-accessible ramp that's clear of snow, probably liberally spread with salt by some public servant in anticipation of the forecast. Lance has little choice but to follow him.

Lance hunches his shoulders so that the collar of Robbie's coat brushes his cheek, and he smells soap, cologne, and something else—spicy, so it's probably not aftershave, considering Robbie is so deliberately unshaven. Does he oil his beard? Does he moisturize?

When Lance sees the familiar truck parked on the curb, he smiles despite himself. The old blue Chevrolet is gathering snow on the pristine curves of its body; with a couple of evergreens in the bed, it would look like something straight out of a Christmas card. It's in the same mint condition that Lance remembers.

"You still have it," he observes. Robbie has his shoulders up around his ears. He's wearing a grey Henley that's molded to his chest—proof, if Lance needed it, that he's still strong and hard-bodied from daily work. His black hat is dusted with snowflakes. The cold is getting to him almost as fast as it did Lance, judging by the red tip of his nose and how hastily he reaches for the truck's driver's side door.

Still, he pauses to shoot Lance a smile. "Yeah, I plan to drive it until the wheels fall off, or somebody steals it. You okay? I'm freezing."

Okay. The concept makes Lance want to laugh. He's never been okay in his life. But he's told this lie a hundred thousand times, and it comes easily enough. "Yeah, I'm fine," Lance says, and he slides into Robbie's truck.

CHAPTER FOUR

Robbie

H e doesn't know what he can do except blast the heat and drive, so that's what he does. He brought the old truck without thinking, even though the new dually handles a little better in the snow. The dually is five years old, not really "new" at this point, but everything is new compared to the Chevrolet.

Anyway, the stock trailer was still hooked up to the dually, and Robbie had been in such a hurry after getting off the phone with Danny, he hadn't been willing to take the time to unhitch it.

That was just a few hours ago. Then, the snow had just been forming a powdery layer that totally covered the grass and soil. Now, it's almost noon, and the wind is beginning to build the snow into banks along the road. He has to focus to keep the truck where it should be, and still they occasionally lose traction and fishtail, but it's all in slow motion, devoid of a real sense of danger.

Robbie is glad he has something to focus on instead of the young man sitting silently beside him, his long, white fingers toying with the oversized buttons on Robbie's jacket, which seems huge and shapeless on his slighter body.

He has so many questions, but he knows better than to fire any of them off. Even if Lance weren't giving off a steady nonverbal message of *"Don't ask,"* Robbie would remember how Lance was as a child. Secretive, so guarded about any pain. That secretiveness used to make Robbie crazy, worrying that something horrible would happen or was happening in Lance's life, and that Lance would refuse to ask for help. Robbie had done all he'd felt he could do, under the circumstances—he'd made sure there was always an extra pillow and blanket on Danny's bed and an extra plate at the table in case Lance showed up. Caring about Lance had been like taking a shine to a lone wolf, even back then. He was never going to let you take care of him the way you wanted, but he'd occasionally appear for a small dose of kindness before disappearing back out into the dark.

"Is this really okay? Me staying with you?"

"Yes," Robbie says with a quiet vehemence. It bothers him that Lance feels the need to ask, or could ever think Robbie wouldn't welcome him.

"Megan won't care?" he presses.

For a second, Robbie doesn't understand the question. Then, he huffs out a laugh and rubs his jaw. "No. Megan won't care." Well, she probably *will* have *opinions*, but they aren't relevant in the way Lance means. "We broke up a couple of years ago." And because he and Megan were famously on-again-off-again from the ages of fifteen to thirty-two, he clarifies, "For good, this time."

If Lance is surprised by the revelation, it doesn't register on his face. He nods a couple of times and looks out the window, and the cab falls silent again.

Robbie continues to hold back the questions burning in

his mind. *What happened yesterday? Why were you in Dell? Why were you in* jail?

He has other questions, too. *What happened six summers ago? Where did you disappear to? Why didn't you call?* Danny had been outright miserable for the rest of that school year.

In fact, Danny still winces whenever Lance's name comes up. Robbie has never been able to get Lance out of his head, either. That sweet, shy kid. That lovely boy, who bared his heart and soul to Robbie so bravely on that last, awful day....

It's hard to reconcile *that* Lance—a painfully thin slip of a thing, all wild brown hair and big blue eyes, his head barely coming to Robbie's chest—with *this* Lance. The eyes are the same, even if the open expression has been replaced by something unfocused and distant. But otherwise, Lance is transformed. He's still slender, but no one would call him scrawny; he has the long limbs and elegant proportions of a dancer. He's probably six feet tall or even just a hair over, based on how close he seems to stand to Robbie's six-foot-two. And, though his clothes are wrinkled and his jacket has a big tear in the sleeve, even Robbie can tell they're designer quality.

But though the outward changes in Lance are stark, Robbie can plainly sense there's more to it than Lance having simply grown up. The more glances Robbie steals across the cab, the easier it is to see the *physical* traits of the boy he knew, now grown into a young man.

But the boy from across the creek had a warm energy that filled a space, a smile that could endear the coldest heart, and a basic sweetness that Robbie had never seen rivaled before or since. There's only been the merest glimpse of him today, when Robbie pulled Lance into his lap after he collapsed in the hallway in the courthouse. As his fluttering lashes lifted, on the verge of unconsciousness, he had the same look on his face that Robbie remembers from the very last time they saw one another—like Robbie could see straight into Lance's when he looked him in the eye, every feeling and hope boldly on display.

There's hardly an echo of that boy's bright presence in the shuttered young man presently sitting in Robbie's truck.

The truck's rear tires suddenly lose their grip on the snow and veer sideways, so that for a second the truck is coasting down almost perfectly perpendicular to the road. The entire view out the windshield is the slope of the ditch and the old barbed wire fence stretched between hedge posts, frosted with snow like Christmas tree garland.

Lance makes a low, alarmed noise. Without thinking, Robbie takes his hand off the gear shift to give Lance's shoulder a quick, reassuring squeeze before putting both his hands on the wheel, guiding the steering column slowly back to the right while gently massaging the brakes.

The brief touch fills him with a buzzing energy, even though all Robbie felt was his own coat under his palm and the suggestion of a hard curve beneath. Still, he's strangely aware that all of the warmth emanating through the fabric came from Lance.

When the truck eases back to forward-facing on the road, Robbie looks over. "Okay?"

Lance is semi-plastered against the door, one hand braced on the dash. He slowly relaxes his limbs, giving Robbie a flustered smile. "I forgot what these roads are like in the snow," he admits.

Robbie blinks, a little taken aback by the sudden light of his grin. He rubs his beard and smiles wanly in reply, looking straight ahead while he gives himself a moment to gather his thoughts. "Should be about two days of this," he says eventually, wondering how obvious his uneasiness is—if Lance will know, like a horse would, that his calmness is a facade.

"Forecast said no more than a day," Lance says.

Robbie glances at him with a raised brow. "You've been

watching the weather?" His tone is light, but the implication isn't. There likely wasn't a television in the one-cell jail on the third floor of the courthouse.

Lance shakes his head. "No," he says, drawing out the word in a "duh" tone that makes Robbie smile. "Tim had an app on his phone. We have nothing in common, and talked all night, anyway, so the weather came up more than once."

Robbie's smile vanishes and his eyes narrow. "Why was he with you all night?" He gives Lance a sharp look. "He didn't—was he bothering you?"

Lance's hand slips over his mouth before Robbie can see his expression. His fingers are long, his palms narrow, and the backs of his hands are smooth-knuckled and hairless. Robbie can't remember ever noticing someone's hands like this before. But the long-lost boy-next-door has never reappeared in his life on the wrong side of a jailhouse door. Maybe strange and random reactions are par for this unfamiliar course.

"No," Lance says eventually, turning to stare out the window. "I was about to freak out—no, I *was* freaking out—over spending the night in the cell, and he could tell. Must have been the fact that I was pacing around and almost hyperventilating. So, he stayed with me; made small talk. He's a pretty good guy, actually."

"I'm so sorry that you had to be there all night." Robbie said it before, but it bears repeating.

Lance makes a little, dismissive gesture, and then his hand falls heavily into his lap like his arms are too tired to stay raised. Maybe they are, after the night he's had.

"So," Lance says more brightly, "what makes you disagree with the weatherman?"

Of all the things they should be talking about, Robbie thinks with mystification, they're really going to discuss the *weather*. Though, it's more of an immediate concern than usual, he supposes. The truck dives through a low place on the road where the snow is particularly thick and sends up a billowing cloud that reaches the windows.

"It's an old farmer's almanac thing," Robbie says, shrugging and feeling oddly shy. "My dad used to say it. 'Three months after a heavy fog, you'll get rain or snow.' And we had three days of fog, three months back."

Lance glances at him. "Your dad," he murmurs. "I guess you remember him, huh? Danny and Johnny never talked about him, but they were pretty little, when...?"

The flash of pain at the thought of that time is duller than it used to be, but still there, never gone completely. "Yeah," Robbie says, "Johnny was eight, and Danny was four."

A tractor had pulled onto the highway off of a gravel road, not seeing Robbie's dad coming, and it had been too late for the truck to get stopped. Robbie's dad had wound up in the ditch. At least it had been quick. The tractor hadn't even needed major repairs.

Robbie had been at school when the wreck happened; by the time he knew, the scene had been cleaned up. But later, he'd found the zigzagging tracks left by the truck's tires, and in the ditch they'd pulled the truck out of, there'd still been a pool of crushed window-glass like a thousand worthless diamonds.

Robbie pushes the thoughts aside with a swallow. "I don't think Danny remembers him at all. Johnny remembers some, but he's not one to think about what can hurt him, you know?" He doesn't know why, but instead of steering the conversation somewhere else, Robbie admits, "I think about him all the time, though."

He can feel the weight of Lance's eyes on the side of his face, but he doesn't turn. Before Lance can say anything, they round the curve an eighth of a mile from Robbie's driveway and four cows appear, standing in the middle of the road in the drifting snow.

Robbie swears, hits the brakes as hard as he dares, and holds the wheel in a double-vice grip. The truck slows abruptly, its brakes vibrating as the tires skid on the packed snow, and then they slide a solid four feet even with the brakes locked. The closest cow, a big, black creature with a band of white around her midsection, stares at them placidly like she's well-versed in the laws of physics and knows she's safe, but Robbie's heart is in his throat until the moment the truck is still.

His hand is back on Lance's shoulder. Robbie realizes it, then looks over without taking it away. This time, his forefinger extends past the collar of the coat, and the pad of his fingertip just brushes the warm, smooth skin of Lance's neck. Lance is looking back at him, his lakewater eyes wide, and his lips are parted. Robbie doesn't remember his lips being such a delicate, deep pink, but now his gaze is fixed there, where he can also see small white teeth, one slightly crooked lower incisor, and the tip of a red tongue.

The cow moos loudly at them and Robbie jumps, taking his hand off Lance and pushing the heel of his palm hard into the middle of the steering wheel, all in one motion. The horn blares, and the cows hike up their tails and scatter. Robbie tests the gas, and is pleasantly surprised when the truck inches forward. Not stuck, then. He reaches into his jeans pocket for his phone.

"I don't remember anyone having cattle around here." Lance's voice sounds steady, but maybe a little quieter than it was before, like he feels the charge in the air from moments ago as keenly as Robbie. Robbie hopes not. He hopes he's alone in this strange awkwardness, which he ascribes mostly to how he's tripped all over Megan's old rules where Lance was concerned: *Don't touch him too much. Don't spend too much time alone with him.*

Don't encourage his delicate young feelings—that had been the spirit of the rules. But the rules seemed silly back then, and they seem even sillier now. Then, he capitulated mostly because he wanted to appease Megan. Robbie himself always knew that Lance would outgrow his crush on his own, and he'd been right. Look at Lance now. Though Robbie hesitates to say it, even in the relative safety of his own head, Lance is objectively beautiful. 'Handsome' isn't quite the right word, though that works, too. Anyway, he's not at all the sort of person who needs to pine for anyone; instead, he's the sort of person who only has to crook his finger to bring anyone he wants running.

Robbie eases the truck to a stop and puts it in park. He doesn't expect any traffic on this road even in good weather, but just to be safe he flips on the hazard lights.

"The old Cane place changed hands a few years ago, and the new owner runs some cows." Robbie gives the careful, political answer, and then, considering how long he's known Lance, relaxes enough to add, "If you want to call it that. He's kept them alive, and they're in the pasture slightly more often than they're out." With a sigh, he rubs his palms on his thighs. "Can I borrow my coat?"

"Oh, sure," Lance says, cheeks going a little pink. He leans forward and struggles to get his long arms out of the sleeves in the cramped cab, like he's no more accustomed to being tall and lanky than Robbie is to seeing him that way. When he hands over the coat, Robbie is careful not to let their hands touch, and then he ignores the fact that the lining is warm from Lance's body when he puts it on himself and gets out of the truck.

He's more than a little baffled by his physical reaction to

Lance. That's as new to him as Lance's short hair and sudden height, and he doesn't know what to do with it.

You're just lonely, he assures himself, and feels better for about a half-second before an inner voice adds snidely, *and sex-deprived.* He trips a little and blames it on the snow, catching himself with one hand on the hood of the Chevy. Then, pushing all thoughts of the young man waiting for him in the truck from his mind, he focuses on guiding the cows that are lingering in the ditch toward the low place in the ancient barbed wire that they stepped over to get out.

CHAPTER FIVE

Lance

With the heat blasting, the Chevy's cab is perfectly warm, but Lance still misses Robbie's coat.

While Robbie trudges after the cows, Lance rummages for his phone in the plastic baggie from the jail. Not because he expects to have missed any important calls, but because if he doesn't do something to distract himself, he'll just stare out the window and watch every move Robbie makes. Staring at Robbie will only make managing his turbulent emotions harder.

And he *has* to get himself under control. He can't humiliate himself with Robbie. Not again.

When he rolls his thumb over the screen to bring it back to life, though, the first thing he sees is a bolded notification. **No service.** The low-battery warning is blinking, as well as a notification for one missed call and two texts.

Danny: I talked to Robbie, and he's coming as soon as he can get there.

Danny: I just realized you might not be getting these texts.

If you are, will you text me back? I called and left a message too, but you can ignore that if you want.

Lance bites his lip at that roundabout reminder that he hasn't returned any of Danny's calls in approximately five years. He isn't sure how he would reply even if he could, but the question is moot. Unsurprisingly, considering Niall reported the car that he gave Lance as stolen, he's already shut off his phone service, too.

He tucks the phone in his pocket just as Robbie climbs out of the ditch and comes back toward the truck.

Tension fills him at the prospect of sharing the tiny space of the Chevy's interior with Robbie again in just a few moments. He isn't sure how much longer he can control himself in this kind of close proximity. They're just a couple of minutes away from Riverside now, though, and when they get to the ranch, he'll at least be able to put a closed door between them.

Will Robbie put him up in Danny's room? He hopes so. The memory of being tucked safely into that lumpy double bed is one that Lance has held close over the years. He hopes that Danny left up all of his dumb childhood posters that he still hadn't gotten around to taking down by the time they were teenagers. Lance remembers that strange, incongruous wallpaper fondly: Teenage Mutant Ninja Turtles and Nintendo characters half-plastered-over with more recent band stickers, movie posters, and concert flyers.

Robbie climbs in, accompanied by a blast of cold air and icy snow that makes Lance shudder. He pulls out his own phone, which looks enormous because it's in one of those practically bombproof cases. "He needs to fix his goddamn fence," he mutters to himself, then frowns while, presumably, the phone rings unanswered several times. Then he sighs, pushes another button, and drops the phone on the dash. He casts Lance a quick glance as he puts the truck in gear. "Okay?"

Lance nods, clutches his knees, and tries to smile. "Yeah."

They bump down the driveway without speaking to each other, but though Lance is still wrestling with his feelings, the silence isn't uncomfortable. Robbie has never been much of a talker. Maybe that's because his younger brothers didn't know how to be quiet, between their fondly antagonistic banter, Danny's endearing, know-it-all observations, and Johnny's constant quips. The handful of times Robbie and Lance happened to be alone together for some odd reason or another, it was like this. Quiet.

Memories of that quiet companionship have led Lance through some of his darker moments, in fact.

The Chevy glides through the snow around the last bend in the long driveway to Riverside, and Lance's heart speeds up. His gaze can't help wandering to the tree line that clogs the slope down toward Chase Creek. How many times did he hike through that stretch of forest, wade through the shallow spot in the water or shimmy across the fallen tree that bridged the banks, and escape from his side of the creek to the creaky farmhouse and the Chases, safe on the other side?

It's impossible to see the creek, named for Robbie's ancestor, that forms the property line, let alone the house where Lance grew up, but Lance can *feel* it—out of sight, but summoning his attention, anyway. He can trace the route from here to there in his mind's eye, imagining the scarred surface of its solid wood exterior door and the fear of what waited for him on its other side.

"It'll look a little different to you," Robbie murmurs as they pull into the yard. Lance snaps his head around like he's just been startled from a dream. Maybe he has.

He sees what Robbie means right away. The yard is the same—holding the enormous, old stone barn, the tidy, white-painted board fences, a handful of small stone buildings, and the lean-to with a few familiar horses peering out.

But the house is gone. Where it stood, there's nothing but snow-covered emptiness; all that remains is the old hedge of rose bushes planted by some Chase grandmother along the porch. He remembers sitting on the porch swing in summertime and inhaling their heady perfume. At the moment, they're nothing but leafless frames draped in snow.

Bewildered, Lance looks at Robbie. "What happened?"

His face is pinched with grief. "Fire. Last fall."

Horrified, Lance thinks of the tall, two-story silhouette that he always searched for when he approached the Chases' home. The generous porch, the white pillars—and, seemingly at random, his mind pulls another, specific memory, of the curtains billowing in the kitchen window when Robbie left it open to let out the heat; he had his sleeves rolled up, standing at the oven and reminding them not to run in the house. A rule they never heeded and which he seemed unwilling to actually enforce.

Lance also remembers sneaking up the open staircase, hand trailing along the wood bannister that glowed from the polish of generations of use. Tip-toeing his way to Danny's room.

He's too stunned for tears. He sees an understanding warmth in Robbie's eyes, and for a moment thinks Robbie's hand might land on his shoulder again, where a phantom of his touch has lived, ready to be revived at any moment, sweet and warm under Lance's skin.

Instead, Robbie turns away to look at the place where the house used to be. "We started converting the hayloft a couple of years ago, as an apartment for Johnny, and since he isn't using it, I've been staying up there." He hesitates, looking at Lance again, and this time there's uncertainty in his voice as he says, "I guess I should have said something before I asked you to stay."

It's left unspoken, but Lance understands: Robbie didn't mention the house because, in the end, the details of the offered accommodations weren't material. *Beggars can't be choosers.*

Lance nods, his heart pounding like it could break his ribs. When he was a kid, he'd thought his heart could just bust free and run away from him. The power of his own heartbeat had terrified him. Now, he knows from countless past experiences how much his body can take.

"Let's get inside," Robbie murmurs, and before Lance can protest, he's shed his coat again and thrust it into Lance's lap. Then he's out of the truck and pushing the door closed behind him before Lance can try to give it back.

The cold is an assault the second Lance opens the door to slide out of the truck. He hurries into Robbie's coat as a blast of wind chases him from the truck and through the snow after Robbie, to the foot of a new wooden staircase and deck attached to the old stone barn. They're camouflaged somewhat by the snow, and so he hadn't noticed them when they'd first pulled into the yard. Lance remembers the barn well. He and Danny used to play in the hayloft as kids, and as they got older, they still sometimes stole up there to feel more alone, often with a pile of comics. Once, with a few wine coolers pilfered from Johnny. The hayloft had always felt magically enormous—a stretch of smooth wooden flooring beneath an arched ceiling of exposed wooden beams that had reminded Lance of a capsized ship.

It was never warm up there in the winter, however, and it's far from the cozy bedroom that Lance had let himself hope for.

At the top of the stairs is a new wooden door. The opening was crafted to match the building; it's framed in limestone just like each of the original window openings that are rowed to either side of it. Lance glances over his shoulder and sees the same view he remembers from his youth: the twist of the creek, the sea of trees, the rocky shelves of the hillsides, and then the river, stretching so far it might as well be an ocean.

"Come on in," Robbie says, pushing the door open with his shoulder and making a halfhearted effort to knock the snow off his boots before going inside. Lance follows.

He isn't expecting what he finds inside.

The ceiling is the same, but it seems to glow in a way it didn't before, like someone has conditioned and sealed every board. Other than that, the hayloft is transformed. It's still one open space, but the floor is refinished to a brighter, even smoother gleam, and in the middle of the room is an island of countertops and cabinets—a small but modern kitchen. At the north end of the space, there's a wall that didn't used to be there, with a door that probably leads to a bathroom, considering Lance sees no signs of one anywhere else. On the south end, where there used to be a massive, hinged door designed for the original purpose of pulling in netfuls of loose hay, there's now an enormous glass window filling that entire opening with just a few large panes, and the view it frames of the snowy hills beyond is stunning. In front of the window is a bed, nightstand, and low dresser.

Lance's stare lingers on the bed, helplessly imagining Robbie lying there. Then he hastily looks around the loft again, and it strikes him that the only other place where anyone can sleep is the threadbare couch shoved up against the wall next to the kitchen. A half-built bookshelf leans against the wall next to the couch, and a black cat is curled on the arm. It opens one yellow eye to see who's responsible for interrupting its nap.

He stares back at the cat, still processing the revelation

that this is one living space that Lance will share with Robbie with no possibility of privacy. It's somewhere between a twisted dream come true for his younger self and a nightmare for his present-day self. He rakes a trembling hand through his hair, then slowly goes about taking off Robbie's coat.

Robbie, seemingly oblivious to Lance's internal crisis, has slipped out of his boots and put his hands back in his pockets, watching Lance with a small, uncertain smile. "I know it's not exactly cozy."

It's way too *fucking cozy!* Lance's panicked internal voice snaps.

But, of course, he doesn't say this or anything else. He just offers a quick smile, turning away under the pretense of looking for somewhere to hang up the coat before Robbie can notice how his hands are shaking.

CHAPTER SIX

Robbie

L ance is pivoting slowly in place, his eyes scanning the stone wall next to the door. That spot would be a logical location for a coat rack, or at least a peg, but Robbie hasn't gotten around to putting one in yet. "Here, let me take that," he murmurs, taking the coat and tossing it onto the bench beneath which he just shoved his boots. "You can put your stuff over there." He nods toward the sleeping area. He makes the bed every morning, so it looks tidy, but he notes to himself that he should change the sheets after he's gotten Lance semi-settled in. "There's nothing in the dresser except whatever Johnny left." He pauses thoughtfully. "You can borrow whatever you find in there. I bet you two are about the same size, now."

"I'm not—" Lance begins, and then swallows instead of finishing that thought. Robbie just waits, and after a moment, Lance glances at him, a hunted expression on his face. "I can't take your bedroom."

It's not a *bedroom* so much as just a bed, but Robbie doesn't point that out. He shrugs. "I don't mind."

Lance's gaze flits to the old couch, which Robbie got from

an online classified ad, but shouldn't actually have brought home with him when it had wound up being so much worse in person than in the pictures. He hasn't found a way to so much as perch on it without encountering a spring or mysterious hard spots. It's mainly been used by the triplicats, which is his name for the three black cats who wander between the indoors and outdoors, terrorizing everyone and everything they encounter, including Robbie.

"You won't even fit on that couch," Lance insists.

Robbie laughs. "I'm not going to try, trust me. There's a really good air mattress in the closet. I got it for when the boys come." He'd used it exactly once, when Danny had been there during Christmas break last month, and before the passing thought can bring back the memory of how badly that visit went, Robbie pushes it away.

He almost expects Lance to argue more; he was always a quiet kid, but stubborn, too, and shy of taking anything from someone that crossed some line he had in his mind about what was too generous for him to accept. But the years or the long night he's had have taken their toll, as Robbie sees when Lance simply gives Robbie a flustered nod and obediently wanders across the loft toward the bed. When he's in front of the big window, he pauses to look out at the view of the ranch from there.

Robbie leans against the edge of the kitchen counter, watching him. "Pretty nice, isn't it? That was Danny's idea, actually. The window."

Lance glances over his shoulder. As Robbie would have predicted, he's smiling at the mention of Danny. But it's a smile that's still very uncertain, giving Robbie the sudden urge to give him space.

"I'm just going to head outside for a bit." He rubs the back of his neck, trying to invent a task that will sound credible. "Make sure the horses have water," he decides, even though their tank was full and the de-icer was working perfectly when he checked four hours ago. "You just settle in. The bathroom is kind of primitive, but it's through there." He points to the only enclosed room in the loft. "Feel free to shower if you want. You'll see where the towels are." They're hard to miss, being stacked on a shelf in the unfinished closet right by the sink. Robbie winces, suddenly seeing the place through someone else's eyes. "It's all kind of a work in progress," he says by way of apology.

Lance turns from the window, his expression solemn. It's still strange, seeing his adult self overlaid against the teen that Robbie last knew him to be. But the two pieces are beginning to merge for Robbie. Lance doesn't look like a stranger now, with his blue eyes earnest and wide, and his voice so serious as he says, "Thank you for bringing me and asking me to stay. It's like..." he hesitates, his eyes darting away.

Robbie waits.

Lance swallows, and for a long moment, Robbie doesn't think he's going to finish. Robbie's about to show himself out the door and let Lance off the hook, but Robbie's patience is rewarded a moment later when Lance's eyes rejoin his.

"It's always been like home."

There's no stopping Robbie's grin, even though he doesn't want to spook Lance, and senses how easy it would be to do that.

"I'm really glad you feel that way," is all he lets himself say. Just those words are enough to make Lance's cheeks fever-bright. Robbie remembers that about him. That his face was always so quick to flush, the hollows of his cheeks turning the deep pink of rose petals. But the effect on his adult face is entirely new. "So," Robbie says, and clears his throat, "I'd better finish those—chores." He's already forgotten what he said he was going to do outside. "I'll see you in a little while."

Robbie takes the coat he just wadded up on the bench

and puts it on, even though it isn't waterproof and the wet snow has penetrated the cuffs of the sleeves and the collar, feeling shockingly cool against his flushed skin. But he barely registers that before he's shoved on his boots and stolen back outside, where he leans against the door for a moment after closing it behind him.

When he trusts his legs to be steady enough, Robbie trots down the stairs and opens the door that's directly below the one he just left. This one, though, is original to the old barn.

The barn is about as tall as a three-story house, with the hayloft taking up two-thirds of its height. Below, where there would originally have been housing for all variety of animals and equipment, there's an open area for storage and eight modern, steel-framed horse stalls.

The stalls have been clean-swept and empty ever since Robbie quit the training business. But sometimes when he comes in, for a moment, he still expects to see certain horses he rode in the past. The ones who left impressions on him for various reasons. It's like the memories fill the stalls with ghosts for a moment, so Robbie tries not to look at all. There are more good memories for him down here than bad ones, but the bad ones are like quicksand, pulling him under and making him blind to the rest.

He still uses one of the stalls on the end for his own horses, but only occasionally. It currently contains Poco. After pushing the horse to get back to the house after Danny's call, Robbie unsaddled him and put him in the stall under a fleece cooler to let his body slowly cool down while Robbie jumped in the truck.

Poco lifts his head from the pile of hay in the corner, and seeing that Robbie isn't coming his way, resumes eating. Robbie leans against the wall and fishes his phone out of his pocket. Danny has been calling nonstop for the past hour, but Robbie didn't want to answer in front of Lance.

Lance, who's above him, mere feet away. Robbie peers up at the floorboards that make up the ceiling from where he stands, suddenly cautious even though he knows from experience that sound doesn't really carry through those thick old planks.

Danny answers on the first ring.

"Finally! Did you see him? Is he okay? What——?"

"Slow down," Robbie tells him, keeping his voice down, just in case. "Yeah, I just went and picked him up. He's—he's in the hayloft. I think he's fine."

There's a long pause. *"He came home with you?"* Danny asks at last, his tone guarded.

Robbie has never been entirely sure what Danny knows about the events of the night before Lance left town, six years ago. It's never seemed right for Robbie to tell Danny if Lance didn't want to tell Danny himself. But the not knowing has led to a lot of awkwardness whenever the subject of Lance comes up.

Over the years, it's also become more than clear that Megan wasn't the only one who was aware of Lance's crush on Robbie. Sometimes Robbie thinks that he himself was the absolute last one to know. Johnny mentioned it a couple years back and acted surprised it was any kind of secret. Danny must have known, too.

"Yeah." Again, he has a strange urge to protect Lance's privacy, but it seems nonsensical, considering that Danny knows Lance better than Robbie could ever hope to, despite their estrangement, and besides that, Danny is Robbie's brother. "It didn't seem like he had anywhere else to go," Robbie admits.

"I was afraid of that. I mean, he called me for the first time in how long? He had to be desperate," Danny replies quietly, and then takes an audible, deep breath. *"So, what's he...I mean,* how *is he?"*

Robbie smiles despite himself. "He's grown up. He's almost as tall as me."

"*What?*" Danny sounds indignant.

Robbie's grin widens. "That's right. You jealous?"

"*God damn it,*" Danny growls, and then launches into a familiar and very unconvincing rant. "*I don't care about that. You know I think our culture's standards of beauty are bullshit. And I'm not, like, a victim of the American height obsession, okay?*"

"Yeah, you don't sound like a victim at all. You sound completely unbothered."

"*That's right,*" Danny says, still growling, "*because I'm not. You know, in some cultures—no, I'm not going to get into this with you. But even if there was such a thing as an objective standard of beauty, it would still be a meaningless measure of worth.*"

He goes on from there for a while about how the beauty bias comes, at best, from the hindbrain, and then delves into a commentary on ableism that feels only tangentially related to the original topic. Meanwhile, Robbie listens and makes sure he doesn't laugh. For a minute or two, it feels like old times—Robbie baiting Danny into a dissertation in just the way he has so many times before, then being just as proud as he is amused by Danny's offhand insights.

"*...Which is why half the people back home still won't let their sons wear pink.*"

That's apparently Danny's closing statement, because he falls silent. With the cell connection suddenly quiet, a few strained seconds pass. Then Danny says in a different, tentative tone, "*I wish I could come back.*"

"Your semester just started." Robbie knows Danny doesn't need the reminder, but he says it anyway, just in case. "I'll... take care of him." For some reason, the words make his face heat.

Robbie swallows. *You're just lonely,* he tells himself again.

"*I know,*" Danny says softly. "*Thanks.*"

"You don't have to thank me. I care about him, too."

"I know. Hey, I tried calling and texting him. Maybe he just doesn't want to talk to me." He laughs, short and mirthless. *"Anyway, will you tell him I said hi, and that if he wants to talk, I promise not to ask him about anything except his feelings about the movie adaptation of* The Team*?"*

"Those awful magazines you used to be obsessed with? What idiot thought that would make a good movie?"

"They're comics, and they're—you know, they're actually a cult classic!" Danny snaps. *"They're deliberately ironic, and fuck you, did you just do that on purpose?"*

"Definitely not," Robbie promises, swallowing his laughter.

"You're worse than Johnny."

"You wound me."

Robbie hears a voice in the background and a moment of static, like Danny just breathed hard into the receiver. Then his brother is back, speaking a little faster than he was a moment before. *"I have a class starting. Are you sure…?"*

"Yeah, I've got it. And I'll tell him what you said."

"Thanks, Rob."

"No problem, Dan." He hesitates, picking at a loose thread on one of his belt loops. "Maybe we'll talk soon?"

"Yeah, I'll call and see how he's doing tomorrow."

Robbie huffs. "Okay, right. I'll update you then, I guess."

"Gotta go. Bye." Then, right when Robbie's heart feels like it could break, he adds, *"Love you,"* and Robbie's next breath comes a little easier.

"I love you, too."

Robbie lets himself into the stall with Poco and runs his hand under the fleece. The fabric is damp over his back, but his coat is dry. The cooler has done its job of wicking away all the moisture from his sweaty skin instead of letting it freeze in his coat. Satisfied, Robbie pulls the cooler off and drapes it over the stall door to dry, then cups his hand under Poco's jaw and guides him out the barn door, across the snowy driveway, and back through the corral gate. Poco heads toward the shed to join his buddies. A trail of tracks through the snow to the hay feeder, and another to the waterer, prove they've ventured out as necessary.

Robbie takes his time, double-checking things that don't need checking. He wants to give Lance as much time as possible to settle in without him there to make Lance feel like he's in a fish bowl in the single, open space.

And to be honest, Robbie could use the respite, too.

Just lonely, he insists to himself. Surely, his reaction to hearing Danny's voice is proof of that.

But if it were Danny up in the hayloft, Robbie would be glued to his side, hanging on his every word, studying his face for every little recent sign of maturation. He can't say he's less interested in looking at Lance, but when he looks, it isn't brotherly affection that he feels.

Okay, Robbie thinks as he shuts off a water hydrant after filling an already-brimming stock tank another inch. *I'm attracted to Lance.* He can admit that. Robbie's a grown man, and so is Lance, so there's nothing fundamentally wrong about Robbie noticing him in that way. And even if there was, Robbie knows from experience that deliberate emotional ignorance never did anyone any favors in life. Maybe it took Megan and him a while to figure that out, but it's not a lesson he'll be forgetting any time soon.

He had *not* been attracted to Lance when he'd been a teenager, thank God, or else he'd have a whole new level of self-hatred to work through. But he definitely is attracted to him now.

Back in the saddle shed to check the cats' water, Robbie tosses the little circle of ice that's in the shallow plastic dish into the snow and refills it from a jug.

Robbie has never so much as flirted with a man. Not for lack of interest, but rather for lack of opportunity. He spent his teenage years assuming he was straight. He liked girls well enough, and he liked Megan especially, and thinking about anyone else—male or female—had always been unnecessary and made him feel vaguely disloyal.

And then his father had died, and he'd had Johnny and Danny to think about. And he'd still had Megan, even if their relationship had been on-again, off-again. During his single periods, picking up women was safer and easier, not just because it was more within his comfort zone, but because he was doing it in the various small towns within driving distance of Trace County. He was fairly certain that if he flirted with the wrong man in rural Nebraska, getting into a fistfight was a real possibility.

Anyway, it's natural for him to register that Lance is attractive. Perfectly natural, even if it would be wildly inappropriate for him to act on that attraction. Even if they didn't have their particular history—even if they'd just met—Lance is Robbie's utterly dependent house guest, trapped with Robbie with no means of escape. He couldn't even hitchhike off the ranch at this point, given the snow and his lack of anything as basic as a coat.

Just because Robbie's noticed that Lance has grown into a beautiful adult doesn't mean that Robbie has to do anything about it. Thoughts aren't actions. He has nothing to feel ashamed about.

His ruminations are interrupted by his cell ringing again. He might have ignored the call, but he recognizes the number as his newest neighbor's. Even though all of his neighborly advice has been ignored in the past, he still can't resist the opportunity to suggest, again, that he either fix his fence or move his cattle. So, he answers.

"Hi, Ed. I got a few of your cows back in a half hour ago. Saw them out on the road by my mailbox."

"Thanks for doing that, Robert! I'm out of town this weekend, actually, so I appreciate you keeping an eye on things."

Robbie pinches the bridge of his nose. "I wouldn't go that far, Ed. I just walked them back through the fence they stepped over. I'm not exactly farm-sitting."

"Still, puts my mind at ease knowing you're there! Thanks for doing that. Those new cows don't know the lay of the land yet. I bet they'll settle in after a week or two."

"You got someone setting out hay? We're getting a hell of a lot of snow." As soon as Robbie says it, he sees the trap he's laid for himself.

But, miraculously, Ed doesn't ask him to do his chores or check on his cattle.

"Oh, yeah, my nephew's staying at the house. He'll make sure they have the essentials. Thanks, neighbor."

Just five or six seconds after the call is over, Robbie hears mooing.

When he was a kid, Robbie's dad ran cattle at Riverside, just like his father did before him. Robbie has fond memories of riding through the meadows to check the herds, and he remembers the cattle as gentle, docile creatures.

But either his memory isn't as reliable as he thought or Ed sources his cattle directly from hell, because the animals that wander on and off of his property are absolute pests. Robbie comes out of the shed to find a trio of cows. Two red cows are flanking the familiar black, white-belted cow, who has her head wedged determinedly through what had before been a small crack between the closed doors of the metal hay shed up the hill, pushing with all her might.

"HEY, YOU, GET!" he calls, heading toward her. Significantly handicapped by the depth of the snow, he waves his arms. One of the cow's posse looks over her shoulder with absolute unconcern as Robbie approaches, and then swings her head back around, unbothered, to watch her friend try to crack open the doors on the building. Miraculously, busting through the steel frame seems to be within the cow's powers. She digs in with her hind legs, tail whipping back and forth like a rudder, and the metal groans.

"God fucking damn it!" Robbie roars, staggering through the snow. Whether it's the volume or the profanity, this call finally gets the entire trio's attention, though the instigator needs a solid second to unwedge her head from between the doors. Then, she springs around in a one-eighty, her belly swaying. She's definitely the same cow he saw in the road. He knows her by the band of white around her belly. A belly that's suspiciously large, too, like she's about to drop a calf. But surely not—surely, not even Ed would have a pregnant cow running loose on winter pasture where no one could check her.

"Go *home*," he tells the trio firmly. But in the back of his head, the same soft-heartedness that keeps him from poisoning mice is making him wonder if Ed's nephew is as much of a deadbeat as Ed, and if that's true, whether or not he *actually* put out anything for the cattle in the midst of all this snow.

He's not sure, which is why he winds up spending the next hour filling a feeder in the empty corral with hay, dragging out a stock tank to fill, finding a de-icer, discovering something chewed through its wires, then rewiring it on the workbench, and finally filling the tank with water that won't freeze, all under the watchful eye of the belted cow.

Then he calls Ed, gets his voice mail as usual, and tells him that when he's back in town, he can come pick up his strays.

By the time Robbie climbs back up the steps to the

hayloft, he's soaking wet, freezing cold, and exhausted. Still, he hesitates at the door.

"Just do what you told Danny you would," he mutters sternly to himself. The three black cats appear from various invisible portals to other realms to crowd around his ankles, eager to go inside. "Just take care of him."

With that, he goes inside, braced to face Lance with strictly brotherly care.

And he immediately relaxes—because, instead of climbing the walls, or having disappeared again without explanation or a trace, Lance is curled on his side in the middle of Robbie's bed, fast asleep.

Robbie slowly removes his boots, and then his hat, gloves, and coat. He walks sock-footed across the loft, slow and careful so the floor won't creak.

Asleep, Lance looks younger, except there's stubble on his jaw, so fine and soft it's silvery in the sunset light slanting brilliantly through the window. There are shadows beneath his eyes like purple thumbprints. He's wearing some clothes of Johnny's that he must have found in the dresser, and his hair is damp against the pillow.

I can take care of him, Robbie thinks to himself, a little frightened by how badly he wants to do it. *Yeah. I can do that.*

CHAPTER SEVEN

Lance

Fourteen years ago.

Since that first day of school, Danny has looked for Lance every time he climbs to the top of the bus's stairs, and Lance has made sure there's always an empty seat next to him.

Over the first couple of weeks, they sometimes didn't speak—just took turns casting shy looks at each other and then hastily looking away. Gradually, they spoke more and more. First, they talked about *The Team*, then other books, and then their teachers and classmates. By September, there were no more shy looks, and they were together as much as possible both on and off the bus. It filled Lance with his first taste of joy, something so bright and incandescent that he didn't know how it could be caused by just one person.

By November, Lance is running out of excuses for why he has to turn down Danny's daily invitations for getting together outside of school.

But we're neighbors, Danny would exclaim, *and Robbie already said okay!*

So, Lance comes up with a plan.

There's no way his father will tell him that he can go to the Chases' house for a playdate, so Lance hasn't bothered to ask. But, on Saturdays, his father almost always sleeps until noon, and Lance has been playing in the woods without his father interfering for as long as he can remember. Lately, he's done so with more purpose, exploring the property line. He knows the spot where the trees break and he can see up the far bank to the tight strands of wire fence that border the Chases' spread. He's pretty sure he can walk there, cross the creek, get to Danny's, and be back before his dad wakes up.

He's told Danny his dad will drop him off—a lie he'd rather not have told. What he and Danny have feels too precious to jeopardize with untruths, like even a small betrayal could poison the pure, perfect thing between them. But, he has a feeling that certain truths could kill it, too. Danny looks at Lance with the biggest grin, the brightest light in his eyes. Lance has no idea how he earned Danny's attention, or why Danny enjoys being around him as much as Lance enjoys being around Danny, but whatever cosmic misunderstanding is working in his favor, he wants it to last as long as possible. If Danny knew the dirty, ugly truth about what Lance goes home to, he'd see Lance differently.

So, Lance is willing to lie, but only when he absolutely has to.

The first part of the walk is easier than he thought it would be. He reaches the creekbank, stepping across where the silt is piled high in waves like squishy stepping stones. He doesn't get his socks wet, which is an accomplishment in his old boots. Even though he's patched them up with tape and glue, they still have a zillion tiny holes in the soles. He has to wear two pairs of socks just to keep every rock he walks over from making him wince.

Once Lance has safely crossed that obstacle, heart thudding, he realizes that the hardest step is still before him. The bank is steeper on this side than the other. It towers over his head, studded with roots and stones, but he knows by the loose look of the soil that those will be poor footholds.

He has to trek downstream about a quarter-mile before he finds a better approach, a slope he can almost walk up, leaning far over his knees; two small trees grow out of it, and he grips their trunks like they're rungs on a giant ladder and vaults himself upward as fast as he can.

He's almost there when his feet lose traction and he lands hard on his knees, skidding in the damp dirt, which is wet enough that he instantly feels it seep through the worn-thin knees of his jeans, cold on the skin beneath. Scrambling up, he grips the top of the ledge with hands like claws and drags himself the rest of the way with a desperate gasp.

He rolls over onto his back at the top. He's made it. The sky is blue overhead, and the air is misty and cool—a stark contrast to his body, which was heated by the climb. Sweat dries fast and tacky on his forehead. He can feel something rough against the back of his head, and, grimacing, he sits up to find that he now has a clod of mud and a few twigs in his hair. He tugs them loose as he gets to his feet and walks slowly toward the tree line. He's disoriented, but he thinks he should still be pretty close to the Chases' place.

And he is. He wriggles through the fence and finds himself in a narrow pasture that wraps around smaller, dirt corrals attached to a massive old barn. He's seen stone barns before—they're fairly common—but never one this big and meticulously preserved.

Similarly, lots of people keep horses, but he can tell instantly that there's a higher standard of care going on at the Chases' as he takes in the pens of sleek animals about fifty yards away. Set apart from them is a working round pen, where a horse the color of a sunbeam, pale gold with a silver mane and tail, trots in a circle. In the middle of the pen, pivoting to watch the animal's every move, is Danny's brother Robbie.

On the top rail of the fence, Johnny is perched, watching Robbie carefully. Lance can hear the low murmur of their voices but not their exact words. Wherever Danny is, he's out of sight.

Lance thought he'd emerge from the creekbed further from the Chases' home, but because of the curving orientation of the creek, he's actually nearer. He's also opposite the property from the driveway, where he'd planned to appear and claim his father had dropped him off at the road, like the school bus would have.

He realizes his mistake too late. Before he can escape back into the trees, the golden horse sees him. It shies violently, kicking out with its rear legs and veering so closely to Robbie that he has to step back.

Then, both Robbie and Johnny are looking to where the horse looked, and Lance is caught lurking in the trees with muddy knees. He curses himself, filled with the urge to cry or run and never come back. He'll just look down the next time Danny gets on the bus. He'd rather do that than try to explain what he's doing in this moment. Even if things had gone exactly according to his plans, though, would it really have worked? *I'm an idiot*, he thinks bitterly, beginning to backpedal.

Before Lance can turn and run, Johnny raises his arm in a friendly wave, jumps off the fence, and lopes toward him. Robbie climbs out of the round pen and follows Johnny at a regular walk, the horse's halter dangling from his hand.

Johnny reaches Lance first, smiling. "Hey," he says happily. At thirteen, he's already as tall as some of the high-school kids who ride the bus. And he's—well, there's no other word for him, really, but *pretty*, with his wavy, dun-colored hair and the bold lines of his face and his sun-kissed skin. Every girl who Lance has ever seen in Johnny's presence whispers and giggles as he passes by, and their voices get high when they talk to him. Today, like most days, he's wearing a denim jacket and his usual easy smile. His glance skims over Lance's knees and his smile turns wider—knowing. Lance freezes.

"You walked over, huh? That's smart. It's not even that far. I told Danny that you live so close, he should just walk to your house if he wants to see you so bad, but he didn't believe me. He thinks he knows everything, but he has no sense of direction. Absolutely none. You should see him play that 'pin the tail on the donkey' game. Or even worse, with a piñata." Suddenly, Johnny's arm is hooked around Lance's neck, and Lance doesn't even know how it happened. But he's falling into step beside Johnny, who's taking small, slow steps that don't fit his much taller, leggy body, and which make it obvious that he's guiding Lance along. "Glad you're here. Danny's been even more annoying than usual all morning. '*When will it be ten? What does it mean when he says 'around ten'? Do you think that means he could be earlier?*'" He rolls his eyes, grinning all the while, until Lance, helplessly, finds himself smiling, too.

That was actually a pretty good impression of Danny, Lance thinks, but obviously he'd never admit it. He likes Johnny, but Danny is his best and only friend. Lance will always be on Danny's side.

Robbie has made his way over to them and the sun is right behind his head, so Lance has to squint at him for a second before his face comes into focus. When it does, Lance's heart skips a beat.

His heart hasn't done that before. It's frightening, like something just snuck into his chest and closed a tight fist around his heart, seizing it briefly, and it has to hammer to catch back up to its usual tempo. The moment steals his breath.

Robbie is smiling at him the way Lance has seen him smile at his brothers. It's like his heart is in his eyes. Lance has imagined it before, inserting himself into the space occupied by Danny and Johnny when their brother looks at them, so many mornings at the end of the Chases' driveway. But the reality is something else. Something beyond imagining.

"Lance," Robbie says, his voice soft, like the wind in the lilac hedge. "I've heard so much about you. I'm glad to meet you." He passes the halter from his right hand to his left so he can hold it out to Lance for a handshake.

When his heart is done short-circuiting, Lance blinks and solemnly takes Robbie's extended hand. He's never shaken anyone's hand before, and his is so much smaller than Robbie's. He more or less clutches Robbie's warm, work-rough fingers, never reaching his palm. Lance blushes, but just as Johnny put him at ease about emerging dirt-stained from the trees like a wild animal, Robbie's smile ensures he's unselfconscious about their handclasp.

For once, the words that Lance has to say come out easily —perhaps the only time they have in the presence of a grown man. Maybe that's because he already thought Robbie was as different from his father as a man could be, but now he knows for sure. "I'm glad to meet you, too."

Today.

Lance wakes up face-down on the most comfortable mattress he's ever slept on in his life, which is saying something, considering that three weeks ago he was living in the penthouse of an upscale apartment complex in Chicago.

But he doesn't smell Niall's starched linens and furniture polish. He smells—

Robbie.

With a jolt, Lance wakes up fully, pushing himself up so that he's sitting on his heels, blinking into what looks at first like a wall of sunshine. After a second or two, he realizes it's actually the glass panels over the bed in the hayloft of the Chases' barn.

He tries to orient himself, still not entirely sure which of the events floating like wraiths in his recent memories are real. Apparently, in the 'real' column is the one where Robbie retrieved him from the Trace County courthouse and drove him through a snowy oblivion to the hayloft of the old barn.

Now that his face isn't planted firmly into the sheets, Robbie's particular, natural cologne isn't the only thing Lance smells. He can also smell coffee, and when he twists around to look for the source, he finds Robbie himself leaning against the countertop in the kitchen area directly behind him, sipping from a mug.

"Hey," he says. "You sleep okay?"

Lance wrinkles his nose. Sometimes, right after he wakes up, words are even harder to get out than usual, but after he swallows, he finds to his own surprise that he can speak easily. "Yeah. Great." He doesn't have to pretend otherwise to be polite; it's the truth. "This bed is amazing," he adds.

Robbie laughs. "Coffee?" When Lance nods, he turns toward a pot next to the sink, reaching into the cabinet underneath and straightening back up with an empty mug. "The only thing up here that I actually bought at a real furniture store was the bed. There are some things I'm just too old to get chintzy about, and a mattress is one of them."

"You're not old," Lance says automatically, and then adds thoughtfully, "but you seem old when you say things like 'chintzy.'"

Robbie turns back, his grin wide and making Lance's heart wobble. "Nice. Johnny would be impressed."

"How is Johnny?"

A complicated look passes over Robbie's face, like a cloud skating over the sun. "I think he's doing just fine. He's definitely doing whatever he wants to do. Can't be anything too unpleasant about that."

Lance thinks about what he knows of Johnny's life just from what's on the internet, and wonders. But then again, Lance's own internet presence hardly paints an accurate picture.

He chooses his words carefully. "You said you set up the hayloft for him?"

Robbie nods. "Yeah, got about this far with it before he decided to take off. That was two years ago. He's an actor now, kind of. Did you know that?"

Lance nods, concerned he's going to have to confess to the occasional, guilt-stricken internet search of all three Chases. But in Johnny's case, there'd been some news Lance hadn't had to go looking for.

Robbie nods with a strained smile. "I'm not sure, but... well, I hope he's happy, that's all. And that if he's not, he knows he just needs to pick up the phone." Robbie fills their mugs, then scoots one of them across the counter in Lance's direction.

Lance forces himself out of bed. He's wearing some of the old clothes of Johnny's that Robbie offered, and they're loose and comfortably soft. "Only coffee could get me out of this bed," he murmurs, hoping a stupid joke can lighten the melancholy mood that fell during the subject of Johnny. "Seriously, it's the best."

Robbie laughs again, this time sounding a little more self-conscious. "I tried a bunch of mattresses." He steps back and leans against the counter behind him. The kitchen is sort of galley-style, but without walls. It just has two parallel stretches of countertop over lower cabinets, but no uppers. The materials all look high quality, but Lance notices that there aren't drawer pulls or knobs on the cabinets, and where a dishwasher is probably meant to be, there's just a chasm.

"It's a work in progress," Robbie says, apparently noticing the direction of Lance's gaze. He said the same thing the day before, Lance remembers, when Lance first saw the hayloft.

"I think it looks amazing," Lance says honestly, perching on a stool and picking up the mug. He inhales the steam and groans. His eyes fall half-closed in dreamy anticipation, but he happens to see Robbie's face over the rim of his mug, how his lips part and his gaze zeroes in on Lance's mouth as he tips the mug against his lower lip to drink.

It's almost like—

No, Lance tells himself viciously. *You're not going to slip back into* that *alternate reality*.

But he's not imagining the look of utter fixation on Robbie's face. Lance knows that look. He knows it very well, and when he's seen it on men in the past, he hasn't hesitated to use it to his advantage. He knows exactly how he'd play this moment with someone he wanted. Well, someone he wanted who *wasn't* Robbie. But with a little, terrible thrill, he suddenly has the urge to play it that way for Robbie, too.

Just to see. Just in case.

"God, it's been a long time since I've had a cup of coffee." He lets his eyes drift fully closed, only half-exaggerating what he imagines as a semi-rapturous expression, and takes the first swallow. After the hot liquid slides down his throat, he lets out a moan of appreciation.

If he wasn't braced for it, carefully attuned to Robbie's response, the sudden crash might have made him topple his own coffee into his lap. But as it is, he only flinches, managing to set the mug down without spilling a drop as Robbie swears.

"Sorry. Fuck. Sorry," Robbie is muttering, grabbing a dish-cloth and bending down to mop at the floor. "It just...slipped out of my hand." He picks up the jagged pieces of ceramic that were previously his own coffee cup and mops up the spilled liquid. The back of his neck is bright red.

CHAPTER EIGHT

Robbie

So much for Robbie's resolve to control himself, despite his inappropriate feelings and thoughts. He blames his discomposure on having slept on the horrible couch, contorted to avoid both the hard places and the cats. He could hardly have run the air compressor for the air mattress with Lance sleeping only feet away, but in hindsight, he would have been better off on the floor with a pillow and blanket.

At least his dropped mug didn't shatter into a thousand pieces, making him worry about stepping on a stray shard of ceramic for weeks. Instead, there are just four or five big chunks, which he carefully gathers and wraps in an empty plastic bag. When that's in the trash, Robbie moves to finish cleaning up the floor so that he'll have a good excuse not to look at Lance.

But, mercifully, Lance doesn't seem bothered by Robbie's temporary loss of sanity. He's drifting over to the couch, where two of the triplicats are rowed up like something out of a modern art magazine, their paws close together and their tails curled around their bodies in a monochrome row.

"What are their names?" Lance asks.

Robbie stands up, coffee-saturated rag in his hand, and sees Lance presenting his knuckles to Two. Before Robbie can warn him, she flattens her ears and tries to sink her fangs into Lance's hand, but he jerks it back, laughing, just in time.

"Um," Robbie drops the rag in the sink and rubs the back of his head wryly. "Their names are Two and Three."

Lance gives him an unimpressed look that's ruined by the obvious fact that he's fighting a smile. "So, you haven't gotten any better at naming animals, then."

Robbie crosses his arms, but smiles. "I haven't gotten any better at anything." It comes out sounding a little more serious than he intended.

Lance's smile twists, almost wistful. "No, you're exactly the same," he murmurs, and looks down at the cats. Three, who has the two white front paws, has dropped to the floor and is skimming his sides against Lance's calves enticingly.

"Don't fall for any of that," Robbie advises. "He'll bite you, too."

Lance's chuckle makes Robbie feel like a time traveler, because although his voice has changed, deepened, in concert with the taller, bigger body he's developed since he was a half-wild teenager clambering across the creek every day, his laugh is still the same. A little high and a little breathy, like he's surprised that he has the urge but couldn't stop himself if he tried.

Uninhibited, is what it is; that's a word that Robbie once would have used for so many aspects of Lance, but now he isn't sure.

"Maybe I haven't changed, but *you* have," Robbie says, shooting for matter-of-fact and landing somewhere between simply fond and hopelessly fond, which earns him another quick smile before Lance goes back to watching the cats. Now, both Two and Three are at his feet, sniffing his shoes and circling. One's head briefly appears from beneath the couch, her favorite hiding place. Her mirror-like eyes flash before she vanishes again.

Lance frowns, as though struck by a sudden thought, and then turns to Robbie, accusing. "Wait, did you sleep on this awful couch?" He looks around the room, presumably searching for that deluxe air mattress Robbie mentioned the night before.

"Well, yeah," Robbie admits. "The air compressor for the air mattress is loud as hell, and I didn't want to wake you up." He rubs the small of his back with a grimace. "I'm regretting being so kind and thoughtful now, though, let me tell you."

Two leaps back onto the arm of the couch, cocks her head, and meows in a very pathetic, plaintive way. Robbie watches Lance's reason vanish in the face of her adorableness, the sucker. As he reaches out to pet her, Robbie, smirking to himself, reaches for another coffee cup.

"Ow!" Lance exclaims a second or two later, and Robbie looks over to find Lance disentangling himself not only from Two's teeth, but the extended claws of both her front paws.

"Yeah, she's the worst of the bunch," Robbie says. "You can't fall for her, no matter how cute she looks. Hey, hellcats, maybe it's time for you to go outside and terrorize the local wildlife instead, huh?"

Two and Three trot over happily as he walks toward the door, and they're followed a few moments later by One, who shoots out from beneath the couch and straight out the door after it's opened. Robbie hastily pushes the door closed behind them. Even in that short time, a rush of air has penetrated the cozy sanctuary of the hayloft, and when he turns back, Lance is hugging himself with one arm and shivering, taking another slug of coffee.

"Brr. But, mostly, it stays so warm in here. I wouldn't have thought that, with the rock walls."

Robbie nods toward the wood stove humming away

between the bed and the kitchen. "The power of a wood stove. I think I've burned ten or fifteen acres' worth of trees this winter."

Of course, all he's burned is about half the hedge from one young stand that was crowding a place along the river-bank where the horses often drink. But still, his supply is running low despite his having split almost twice as much as he'd expected to need. "It's been a long winter."

Lance laughs again—another one of those half-involuntary sounds that reveals so much emotion, it's like a glimpse into his heart. And what Robbie sees this time makes his own chest ache in sympathy.

"You can say that again." He turns, staring down at his coffee, his curls so much shorter than he kept them as a kid, but still long enough to make a messy tumble when he's just out of bed.

Admiring Lance's bedhead, which he acquired in *Robbie*'s bed, isn't doing anything helpful for Robbie's intrusive thoughts. He sternly reminds his subconscious who Lance is to his family, how damaging his past feelings for Robbie were, that those feelings are *in the past*, and that even if they could be resurrected now—that is *not* the way to 'take care' of him.

And he's promised Danny, like he's promised himself, that he'll take care of Lance.

"You hungry? I've got cereal and bread and—" He checks the mini fridge. "Yep, eggs," he adds, feeling a little triumphant, and then tips back the lid on the foam carton and frowns. "Oh. Not 'eggs,' plural. 'Egg,' singular." He sighs. He'd been planning to stock up yesterday, before the weather came in, but of course his trip into Dell turned into a rescue rather than a grocery run.

Lance laughs again, but he doesn't sound remotely sad this time. Robbie decides he's content with the pathetic state of his pantry, if it makes Lance laugh.

"Toast is okay," Lance says, sliding back onto the barstool he left a minute before and draining his cup. Robbie reaches out with the carafe and refills it, only meeting Lance's gaze for the briefest moment, and only because not to do so would feel unnatural. Yet, he feels like he's stolen something by catching sight of Lance's face, illuminated to an unearthly silver pallor by the winter sunlight, like a marble statue breathed to fragile life, his dark chestnut curls softly haloed.

Robbie's hands are unsteady as he sets out the toaster and unwinds the end of the plastic sleeve holding the bread. It's not Wonder, but it's some kind of small-grocery-store equivalent, and he shoots Lance an apologetic glance as he feeds two slices into the toaster. "Nothing fancy."

Lance puts his elbows on the edge of the counter and props his chin in his hands. "I don't need anything fancy."

"You sure?" Robbie keeps his tone as light as he can. "I'm pretty sure the clothes I threw in the laundry this morning are dry-clean-only. They're probably screaming in French about the indignity of being machine-washed."

He expected Lance to laugh, or to be annoyed, but realizes his mistake at once. Maybe his brothers roll their eyes or raise their hackles when he pries, but if Lance has a temper, Robbie has never seen it. This seems to be as true in the man as it was in the boy. Lance's cheeks flush, but he looks quietly troubled instead of defensive, spinning his cup in a slow circle that makes its contents rise up toward the lip like a small, dark whirlpool and causes the faint steam to curl.

"I do like fancy things," he admits at last, his voice hesitant. He shoots a look up at Robbie. Lance's eyes are wide and soft beneath his eyelashes—showing that emotional fearlessness that Robbie remembers, which always touched him. Lance was mistreated throughout his entire childhood, and yet was so eager to go around handing his heart to people. It always made Robbie crazy with the urge to protect him, all too aware of how easily someone could take advantage.

He feels that protective urge now, too. It doesn't matter that Lance is grown up and presumably better-equipped to protect himself than when he was only a slip of a thing, running the trails with Danny. And now, there's another element to the old feeling that's making Robbie's pulse speed up. It's the idea of Lance easing his long limbs into fancy clothes, the brush of fine fabric against his fair skin, perfumed by expensive cologne—

The toast pops up, yanking Robbie out of his brief visit to unreality. The bread is supposedly whole wheat, but from what Robbie can tell, all that means is that the thin slices are an unappealing shade of light brown instead of white. Robbie wordlessly puts the toasted slices on a plate and slathers them with butter. Then, he reaches into the cabinet where the little-used spices and seasonings are gathering dust. He isn't sure he'll have what he needs, but whistles softly in triumph when he finds cinnamon, the seal still on the bottle. Most of the miniature spice rack is in the same dusty condition. It was Megan's house-warming gift to Johnny when the loft got to the point that it was habitable and he relocated from the house.

"What are you...?" Lance starts to ask.

"I don't have any of that cereal you used to eat by the box that was all dye and sugar," Robbie says, flashing him a grin, "but I have something that might be even better." Robbie fishes two paper sugar packets from a drawer that also contains a handful of ketchup and mustard packets, four sets of plastic silverware, and three fortune cookies. Robbie tears open the sugars, pours them carefully out on a saucer, and then adds a dash of cinnamon and stirs. Lance has gone quiet. Robbie's hands are starting to tremble again when the mixture is ready to be spooned up and sprinkled carefully over each piece of buttered toast.

He slides the plate toward Lance before looking up. As he meets Lance's eye, Robbie realizes he's adopted Lance's ridiculous and inadvisable behavior—that he's opened his chest and exposed his heart in this small gesture, this callback to the past; if Lance doesn't remember, it will hurt.

But when he glances up, Lance is smiling back, with his whole heart out, too.

Robbie forgets all of the internal speeches he's given himself over the past twelve hours and loses himself for a while in the bright warmth of that smile.

"You remembered," Lance says happily, breaking eye contact first so he can drag the plate closer and snag a slice. His enormous bite consumes about half of the first piece, so Robbie, smiling to himself, turns to reload the toaster.

"Yeah," he says so quietly that it's possible Lance can't hear over his enthusiastic chewing. "I remember everything."

He knows he should press Lance a little more. Ask the questions that have gotten even harder to ignore since yesterday. But, he doesn't want to disrupt this moment, or that smile. So, he lets the peaceful, companionable quiet fall and spreads a careful layer of cinnamon and sugar over the second serving of toast after it pops out. When he scoots it in front of Lance, Robbie sees that, over Lance's shoulder and through the big window by the sleeping area, the snow is falling again.

———

An hour later, Robbie is pulling on his coveralls and boots when he catches Lance watching him wistfully. He's confused for a moment, but then he understands. It's like the cinnamon toast all over again, convincing him one step at a time that there isn't that much difference between this new Lance and his old Lance—not as much as there appeared to be yesterday, anyway.

"I've got a few spare coveralls and coats. And there's a new pair of boots Johnny didn't get around to wearing." He nods toward a storage chest on the other side of the door; there are two plastic tubs set on top of it, both full of stuff he hasn't gotten around to unpacking yet. He hasn't needed any winter clothes except his own, and judging by how long Johnny's been gone, maybe he won't be unpacking them at all.

Lance perks up. "Yeah? It might be nice to go for a walk. Maybe out to the wooden bridge. If that's okay?"

Robbie smiles reassuringly. "I wouldn't have offered if it wasn't okay." He hesitates with his arms halfway into his coat and catches Lance's eye again, more seriously. "Anything you need around here, it's yours. Anywhere you want to be, go there. That hasn't changed, okay?"

Lance hesitates for a moment, then nods slowly.

When Robbie gets out the door, he feels both eager and loath to leave the warm bubble in the hayloft. Even after just one night, the place is permeated with *Lance*. Robbie doesn't know how to describe the change, exactly, except that the whole space feels warm, in a way that has nothing to do with the temperature.

These thoughts lead Robbie into a cycle of waxing poetic and then berating himself for being an idiot at best and a predator at worst, which leads in turn to a lot of muttering, even though Megan has told him that the more he talks to himself, the more she worries about the side effects of social isolation.

He checks the horse pen first. They're in a semicircle at the round bale, though only Poco looks content; the others are eating as fast as possible while snow collects down the broad lines of their shoulders, backs, and hips. Poco jerks his head up at the sight of Robbie, looking hopeful, but when Robbie only checks the water tank and doesn't move near the gate, he goes back to his hay without coming over.

Robbie probably does spend too much time alone. That has to be part of the reason why he's reacting so powerfully to Lance's pretty face. Not to mention his pretty...everything else. But it's not that Robbie *wants* to be all alone out here, as he told Megan plenty of times. Who's he going to make an effort to go and see? The few of his old friends from high school who still live around here? They never had much in common except that they were born in the same place. It was no hardship to stop spending time with them in favor of keeping the ranch going and taking care of the boys. The boys were company enough.

Then the boys left him, one by one.

As Robbie treks over to check on his neighbor's runaway cows, he's so lost in his thoughts that he stares at the dark spot in the snow inside their pen for a solid second before he registers what it is. When he does, he breaks into a run, leaps over the board fence, and skids to the ground on his knees next to the unmoving shape, hoping he's not already too late.

CHAPTER NINE

Lance

L ance feels a familiar satisfaction at getting bundled up in the kind of clothing that can conquer the weather. His earliest memories of winter in the little house with his father are of loneliness and cold. After he and Danny became friends, though, Lance quickly learned to enjoy the snow and ice. The Chases offered him clothes year round, but it was in winter when he was hard-pressed to say yes. Robbie always claimed they had plenty of extra coats and boots and snow pants that Johnny had outgrown. Lance pretended not to notice that most of these items had a suspicious lack of wear, and once Lance even found a tag in the inseam of a pair of fleece-lined jeans.

Armored with all of the appropriate gear, he and Danny were able to spend hours out in the woods during even the coldest months, tunneling in snow drifts, building snowmen and towers and forts, and packing snowballs and throwing them at each other with remarkably terrible aim.

Maybe it's those memories that lead Lance into the trees by the creek, instead of up the driveway toward the road and the bridge.

When he went to live with his aunt right after his sixteenth birthday, he had to get used to living in a town, on a cultivated street where there wasn't a flower blooming that someone hadn't planted, or a tree that wasn't ringed in mulch. He missed the wildness of Trace County fiercely at first, though it was hard to separate that feeling from all of the other grief. Lance missed *home* in all the meanings of the word—the creek sound, a steady background music he could hear whenever he paused and really listened; Danny's laugh; the smell of horses lingering on the jackets Robbie and Johnny left on pegs by the door on the porch; the rumble of tires churning gravel when a vehicle was still miles off; the way the creekbanks clotted with decaying leaves and pine needles to form a fragrant, slick hazard; Robbie's face and the warmth in his eyes when he smiled at Lance.

Lance has reached the creekbank before he realizes it's even in sight. It's masked by ice and snow. He presses his palm against the rough bark of a tree that's dry-brushed with dark green lichen. He knows the water is still moving invisibly and silently under the shell of ice. He knows it like he knows his own heart is beating without checking his pulse.

Close to the creek's edge, he can see a jagged-edged oval of darker, thinner ice where an animal must have broken through to drink and that crusted over again but hasn't frozen solid yet. He studies the bank for clues and sees one clear, cloven hoofprint, but it's too large to be that of a deer. With a frown, he squints up and down the stretch of the creek, just in case someone's loose cow is still close by. He remembers the cattle in the road yesterday when they were driving in. The memory is surreal, like that moment should have been longer ago. He feels like he slept a hundred years last night, and awoke as someone else. Not someone new, though. An old self...one he left here in the now-burned farmhouse on the night he ran off and never came back.

He walks along the icy edge of the creek, frozen mud crunching under his loaned boots. Johnny has big fucking feet, he's learned, and he wishes he'd put on two pairs of socks to keep his feet from shifting so much inside the boots' stiff, wool lining. He's already courting blisters.

It's not the first time he's wondered what Johnny's whirl-wind tours of Las Vegas, New York City, and Los Angeles mean for Robbie, especially with Danny gone off to school. It's been hard for Lance to picture Robbie alone.

Before yesterday, he'd hoped—or feared, it was hard to say which—that at least Robbie had still had Megan. And that maybe with the boys fully raised and out of the house, he'd really given Megan a chance, the way he so obviously hadn't in all their prior years together.

Robbie claimed that he and Megan had really ended things. That's hard for Lance to imagine. Megan was the villain in all of Lance's fantasies, which was ridiculous because she was—and probably still is—one of the kindest people alive. And she's beautiful, patient, and practical. If Lance had been asked to invent a woman who was worthy of Robbie, Megan would have come closer than anyone he could have made up.

But she isn't here. And Lance has a vivid memory of the way that Robbie was looking at him in the kitchen that morning, and the coffee mug tumbling out of his hand.

Lance hadn't imagined Robbie's stare in those moments. And if it meant what he would have assumed it did, if the man had been anyone but Robbie...well, if Lance's suspicions are correct, then, incredibly, he doesn't know how to feel. His sixteen-year-old self would have flung himself at Robbie at the merest glimmer of interest, overjoyed.

Now, though—well, it's been a long time since he was surrounded every day by Chases, never given the chance to doubt he was loved. Back then, if he'd had to choose between

Robbie loving Lance like he loved Johnny and Danny, or *wanting* him, he would have chosen *wanting*. But since then, he's had a lot of opportunity to learn just how rare and important love is, and he's no longer sure he could choose so easily.

Winter was always the only season when he and Danny could walk the creekbank without risking losing a shoe in the silty mud. In warm months, they used to bait danger by wading down the center of the creek, where the regular depth was to their waists, but the rocky bottom occasionally fell out beneath them and they'd dunk themselves to their chins, or sometimes go all the way under.

He likes walking here along the bank, the frozen mud not sucking him down, so that his steps are easy. *Walking on water*, he thinks with a smile. The snow is a white blanket over the creek's ice. He takes a sideways step and shifts his weight onto the foot that's resting on the ice. When the ice holds, Lance walks on across its center, the thick, powdery snow giving him traction. It's like the forest paved the creek for him, offering a path he can walk alone to the end of the world —or, more accurately, to the creek's mouth, where it meets the river in a broad triangle of shallow tributaries.

Lance remembers winters past when they used to skate the creek. Though Lance wasn't much of a skater, mostly wobbling and straining not to fall, ending the day with bruises and aching calves, he liked it when Robbie and Johnny each took one of his hands and towed him. They'd pick up so much speed that the creekbanks became a blur in the corners of his eyes; only their faces were in focus, taking turns glancing over their shoulders to grin at his expression. By the time they wound the entire distance from the yard to the river, his face would be streaked with tears from the cold air and his chest would ache from breathless laughter.

He walks until he can't feel his feet. Even good winter gear can only keep you warm for so long; when the reservoir of body heat is spent, it's best to get back to somewhere warm. That lesson is too deeply ingrained for Lance to forget it, so he's turning back almost without deciding to when he hears an ominous crack. The ice is splitting under his feet.

He scrambles to the bank, but in his haste, he goes to the wrong one. He looks up and instantly recognizes the specific crook in the trunk of one of the big trees.

He knows exactly where he is.

If he leans into the climb and walks up the bank, he'll emerge into the little weedy clearing with the small, square house.

Lance trembles not from the cold, but from an urge he can't name. It's like the indecision in his heart over Robbie and the suggestion of interest he saw in the kitchen. Does he want to go toward it, or veer away?

His head doesn't have an answer, but apparently his feet do, because suddenly he's climbing up the bank.

It's easier than he remembers. He's bigger and stronger, after all, than he was at sixteen. It just takes six long, careful steps, like lunges on an incline, and he's up. The burn in his thighs is faint, almost pleasant.

The tree line is more dense than he remembers. The natural consequence of lack of maintenance, he supposes; opportunistic evergreens and young oak trees have created a waist-high underbrush that he has to paw through, and it snags in the coveralls and coat he's wearing, distracting him so that he doesn't get his first look at the house until he's already a dozen feet from the tree line.

Lance had vaguely assumed that the empty house would be moldering, like the old farmsteads in various stages of disintegration on the Chases' property. The places that had been in half-decent shape had been frequent playgrounds for him and Danny. In hindsight, they'd been lucky never to break their legs in a cellar cavity camouflaged with brush, or trod on a rusty nail as they'd climbed through various newer ruins.

But the house isn't derelict. Or, at least, it's not in much worse shape than in all of the years Lance lived there. Also, the house isn't empty. There's a path through the otherwise unmown yard to the door, obvious even beneath the snow. And there's an unmistakable light in the small square windows that stare at Lance like eyes, just as they always used to when he skulked home reluctantly after a day or days of respite with Danny and his brothers.

The last thing he notices is the strange, skeletal shape of a snow-draped bike with training wheels before he unsticks his feet and retraces his steps, fast. Around here, people are likely to point a gun at a stranger who comes out of the trees, and they're very likely to shoot rather than ask questions.

Lance does have questions, though. Who's living there? How did he not know? He curses his father, imagining some strange under-the-table deal, though that seems absurd under the circumstances. He'd seen the man himself, five or ten minutes before his arrest. He was hardly in a position to be acting as a landlord.

Maybe they're squatters? But then, how did they get the utilities on?

Maybe the light was just a trick of the eye.

For some reason, it's that bike and training wheels that Lance can't get out of his uneasy mind. He rushes across the ice, which doesn't show signs of splitting this time, but he still feels like the earth could drop out from beneath him at any second even when he's safely on the other side. He breaks into a run, like a spooked horse fleeing blindly to the last place it felt safe. He doesn't break stride until he's crossed the Chases' meadow and rushed up the deck stairs to the hayloft, where he leans against the hayloft door.

There, he stops and thinks, breathing hard. He doesn't

want Robbie to remember how irrational Lance can be, so he needs to act normal. He recognizes that his reaction to finding out someone lives in his father's house, someone he didn't know about, is out of proportion. He shouldn't care. It's barely even his problem. What difference does it make if it's empty and rotting or if someone's living there?

Someone with a kid the right age for that bike.

He goes inside, hurrying out of his borrowed coat. He doesn't see Robbie, but hears water running in the bathroom. He frowns when he finds the bathroom door ajar. Would Robbie be *showering* with the door open?

All of the confusing, mixed emotions Lance has been avoiding with respect to Robbie come crashing back down. Just like when he went up the creekbank toward his old house before he consciously decided to move, he finds himself stepping out of his coveralls, kicking off his boots, and walking toward the bathroom, through the haze of light and steam emanating from inside.

When he steps into the doorway, what he sees is somehow the last thing he expected.

"Is that a *calf?*"

CHAPTER TEN

Robbie

Twenty-three years ago.

"Here, son," says his father, reaching out with a hand that's scraped raw on the knuckles. His father, for some reason, never wears gloves, but he always makes Robbie put them on. *You need to get in the habit*, he'll say. He's just been leaning into the back of the pickup truck, outwardly calm but with a grim expression. There's a steer with his head stuck in the pipe-post fence.

Robbie takes the wire-cutters and then trots after his father, who's carried by much longer legs at a brisk walk. The center and top bars of the fence around the feed pen are pipe, but it also has three rows of sucker rod, including the two closest to the ground. The sucker rod is just flexible enough that the steer, trying to reach for the green grass on the other side of the fence, could worm his head through like someone cramming their fist into a jar. Now he's stuck tight, wailing, tail lashing back and forth.

The whole scene makes Robbie's heart pound, but his dad is matter-of-fact as he bends down. The steer rolls its wide eyes toward them, fighting hard for another second. Then, he abruptly goes limp. Another long, low bawl escapes his muzzle, where a thin foam of saliva has built on the fine hairs around his lips. Then, he's silent as well as still.

Robbie's father swears, grasping one piece of the sucker rod in each hand. He pushes and pulls at the same time, using so much of his strength that his shoulders tremble. He widens the gap in the rebar rungs enough that they aren't biting into the steer's neck quite so hard, and the steer's eyes refocus, but still he doesn't move.

Swearing again, Robbie's dad gives the steer's snout a hard nudge with his left knee, but at his angle and with so much of his effort dedicated to bowing the rebar, it doesn't have any force. The steer doesn't even seem to notice as his eyes drift closed again.

"Pop him with the handle of those wire cutters," he tells Robbie, his voice short with effort.

Robbie gives him a wild, pleading look.

"Do it," his dad insists, his voice rising. "Hard as you can. Now!" He's never terse with Robbie, but he almost shouts the last word through his gritted teeth.

Robbie's hand spasms, and then he pulls his arm back before he can think about it. He closes his eyes when the rubber-covered metal of the handles strike the steer's snout with a crack.

The steer wakes up completely at that, letting out the loudest and most blood-curdling bawl yet. He wrenches himself backward, forehooves scrabbling in the dirt. Robbie tumbles backward and lands on his butt in the grass, staring. For a moment, Robbie thinks the steer still won't get free. Then, the panicked animal happens to turn his head to just the right angle, and he pops loose. He staggers a short distance, shakes his head, bawls again, and turns and high-tails it away from the fence. Robbie's dad lets go of the sucker rod and slides to the ground beside Robbie, breathing hard.

He fixes a steady look on Robbie, then reaches out and squeezes his knee. "You did good, son."

Robbie shakes his head and rubs a wrist under his eyes. His glove is slick leather, though; it doesn't absorb anything—just moves the wetness around on his cheeks. "D'you think I hurt him?"

His dad snorts. "Of course, you did. But nothing that won't fade. And if you hadn't, he would have just given up and died on us right there. I've seen it happen before." He rests his forearms on his bent knees. "Look at me, kiddo."

Robbie doesn't want to, but he does, his lower lip snagged between his teeth so it won't wobble.

"Don't beat yourself up. He'll be just fine now."

"It's not that," Robbie says, letting out a ragged breath. He tucks his chin again because it's easier to keep from crying when he isn't looking at his dad, even though there's only kindness in his eyes. Somehow, that makes it harder. "I just wish I was...tougher, you know? Like you."

For a long time, his dad doesn't say anything, but Robbie is used to these stretches of quiet with him. He chances a glance, and when he sees that his dad is looking out into the distance and not at Robbie, he lets his gaze linger on the side of his familiar, beloved face.

There's a dash of silver in the dark blond stubble on his jaw where he has a scar. Robbie was there when he got it, four years ago. The colt he'd been riding had spooked, then somersaulted down the creekbed. Robbie had been riding along just feet away when it had happened. Those slow-motion seconds are burned into Robbie's memory, the ultimate proof that his dad is superhuman. He'd stayed in the saddle the whole time, defying force and gravity alike, even as the colt had succumbed and struck the muddy water. And when the colt staggered back to his feet, trembling and dripping with creek water, his father had simply leaned over his neck and stroked him with a hand as steady as when he poured coffee at the breakfast table. Even with blood pouring from his face in three places, his first concern had been his frightened horse.

"There's nothing wrong with gentleness," he says at last. He squeezes Robbie's knee again, smiling with unmistakable pride. "You shouldn't compromise with your heart, son. Not if you can help it."

It's a conversation that Robbie will think back on again and again. One of those moments in youth that strikes your heart in ways you're not yet ready to grasp, so your mind holds onto the memory for you, until the day comes when you're ready to learn the lesson it was waiting to teach you.

Today.

Lance's voice from the bathroom doorway startles Robbie so much that he nearly loses his grip on the slippery calf, but he keeps her positioned after a moment of unsteadiness.

Robbie is kneeling on the floor with his sleeves rolled up to his elbows, his coat discarded on the floor. The bathtub is half-full of steaming water, and Robbie is carefully holding the calf with both hands so that her head stays above water.

He looks over his shoulder with a smile that's probably more like a grimace.

"I remember my dad doing this, but I guess I didn't totally think it through before I started. Can you reach by me and turn off the water? I need both hands to keep a hold of her."

Even immersed in the warm water, the calf is almost totally listless. From what Robbie can tell, the cow delivered her onto the ice and was then unable to do much more than halfheartedly lick her clean while her wet coat fused to the frozen ground. Calves being born on cold ground is a common hazard of winter calving, but if owners have any sense, they keep any cow that might be close to the end of a pregnancy near a good source of shelter and check on her often.

Ed, obviously, has no sense.

That being said, if a cow chooses the wrong spot to drop a calf, even an attentive rancher can lose a newborn. Robbie has a few memories of tiny calves being bundled up next to the fireplace in the old house while his father kept watch from the sofa, a blanket in his lap and a book in his hand. He'd stay up late into the night after everyone else was in bed, occasionally carting the calf out to drink from its mother, or hydrating powdered milk in the kitchen sink and pouring the concoction into the calf with a tube.

Those memories are the closest thing Robbie has to training when it comes to something like this. They've hardly prepared him to save a calf himself.

Lance reaches past him and turns the hot water tap to the right, leaving just a trickle of cold that feels like ice where it hits Robbie's steam-warmed elbow. Lance grasps the other tap, standing at Robbie's back and leaning over him. His body is long and hard, and might as well be spun from lightning, the way Robbie feels a jolt of heat under his skin everywhere they brush against each other.

Luckily, he's too distracted by the slippery throat in his hands and the smell of wet fur for the passing touch to have its full effect, and then Lance is stepping away and Robbie can think straight again. His heart only skipped a few beats.

"She was just born, out in the snow," Robbie explains, looking down at the little slits of the calf's eyes. Her eyes and the small puffs of air coming out of her nose are the only signs of life. "This is the fastest way to warm her up."

Lance comes around on his other side, not close enough to touch from there, and sits on the edge of the tub, one long leg folded under him.

"She's so cute," he says quietly. "Is she going to be okay?"

"I don't know," Robbie admits.

"Could we take her to a vet?"

"Maybe. My dad would say I should see if the cow will let me milk her so we can try to get something in her belly. Then to just keep her warm, and see."

Lance's eyes are wide and bright, like the fragile life in Robbie's hands is important to him—even though, just minutes ago, he didn't know she existed. Robbie rests his chin on his shoulder, head craned to look up at Lance, and smiles.

"You always had a soft heart," he says quietly. Lance's lips are winter-bitten to red, and his face is flushed from coming in out of the cold. He's unspeakably lovely, especially when he gives Robbie a shy smile and then looks down, his eyelashes dark little veils over his eyes.

"So did you."

"Yeah," Robbie agrees, though it's been a long time since anyone seemed to notice—it shouldn't surprise him that Lance has.

There's not much noise except the soft stirring of the water in the tub, the occasional slow drip from the faucet, and, in the quiet, the audible little puffs of breath coming from the calf. Robbie adjusts the position of his hands, slowly and carefully, just to be sure he's not obstructing her airway.

"I didn't realize you knew about cattle," Lance says.

"I don't, really. Just what I learned from following my dad around."

"He ran cattle out here?"

"Yes. He loved cattle ranching in a way I couldn't really understand." Robbie shifts his body, feeling little bursts of pain from his folded knees, along with tingles in the soles of his feet from kneeling too long on the hard floor. He adjusts as much as he can without moving the calf. Her skin finally feels like it's warmed to a neutral temperature, but the water is still much warmer than she is. "I wasn't cut out for it."

"I can't imagine you as anything except a horse trainer," Lance says comfortably, obviously not realizing how that offhand comment makes Robbie's gut wrench.

"I'm a man of very few skills," he says lightly, before changing the subject. "Did you have a good walk?"

"I...went across the creek," Lance murmurs, like he's confessing a sin. "Had you heard that someone was living there? In my dad's place?"

Robbie shakes his head. "No. It's been empty, as far as I know. You saw someone over there?"

Lance hesitates, then shrugs. "I didn't see any people. But there were lights on inside. Or, I thought I saw lights, but I don't really see how it's possible." He takes a breath. "You know about my father?"

"That he's in the care home? Yes."

Lance nods shallowly. "Yeah. And I don't think he'd agree to anyone living out there for free. And getting something set up with a renter? I don't think he could have done that, either." Lance shrugs, leaning in to pet the calf, his arm almost brushing Robbie's. His expression is distant. "If someone's there, I don't think he knows about them."

Robbie doesn't know the details about Lance's father—not whether he's in the care home due to ailments of the mind, body, or both. Lance doesn't say more. Without the distraction of talking, Robbie's not sure how much more time he can spend with his hands more or less tied while Lance leans close to him, smelling like the cedar trees he walked through by the creek, and Robbie's own shampoo, and beneath that, a sharp note of masculine sweat.

"Hand me that towel," Robbie says, trying to corral his

panic. "We'll get her as dry as we can and set her in front of the fire. Then I'll go see if her mama is feeling agreeable and will let me take a little milk off of her."

Robbie hoists the calf up as the last of the water forms a dirty swirl in the drain, and Lance helps him bundle her in towels. Then Robbie carries her back into the main room. She doesn't weigh much; maybe fifty or sixty pounds. But that's about right for a new calf, and she feels sturdy, her list-lessness aside. He's trying not to set himself up for disap-pointment by thinking she'll live, but he can't help hoping.

Now that she's clean, she's oddly white. Robbie assumes her mother was some kind of Angus cross, but the calf doesn't look like an Angus or any of the other breeds most common in their area. Her creamy coat has a spray of black speckles on her shoulders and hips, and there's a roundness to her ears that's unusual to him.

"She's so still," Lance murmurs worriedly, hovering over Robbie's shoulder while he arranges the calf by the wood stove and then covers her in a second towel.

"Yeah. But that's pretty normal for cattle when they've had a shock." Robbie makes the mistake of looking up and finds their bodies too close again. Clearing his throat, he pushes himself to his feet, backing away. "I better go give milking the cow a try."

CHAPTER ELEVEN

Lance

Ten years ago.

It's spring, and the school year is spiraling fast toward summer, catching Lance up in the whirlwind delight of knowing that long, empty months with no homework are just ahead. He hated summertime before Danny and the Chases came into his life, but now it's his favorite time of year. The long days melt into cool, clear nights, and some kind of magic spell keeps his father from noticing when Lance doesn't come home for days.

But this summer is going to be new in other ways, too, because Lance is changing. Since spring, he's abruptly grown five inches without gaining a pound, leaving him thinner than ever. He can basically wrap the old belt of Johnny's twice around his waist, and has to keep it cinched tight or the jeans that are long enough to cover his ankles won't stay up.

And that's not all. He's got three dark hairs on his chest, and his voice has gotten rough and scratchy.

And that's not all, either. He's been having a certain kind of dream.

Lance isn't totally naive. He knows this sudden rebellion of his mind and body, this new awareness of his own skin and total inability to control his random and inconvenient erections, is all normal. He's maybe a hair ahead of schedule, but there are boys his age who are further down this path. Of course, there are also boys his age who aren't on the path at all—who may not even have the path in sight—like Danny, who's now the shortest boy in their grade and still has the narrow chin and big, glaring eyes of the eight-year-old who first sat next to Lance on the bus almost five years before.

What's *not* normal, Lance also knows, is that the main trigger for all of Lance's new, riotous hormones seems to be his best friend's much older brother.

In addition to finding himself staring and blushing around Robbie all the time, he also has to be careful that he doesn't smell Robbie's jacket when he walks past the coat hooks on the porch, or let their hands touch when Robbie hands him a glass of water at dinner. Or look at the vee in the collar of Robbie's shirt where a few dark hairs curl. *Or, or, or*. If he does any of the things on that growing list, he has to clamp his hands over his lap and get out of sight as fast as possible.

And at night, he feels the worst kind of shame when he grinds against the blankets of his bed, face pressed into his arm and pillow, praying his father won't hear him—and the only thing that can push him past the horrible pressure and into a half-painful release is the thought of Robbie. Not even Robbie's nakedness, which he doesn't know how to imagine, or even his touch or kiss, which would be incomprehensible. Just his smell and his laugh and his outline, and even the way he walks. All of the details that Lance has been storing up for years, as though he's accidentally calibrated himself to only want Robbie in this, the most hopeless of ways.

On the third day of summer, grade cards come in the mail. Parents can check them on the computer, too, but Lance's father doesn't have a computer, and the beginning and end of his effort around Lance's education is to grudgingly enroll him in school every summer, despite the inconvenience of going by the school at the appointed time.

He's either forgotten Lance gets grades or he doesn't care, and the latter is much more likely than the former. Whatever the reason, Lance tucks his grade card into his back pocket and runs for the creek without bothering to tell his father it came.

The Chases fish during summer afternoons when it's too hot for Robbie and Johnny to work the horses. Fishing with them is one of Lance's favorite things—especially when it comes to riding in the back of the truck, bumping slowly over the pasture grass, until they reach the shaded banks of one of the ponds, or walking up the creek to one of the quiet pools that feed it.

Today, though, they're going to the reservoir, and Johnny and Danny even talked Robbie into bringing the rowboat. When they get there, Robbie starts casting into the shaded water near the dock by the boat launch, and Lance casually offers to stay with him while Johnny and Danny take out the boat.

That's how he finds himself sitting on the rocky shore next to Robbie, his shoes and socks off and his jeans rolled up, and his feet stretched into the cool water. For some reason, all he can think about is how badly he wants to show Robbie his grades.

He got straight A's, which is even better than Danny, who argues too much in Phys-Ed and can't make better than a B-minus.

Lance is trying to think of a way to bring up his grade card when Robbie turns with a smile and asks, "Hey, did your grades come? We got the boys' this morning."

Lance nods and sticks his fishing pole between his knees,

already reaching into his pocket. The folded paper is kind of damp from sitting on the bank, but not too bad. Robbie takes it, still smiling, and then sets down his own pole, resting a foot on it to keep it from going anywhere as he unfolds the paper with care.

As Robbie studies the page, Lance can't look away. He has the strangest urge to look over Robbie's shoulder, like maybe he read the card wrong the first time. Maybe there's something he missed, and actually it's a *bad* report card, or—

Robbie slides his arm around Lance's shoulders and gives him a little shake. The sight of his grin is like stepping out of the shade and into broad daylight. "Aw, Lance. This is amazing, buddy. I'm really proud of you."

Lance's heart seems to actually stop. His breath hitches so hard, he makes a little gasping sound. Robbie's smile fades, eyes concerned. Then, searching Lance's face, he squeezes his shoulder gently. "You know that, right?" he asks softly. "You know I'm really proud of you?"

All Lance knows is the fury of his blush—it burns, like that time he got too close to the campfire and singed his eyebrows. He shakes his head mutely, throat dry and tight.

Robbie takes a deep breath, scooting closer and holding Lance against his side. Then, he puts his face down against Lance's head. A kiss, Lance realizes faintly, lost somewhere in the tumble of his curls.

"Well, I am proud of you. And I love you, okay, kid? If you didn't know that already, too."

And that's how they sit, fishing poles more or less forgotten, Lance paralyzed by how much he wants it never to end— Robbie's arm around him, Robbie's hand cupping his shoulder, Robbie's chest against Lance's cheek. But when Johnny and Danny bring the boat back around close enough that Lance can hear them bickering playfully with each other,

Robbie gives his shoulder a last squeeze, unwinds his arm, and reaches for his pole.

"Mind if I keep this?" He tucks the paper, refolded now, into the breast pocket of his pearl snap shirt and winks. "I want it for the fridge."

All Lance can do is nod. And then, to complete the miracle of the afternoon, there's a jerk on his line. He's hooked a fish.

Now.

Lance sits cross-legged on the floor, looking at the calf. She's about the size of a small Labrador, and her big, liquid brown eyes are framed by ridiculously long, inky-black eyelashes that curl. Her nose is a wrinkled black triangle, her ears big and silky. He's starting to understand why people use calves as a metaphor for cuteness. He's never seen anything more precious than her face. The thought that she might die overwhelms him.

She seems to be watching him back, aware of his attention, although she's motionless except for the occasional sweep of her eyelashes when she blinks. He wonders if this is normal newborn animal behavior for creatures that evolved as prey. If she were curled in the grass while her mother left her to graze, a predator like him could brush past, and if she didn't move, he might never know she was there. It's a comfort to think that her stillness doesn't necessarily mean she's sick.

Lance is almost too hot while sitting this close to the wood stove, which makes him worry about the calf. But when he runs his hands all the way down her body over the towel, he can tell her body is still too cool.

From where he sits, it's easy to stare out the big window

over the bed. The snow makes the day outside look bright even through the clouds. It's like the Earth has the same muted glow from above and below, and the trees are low-burning candles.

He catches sight of the folder that Tim gave him, sitting on top of the dresser in the sleeping area. His stomach instantly knots at the reminder of that stack of documents and the hearing date on the citation, which says he needs to be at the courthouse on Wednesday at one o'clock. How is he supposed to travel in this weather back to town for his hearing? He guesses he'll have to ask Robbie to drive him, and that might also mean the end of this strange dance they've been engaged in, where they pretend Lance is just here for a visit and don't ask one another any difficult questions.

Before Lance can stew any longer, the door opens and Robbie comes in, stomping the snow off his boots. The floorboards around the doorway really need to be tiled over, or at least sealed, Lance thinks absently while he watches Robbie emerge from the cocoon of coat and coveralls. He's holding an old metal coffee can protectively against his chest, like it's full of gold.

"Any luck?" Lance asks in a hushed voice, as if he's trying not to wake a baby, even though the calf is a calf, not a human infant, and she's not even asleep.

"Well, she didn't break my legs kicking me," Robbie says, and then grins ruefully. "Just bruised me some."

Lance's eyes widen in alarm. "Are you okay?" He's forgotten to whisper, and he's halfway to his feet before Robbie's voice stops him.

"I'm just kidding," he says hurriedly. "Sorry. Don't worry about me."

Lance settles slowly back down to the floor, then scoots a little closer to the calf so that he can reach inside the towel she's wrapped in and stroke her side. He can feel her ribs through her coat, which is already mostly dry.

Robbie goes to the kitchen, washes his hands, and opens and closes a drawer. When he comes back, he has his coffee can, which is maybe a quarter full of pale liquid, and a small dish rag. He gets down on the floor opposite Lance, sets his supplies carefully to one side, and finally pulls the calf's head and shoulders up into his lap.

Lance rests his chin on his knee, watching with fascination as Robbie's large, gentle hands move—one cupping the calf's jaw, his thumb coaxing down her jaw. With his other hand, Robbie makes a point out of one corner of the rag and dunks it in the milk. Then he puts the wet cloth against the cup of her tongue.

The calf's eyelashes flutter and she struggles in Robbie's grip, but weakly. He holds her firmly, rubbing the cloth against her tongue. When she doesn't seem to get the hint, he slides his thumb down her tongue beside the cloth.

That does the trick. Her eyes go wide and she abruptly clamps her mouth closed around his thumb and the rag, then begins sucking aggressively. Robbie laughs and winces at the same time, tugging free of her mouth after a few seconds.

"Good girl." He dips the rag in the milk again and repeats the process.

By the time he's wrung the last of the can's contents into her mouth, the calf seems exhausted again. Her eyes drift closed. She makes a tiny, contented mooing sound as she lowers her head, draping her neck over Robbie's thigh. He and Lance's eyes meet; they share identical smiles.

"I think I love her," Lance blurts in a whisper.

Robbie breathes out a laugh. He rubs the calf's neck with his splayed fingers. "She's definitely a cute little thing," he murmurs in agreement.

Robbie and Lance pet her another moment, ruffling her

coat, moving their hands in intersecting circles without touching one another. Then, Robbie rearranges her towel nest a bit and slides her back into it. She is as boneless as a plush toy, eyes firmly closed now. Lance positions her legs in a way that looks a little more comfortable, though he's mostly guessing since he doesn't have four legs and he's pretty sure all of the joints on the two he does have are in different places.

"Can I ask you something?"

Lance looks up abruptly. He hadn't realized Robbie was watching him, and now that he does, his hands slow, lingering on the roundness of the calf's little ankles, the absurdly tiny points of her cloven hooves. "Yes," he says without thinking, and then immediately wishes he hadn't, considering all of the things Robbie could ask that Lance really, really wouldn't want to answer.

For a split second, Robbie looks unsure, like he's changed his mind and isn't going to ask. Then, he seems to steel himself, and Lance's dread triples at whatever he's about to say.

"Did you go to school?"

For a moment, Lance just stares. Then, the breaking tension rushes through him and carries with it the urge to laugh. He manages to smile instead. "You mean, college?"

Robbie nods.

"Yeah. I did it in three years, to save money. I had some scholarships, but there were still so many expenses. And my aunt said she didn't mind paying, but I didn't want her to— well, I didn't want her to have to worry about it." He shrugs uneasily. *I didn't want to be a burden*, he doesn't say. He had been a burden on his aunt, but he's come to terms with the fact that it wasn't something he could help at the time. Now, Lance tries not to bother her if he can help it. He already derailed her life for two years when he abruptly showed up at her doorstep at sixteen, practically a runaway.

"What did you major in?"

These questions seem strange, until Lance is revisited by a series of vibrant memories. Robbie overseeing his brothers' homework at the dining room table in the farmhouse, asking detailed questions about school projects and follow-ups to the answers; Robbie doing half of their required reading along with them; Robbie snagging Danny's textbooks when he finished studying for an evening and reading from them like other people read pulp fiction.

Robbie had loved school, and he probably would have loved college, too. Lance already knows that Robbie never went. His dad died his senior year of high school, and he stepped in to take care of his brothers and the ranch. Lance has always known the bare bones of that part of Chase history, but as a kid, he hadn't dwelled on how hard that would have been for Robbie. How young eighteen really was.

"I majored in film studies, and also in photography." He's braced for comments on the impracticality, but instead of disapproving, Robbie looks both impressed and mystified, like Lance has just told him he has a PhD from MIT or something.

"Two degrees?"

Lance nods shyly.

"So, you take photographs?"

"Well." Lance pulls his knees tighter against his chest. "Yeah, but I haven't sold much yet. For work, I wound up on the other side of the lens...you know." He shrugs uncomfortably. Talking about modeling always makes him feel vaguely itchy, especially since what happened with Niall.

"'The other side of the lens'?" Robbie echoes, making it a question.

Lance realizes, with mixed feelings that range from hurt to amusement, that Robbie has never searched Lance's name on the internet.

"I've done some modeling."

"Oh." Robbie's eyes are a little wide, and it seems like he's having a hard time not letting them drift over Lance, as though knowing Lance makes a living out of being looked at makes Robbie want to look, as well. "I, well. That makes sense." He clears his throat. Lance's lips twitch with the effort not to grin as a wash of dark red appears in the line of skin above Robbie's beard and below his cheekbones. "I mean, you're—" He gestures at Lance, then clears his throat again and picks up the coffee can, fumbling it at first so that its metal bottom rattles against the floorboards until he gets a good grip and pushes himself off the floor with his other hand. "You're really...well."

It's like the moment in the kitchen that morning with the spilled coffee, all over again. Awareness of the energy between them rushes through Lance, and he has that irrepressible urge to—*perform*. He stretches his legs in front of him but keeps his feet flat on the floor, easing back on his hands. Not quite a pose, and yet he knows exactly how it makes him look. Just like he knows that when he holds his chin down at this precise angle, then looks up—

Robbie staggers backward a half-step, dropping the can and then catching it in his other hand with remarkable dexterity. They stare at each other, Robbie breathing heavily and his eyes aglow, Lance trembling with the effort to contain the undeterred yearning that ate him alive between the ages of thirteen and sixteen. Maybe it's never stopped eating at him at all.

"I'm gonna wash up," Robbie mutters, his voice as rough as gravel under snow tires. He strides the short distance to the kitchen, drops the can in the sink, and then leans over the counter with his back to Lance, his shoulders high and tight, his head slung low between them.

CHAPTER TWELVE

Robbie

R obbie doesn't have the stockpile of non-perishables he wishes he did, considering that the snow shows no signs of letting up.

That's what he makes himself think about: his proverbial bare cupboards. He times the mental inventory with the drawing and expulsion of his breaths. Deep breath in: three dented cans of tomato sauce. Slow breath out: one jar of sundried tomatoes with the label peeling off. Deep breath in: two vacuum-sealed, one-pound bags of quinoa which Megan brought over to the house, and Robbie hid out here so that he could pretend he'd eaten it. Slow breath out: a few teaspoons of the loose leaf tea that only Danny drinks, barely covering the bottom of a mason jar.

Maybe he should call Danny. Hearing his brother's voice will remind him how many people could get hurt if he lets attraction overcome his better nature.

"I'm going to ride up to the hay meadow and check on the mustangs." He thinks his announcement sounds reasonably casual. He sneaks a glance at Lance to see whether or not his minor crisis has somehow gone unnoticed.

"Mustangs?" Lance looks up from the calf with raised brows, acting normal enough.

"Mustangs," Robbie confirms, and then clarifies, "Danny set it up, for the most part. Welcome to the Riverside Ranch, a Bureau of Land Management-certified, long-term holding facility, and the home of forty-nine horses that are the property of the federal government."

"A long-term holding facility," Lance repeats carefully, like he's committing it to memory. "I've never heard of that. So, the government pays you?"

Robbie nods. "About two dollars per horse per day. The mustangs have free rein of the place, and I keep them fed and watered and try to check on them as much as I can, especially in bad weather. They've been here a few years now, but the winters still baffle them. Most of them were born in the desert."

Lance looks fascinated. "Could I see them?" He immediately flushes and looks at the calf, stroking her faster. "If that's—I mean, never mind—"

"Of course," Robbie interrupts. "We'll get saddled up and ride up there together. But first we'd better move her." He nods at the calf. He remembers the calves his father brought inside being completely lifeless at first, but if she does perk up, he doesn't want to imagine what she could get up to.

Lance helps him put the calf in the bathroom, then he turns down the woodstove, and they get ready to go outside.

This isn't the respite Robbie wanted—not privacy to call Danny, deliver an update, and recalibrate himself somewhere away from Lance. When they're together, Robbie's brain only seems to function at half-capacity.

But he finds he's glad Lance wants to come. It surprises him, but he wants Lance to see the mustangs.

———

Poco is more serious with Dusty along, like she's his supervisor shadowing his shift.

Robbie loaned Lance a hat to help keep the snow out of his face, but it's too big for him and sits low on his brow. He looks good, anyway. Dusty is Robbie's most steadfast horse, but she always has a slight attitude when she's asked to work. Since Robbie has made Poco his primary ride, only using Dusty when Poco is hurt or worn out, she's objected to *every* disruption of her retirement.

When he saddled her for Lance, Robbie worried she might be a little grumpier even than usual, having to cart around a stranger. But so far, though she's let out several opinionated sighs and her ears are permanently pinned, she's behaving herself pretty well. Lance was never a confident rider, and he's more tentative now than Robbie remembers, but he knows what he's doing. Johnny taught him, after all.

"You doing okay?" Robbie calls over his shoulder as the horses clamber up the last slope in the trail before the meadow.

"Yeah," Lance calls back. He sounds sincerely exhilarated. Sure enough, when Poco gets to the top of the incline and Robbie twists in the saddle to watch Dusty and Lance coming up, Lance is grinning with flushed cheeks.

"I forgot how amazing this is," he tells Robbie, leaning over to rub Dusty's neck when she comes to a stop of her own volition beside Poco. Poco turns his head enough to brush his muzzle against hers, and she pins her ears and responds with a snap of yellow teeth.

Robbie smiles at Lance and tightens his reins to keep Poco in his own lane.

"Yeah," he agrees, because even though he rides this trail more days than not, he's still amazed by it, too. "We're almost there," he adds, and feeds Poco some slack and clucks to him. But before Poco takes a step, Dusty shoulders past, apparently pulling seniority-based rank, and she and Lance take the lead for the last short stretch.

That change in position gives Robbie a view of Lance in the saddle, his posture tall and balanced, with that natural grace and sensitivity translating beautifully to horseback, even bundled in winter clothes.

Also, because of this rearrangement, he gets to see Lance react when they spill into the meadow and he sees the wild horses gathered there. All the bands have come together in the meadow, using each other's bodies for shelter. They're a hundred feet away, but all together, they seem to fill the meadow.

"Holy shit," Lance breathes out. Robbie's laugh startles a couple of the nearest horses, who apparently aren't used to hearing Robbie laugh.

The snow has piled up so high where Robbie has the fiberglass posts and wire, they might try to walk over it, or fail to see the wires while they're wading through the snow. Not wanting the fence to turn into a latent hazard, he decides to take it down.

"Can you hold onto Poco a minute?" When Lance nods, Robbie dismounts and hands Poco's reins to Lance. Poco, seeing an opportunity and immediately taking advantage, bumps his muzzle against Dusty's shoulder. Her eyes glow with the promise that later, when they're back in their corral, he'll pay for taking such liberties. Poco is cheerfully oblivious and does it again.

The mustangs quickly move away from Robbie as he comes closer, like a stream avoiding a stone. It's not unheard of for them all to spend time together like this for an hour or two, but the way the snow is trampled down around the hay suggests they've been out here as a group for a while, probably since last night. He coils up the wire and grabs the slender fiberglass poles with the pliers he always has on his belt, wrenching them out of the frozen ground. It takes some time. Robbie knows that without the fence to stop them, the horses will destroy all the bales they can get at. All he can do is try to get back up here as soon as the snow starts to melt.

When he finishes, he walks back toward the saddle horses. Lance's blue eyes are still wide and fixed on the scene around him, his chapped lips parted like he's truly moved by the sight. Robbie takes Poco's reins back and then looks at the herd, trying to see them through Lance's eyes.

They're already pushing toward the hay bales that are no longer protected by Robbie's fence. Their snow-brushed coats are thick, their manes and tails long and wiry. Like most mustangs, they aren't particularly large, and they have the rangy, hardy appearance of animals whose ancestors evolved to survive in rough country, not the show ring. Some people wouldn't be impressed.

But some people look at them the way Robbie does. Those people can sense it—their wildness. Robbie doesn't know how else to explain it. There's an element of spirituality in the way he regards all horses, and he's been around hundreds of them over the years. But there was always something different about the mustangs, since the moment they came off the BLM trailers that summer three years ago.

He's not sure, but the look of focused calm on Lance's face makes him think that Lance might see the horses as Robbie does, too. He swings back into Poco's saddle, putting him at eye level with Lance, who looks at him with a smile. "Thanks for bringing me up here," he says quietly.

Robbie nods, not bothering with words. The feeling inside him—between them—keeps building, like the river when it climbs toward the reservoir gates and threatens to crest the spillway. He's not sure how much longer he can hold it back, or what will happen when it flows over. It's frightening and it's thrilling. His knee bumps Lance's as he turns Poco back toward the trail.

At the third creek crossing, Poco crosses the frozen water in a bound, with no sound but the thud of his hooves striking packed snow. Dusty makes to follow, but when she lands at the edge of the ice instead of cleanly on the bank, the ice breaks under her hooves. It cracks with a sound like a gunshot, flushing a trio of crows out of the bushes by the bank. The birds and the sound make Poco hop around a few times, distracting Robbie. Dusty is a veteran, and it takes more to startle her, but she grunts when her next step brings her fully through the ice, and then she trips and pitches forward onto her knees.

Lance is slung sideways, out of the saddle and onto the snow-covered ice while Robbie watches helplessly. The snow is a cushion, at least, but beneath it, the ice has apparently broken up; as Dusty splashes to her feet, Lance is half-submerged in the freezing water.

"Lance!" Robbie is out of the saddle already, scrambling down the bank. The passage of two horses on the trail has left the snow packed enough to be slick, and he almost slips and ends up next to Lance in the water, but he rescues himself at the last second. By the time he's at the edge of the creek, Lance is on his feet, too, his hat in one hand, catching Dusty's trailing bridle rein in the other.

"I'm f-fine," he tells Robbie, but he's already trembling, and Robbie can see he's wet to the bone over at least half of his body as he steps out of the water and onto the bank.

"Can you ride?" Robbie can't believe how calm he sounds. "We need to get you warm."

"Yeah, I'm f-fine," Lance says again, unconvincingly. "But what about her?" He frowns worriedly at Dusty. She's wet on her legs and up her right side, but Robbie can see plainly that she's fine.

"She'll be all right, if we get her back to the barn and dry her off."

Lance nods. Robbie grips his shoulder. "You're sure you're...?"

"Yes," Lance says stubbornly, reaching for the saddle horn and fumbling a little with the reins in the process. Robbie takes the reins from him and bites his tongue while he watches Lance take three attempts to get his boot in the stirrup. Then he swings onto Dusty's back—but so clumsily that she staggers.

Robbie gets on Poco and they ride back as fast as the horses can manage. Robbie isn't worried about Dusty; he'll put her in the barn and she'll be fine. Horses' bodies are made to survive the harsher elements. It's Lance who has Robbie scared.

As soon as they get into the yard, Robbie jumps off Poco and goes to Lance's side. "Need help?" He puts his hand on Lance's thigh and flinches when he finds the denim stiff with ice.

"No," Lance says firmly, then proceeds to dismount and almost fall over as his feet hit the ground. Robbie snags him by the waist.

"*Shit.* Lance."

"M'okay," Lance insists.

"You're not—listen, let's just get you in the bath."

"Like a calf?" Lance sounds like he's smiling, though Robbie can't tell for sure, preoccupied as he is with towing him up the deck stairs while his head lolls on Robbie's shoulder.

"I think I'd r-rather have a shower. Pretty sure you d-didn't clean the tub."

Is sarcasm a symptom of health or hypothermia? Robbie gets Lance to the door, and he seems steadier. Or, at least, he pushes Robbie gently away and walks inside with his own strength.

"I'm *fine*. Go take care of the horses."

Robbie runs back down the stairs to deal with the horses as quickly as possible. He puts them both in stalls, dumps their tack in the aisle in an untidy heap that would have his dad turning over in his grave, and tosses a cooler on Dusty. He can barely keep himself from running upstairs right then. But instead, he takes the time to hurriedly fill two water buckets and hang them in the stalls.

When he lets himself into the hayloft, the shower is running. He leans against the door.

"Okay in there?" he calls.

"Yeah," Lance calls back.

Reassured that he hasn't collapsed, if nothing else, Robbie wanders around the hayloft nervously. The wood stove has almost burned out, and the triplicats are piled on the horrible couch. He hopes Lance didn't trip over the calf when he went in the bathroom.

A glimpse of the clock on the stove gives Robbie a moment's sense of lost time; it's late afternoon. It's been more than twenty-four hours since he picked up Lance from the courthouse. He forgot to change the bed linens the day before, and he worries about it for a moment, wondering if Lance noticed. He drifts over to the sleeping area with half a mind to change them now, but then he notices the folder on top of the dresser—the folder that Lance brought back from the jail.

Robbie glances toward the bathroom. He can still hear the shower running. His hand lifts. His fingers graze the edge of the folder, which is so worn that it's almost soft. Then he remembers himself, jerks his hand back, and keeps himself busy feeding the stove. He's just closed the wood stove door when the bathroom door swings open.

There's Lance. Lance, in nothing but a pair of worn-thin, light blue boxers that Robbie vaguely recognizes as Johnny's from his years of taking his turn doing the laundry. Steam billows out behind Lance and he's rubbing a towel through his wet curls. Robbie should be making sure that he's okay, looking at him for no reason except to gauge his color and ensure that his feet are firmly on the floor and his balance is steady, and that he didn't lose any digits to frostbite. But as Robbie looks at him, those are the last things on his mind.

He shouldn't have needed to be told that Lance was modeling. What else could he be but someone in the business of being looked at? He's toned with care—obviously no stranger to the gym, but there's no bulk to him, either. He has an unmistakable six-pack, but the muscles are tight and corded against his torso, almost like they were drawn on. His arms are the same, sculpted to reveal the play of each individual muscle, but still sleek. With his hair lying wet against his skull, all of the sharp angles of his adult face are more pronounced. If Robbie had seen him like this unexpectedly, he could have thought him a total stranger.

Then, he smiles lopsidedly, and just like that, he's Lance again. Robbie's Lance.

"Feel alright?" Robbie asks, still crouched on the floor by the stove, but as Lance slings the towel around his shoulders like a cape and walks toward him, rubbing his arms, Robbie stands up.

"Yeah. Still cold."

When Lance gets closer, Robbie sees the signs of lingering chill that he missed while he was struck senseless by the first sight of Lance in the bathroom doorway. His lips are pale and he's trembling slightly.

"Well, get under some blankets," Robbie insists. And since the only way to do that is by sitting on the cold floor or the uninhabitable couch, or getting in the bed, Robbie points toward the bed. "I'll get the fire going a little better. And for fuck's sake, put on some socks."

Lance smiles again, but he goes to the dresser obediently. His towel-clad shoulders are still trembling with faint shivers, but his voice is low and playful when he says, "It's so weird to hear you say 'fuck.' I don't think I've ever heard you cuss before."

"Well," Robbie says tartly, closing the grate on the stove behind another few chunks of wood. Fire leaps up eagerly to consume the fuel, making the view through the transparent plate in the door glow like an ember. "I was probably trying to set a good example or something."

He glances at Lance, who's leaning against the dresser and pulling on socks, his back bowed. The towel slips off of him and hits the floor with a soft sound, and he doesn't bother picking it up again as he changes feet. Robbie can see the knobs of his spine, the exact shape of his hard, tight ass in the fraying boxers, and the cords of muscle in the backs of his long, long thighs.

Robbie steps closer to the woodstove until the heat is almost too much, a welcome discomfort.

Lance turns and gets under the covers. He's still shivering, though. He rolls onto his side and catches Robbie looking at him, then goes very still. "I'm still cold," he says, so quietly.

"I'll get another blanket," Robbie says roughly. There's a faded quilt in one of the plastic storage containers. He brings it back, shaking it out and grimacing at the musty smell, but then spreads it over Lance's body anyway, careful not to touch any of the angles and curves he's formed beneath the covers.

When he looks down, Lance is looking up.

"Still cold," Lance says. He holds up the covers in silent invitation, his eyes unflinching.

Take care of him, Robbie thinks, and gets into the bed.

CHAPTER THIRTEEN

Lance

Nine years ago.

Johnny takes them to school in the Chevy, which he's been allowed to drive in good weather since his sixteenth birthday. As usual, Lance is crowded into the bucket seat between Danny and Johnny. His legs are tucked into Danny's side of the gear shift, and Danny and Johnny are battling across him for control of the radio dial. Johnny is laughing and Danny is growling.

The school day is uneventful until Danny and Lance go out to the parking lot after their last class. They're among the first kids to spill out the back doors into the student parking lot, which is about ten times the size it needs to be for the number of kids who drive. It's a warm afternoon, the sun high and the pavement hot through the thin rubber of Lance's sneakers.

"Where'd you leave off? Issue thirteen, right?" Danny asks, continuing the conversation they've been having in various forms all day. A new issue of *The Team* is about to drop next week, so they've been rereading every issue from Danny's collection.

"Twelve," Lance says, and then stumbles on the first step when he hears a girl's shout ring out from the parking lot.

"Did someone call a teacher?"

Lance and Danny look at one another for a split second, then in the direction of the voice. There are a handful of cars parked in the first few rows, and from there the vehicles are more scattered. But there's a congregation of kids growing in the row where they left the Chases' Chevy that morning.

From the top of the steps, Lance can see over the crowd's heads and spot Johnny, his head of golden waves unmistakable even from a distance. For a moment, Lance thinks he's kneeling on the ground—like maybe he dropped something, and has knelt to pick it up—but then he sees his arm arch behind his head, then fall.

Their school is small. People don't *fight*. Sure, there are arguments in the hallways, and sometimes a few angry shoves. But Lance has never seen anyone get punched except on his father's westerns. It's so alien that it takes him another long moment to realize there's another boy sprawled under Johnny, a boy Johnny is hitting.

Before Lance can unfreeze his mind, much less his feet, Danny lets out a howl and breaks into a sprint, down the steps and toward the scene unfolding a few dozens yards away.

Danny isn't bothering with words—just high-pitched howls, like a mad cat. But Lance understands that all he's trying to do is to distract and startle, like when they've chased birds out of the vegetable garden at the ranch.

Lance scoops up the backpack that Danny just dropped and follows as fast as he can without tripping. As soon as he's at the bottom of the stairs, he can't see the fight for the crowd, but some of the kids have been so startled by Danny's ongoing wails that they've turned away from the fight and toward him. That makes it easier for Danny to elbow his way through, Lance a few steps behind.

When Lance makes it past the other kids, he finds Danny frozen on the inside of their periphery, staring. Lance stares too. On TV, punches sound like gunshots—loud, dry pops. But Johnny's punches sound heavy and wet, like slaps. The kid on the ground is Cade—one of Johnny's classmates, another popular boy who plays football with Johnny. Lance sees two more boys on the football team that he thinks of as Cade's friends, and they're muttering and shoving each other, like they can't decide whether or not to join the fight.

Maybe they don't know whose side they should take.

Then the interlocked bodies lurch and topple sideways, and it's Johnny on his back, and Cade is straddling him. He grabs the collar of Johnny's shirt, snarling as blood runs down his face.

"Fuck you, you pervy fucking pretty boy, I'll—"

"No!" Danny howls, darting forward from Lance's side and pushing Cade's shoulder with both hands. He's about half Cade's size but still manages to shove him with enough force that he's off-balance and startled. He lets go of Johnny's shirt, rolling over his left knee and landing on his butt on the asphalt. Johnny pushes himself to his feet and scowls at his brother.

"Get out of here, Danny!"

It's only at that moment that Lance sees the Chevy, about two parking spaces away from where Johnny and Cade were fighting. Someone painted the word *"FAGGOT"* in bold red spray paint across the tailgate.

Whatever fervor possessed the two older boys seems to have passed. They're glaring daggers at each other and breathing hard. Maybe after another second or two of that, they might have gone at it again, but just then a teacher shouts, *"HEY!"* from the top of the stairs, where Lance was standing with Danny only a minute ago.

"I hope you get suspended," Cade snarls. There's blood streaming from his nose and a red mark on his cheek and jaw; his eye is starting to swell on the same side. Cade turns to appeal to the crowd. "You all saw how he jumped me for nothing."

Two junior girls exchange a glance, and then one of them gives a cool shrug and the other says, "I thought *you* hit *him*."

"Yeah," says her friend. Then, she points at the tailgate. "And you put that on his truck, you asshole. That's hate speech."

There's a general murmur of consensus amongst the teenagers.

Something dark and horribly nervous in Lance's chest solidified the second he saw the word on the tailgate, but hearing the majority of the kids in the parking lot taking Johnny's side makes it loosen, just a little. His next breath comes easier.

Cade backs away from Johnny and Danny altogether. Lance advances into the space he left and wordlessly hands Danny his bag.

Cade is looking around as though bewildered by the lack of support. "So, what, none of you care that—?"

"Kids, what the heck is going on out here?" Mr. Bellows, one of the Math teachers, has reached the knot of students now. He sweeps them with a look, then does a double-take when he sees the Chevy's tailgate. His lips press into a thin line.

"Okay, I'm going to need all of you to stay right where you are while we sort this out."

———

After the teachers have gotten the basics of the story down, they send everyone home with promises that parents will be called. It's silent in the cab of the truck as Lance and the Chases leave town, but as soon as they hit gravel, Danny can't contain himself any more.

"Johnny, what...?"

"No."

"But—"

"I said no, Danny. Goddamn it, can't you just leave me alone?" But before he's finished telling Danny to shut up, Johnny's mind seems to pivot, and he takes the gaze he's had fixed out the windshield and pins it to Danny as they slow to a stop at an intersection. "What were you thinking, running into the middle of that? You could've gotten punched in the face. You want a broken nose?"

Danny shrugs, totally unbothered. "You're my brother."

Johnny sighs frustratedly. But after he puts the truck back in second gear to accelerate away from the stop sign, he knocks off Danny's ballcap with a flick of his hand and musses his hair.

"You're an idiot," he says quietly.

Danny, batting away Johnny's hand, rescues the cap from his lap and puts it firmly back on his head. "So, what—"

"Not right now, okay? Later."

Silence falls. Lance is thinking about Cade and can't stop looking at Johnny, staring at the blood on his lip. He feels hardness around his heart, like roots of stone are spreading, making it hard to breathe.

Robbie must have seen them pull up. Maybe he was watching for them; he gets worried whenever they run even a few minutes late. He comes out of the house at a jog. Johnny, barely out of the pickup, closes the truck door and shoves his hands in the pockets of his jeans, hanging his head.

When he's standing in front of his brother, Robbie ducks

his head to look at his face, and his expression twists. "You got in a fight?"

Johnny pulls his head up, a glint of challenge in his face. He shrugs.

Robbie folds his arms. "Who threw the first punch?"

"He had it coming," Johnny mutters. He brushes his wrist against his split lip, then grimaces as he seems to notice that he's gotten a streak of blood on the cuff of his denim jacket sleeve in the process.

"Robbie," Danny starts to pipe up.

Johnny shoots him a withering look. "Don't."

That remark, of course, has the opposite of its intended effect. Danny bristles more. "You think he's gonna *care?*"

"What are you two—?" Robbie tries, but Danny speaks over him.

"He won't," Danny says with confidence.

"Danny," Johnny growls, "for once, would you mind your own fucking business?"

"Hey!" Robbie snaps. "Language!"

"He won't care," Danny says again. "I know he won't. I've seen his porn."

That shuts up everyone, including Johnny, for a shocked second.

Danny's ears get pink. "I mean, it wasn't on purpose. I was looking for Christmas presents. I guess you can find the wrong hiding place, sometimes. Anyway, there were some naked girls, yeah, but also—"

"How, exactly," Robbie interrupts, his voice a little strangled, "is this relevant to whatever is going on?"

Johnny, who's been gaping at Danny along with Robbie and Lance, now hangs his head again.

Danny takes a deep breath through his nose and jerks his head toward the back of the truck.

Robbie, cheeks still faintly red above his beard, looks

back and forth between them in bewilderment, then follows Danny's silent gesture and starts to circle the Chevy. When he sees the tailgate, he freezes mid-step.

For a long moment, Robbie just looks. Even Danny doesn't break that silence. Then, Robbie retraces his steps until he's back in front of Johnny and puts both of his hands on his brother's shoulders. Johnny hesitantly looks up. When he does, Robbie pulls him into a tight hug that goes on for a long time. Neither of them say a word.

Later, after a quiet dinner where the events of the day aren't mentioned, Lance and Danny go upstairs and sit on the floor wordlessly. The issues of *The Team* are still there in a neat stack from the night before, ready for them to dive back in. Lance reaches for Issue 12, but, for once, even the subplots that feature Mr. Cosmos can't hold Lance's attention.

"Did you really...?" he blurts, but he can't bring himself to actually say the words.

It doesn't matter. Danny definitely knows what he's talking about. He glances up from beneath the oversized bill of his ballcap. "Yes, I've seen Robbie's collection. Or, at least part of it. Maybe he doesn't keep it all in one place. I only saw magazines. He probably has other stuff, you know? I mean, he's not ninety years old, so I assume he has some video—"

"Danny," Lance murmurs desperately, not sure how much longer he can listen to Danny talking out loud about porn— porn that belongs to *Robbie* and that *isn't all girls*—without his head exploding. "Please stop."

"Well, you asked," Danny huffs, but his gaze is lingering on Lance, not returning to the comic book open on his lap. He looks like he's about to say something.

"What?" Lance mutters.

"Why do you want to know?"

"I don't know. It's just—I don't know. Why do you...what

do you...?" Flustered, Lance gropes for something to say that won't be incriminating.

For once, Danny lets him off the hook. He looks down at his comicwith a shrug so casual that Lance wonders if he imagined the intent look in his eyes a moment ago. "Whatever. It's not a big deal. But I guess he's probably bi." He looks up from the page again, a thoughtful expression on his face, and Lance can tell he's about to orally draft another thesis about Robbie's porn habits, or an adjacent topic, before he even begins. "Or, maybe he's pansexual, or autosexual but responsive to different visual—"

"Please stop," Lance insists in a strangled voice. "Please."

Danny shrugs and looks back down at his comic. Lance worries for a second or two that he'll start up again, but he just turns one page, and then a bit later, he turns another.

Lance looks down at the issue he's holding and pretends to read it, too. But there's no way he can focus now.

After dark, Lance leaves out the back door to walk home. In the fading light, he might not even have noticed Robbie around the front of the house by the truck if he hadn't heard the whir of the cordless drill. Lance pauses, unnoticed by Robbie and nearly at the tree line, so that he can watch Robbie loosen the tailgate's bolts to remove it from the body of the Chevy. After he's detached it, he sets it in the bed and stares down, presumably at the painted words. Then he steps back and kicks the tire several times, so hard that Lance hears the impact of his boot on the rubber. That's more like what he'd thought punches would sound like, he thinks absently, as he slowly melts into the trees and makes his way home with leaden feet.

Today.

"I'm still cold," Lance says, knowing exactly what effect those words will have. Still, a part of him can't believe that Robbie steps forward, picks up the corner of the blanket, and slides underneath it.

Robbie is fully clothed, and there's an outside chilliness clinging to his clothing that flushes the bit of trapped body heat out of the shelter of the blankets. Lance shivers despite himself, but when Robbie settles the blankets back around them, lying on his side and facing Lance, but somehow not touching him anywhere, the warmth returns twofold within a moment.

"I'll lend you a little body heat," Robbie says, his voice a low, rough murmur that Lance feels like the soft rasp of wool on his bare chest, his thighs, and his cock. He shivers again. He's at eye level with Robbie, facing him, their cheeks pressed into the same long pillow. It's like being plunged into a dream unexpectedly—and like any plunge, it's as frightening as it is exhilarating.

Robbie rubs Lance's arm through the blanket, murmuring something that Lance can't make out—maybe something about a doctor. But Lance could close his eyes and moan at just the weight of Robbie's hand and the delicious reality of his body warming the bed Lance is lying in.

He wants to tell Robbie to stop touching him. He also wants to grab Robbie's hand and thrust it between his legs. He's paralyzed by these warring feelings.

"Lance? Kid?" Robbie touches his cheek. "Sweetheart, are you crying?" His voice cracks slightly on the endearment. So slightly, like a fissure in varnish with the wood solid beneath it. Robbie's thumb brushes away a tear from Lance's cheekbone.

"I'm just," Lance breathes, "so...*Robbie?*" He's asking for something, but he doesn't even know what. He shudders, but not from the cold. He pushes his face against Robbie's hand, speechless, and then can't contain a little cry when Robbie's other hand runs down his blanket-covered side to his waist and pulls their bodies together under the blankets.

"Lance." His name is a sigh on Robbie's lips, stirring his hair. And Lance's hammering heart is pressed to Robbie's chest, where he can feel Robbie's heartbeat in turn; together, they make a confusion of rhythms, fast and desperate. Then Robbie's lips are at his temple, his beard surprisingly soft on Lance's face. Lance tips his head back, questing, his nose dragging through the bristle of Robbie's beard, presenting his panting mouth. He wants this most forbidden thing: Robbie's kiss. He wants it no matter the price. In this way, he's forever the boy he thought he'd left here, the boy it turned out he could never leave behind after all. The feeling he had of conflict—Robbie's love, or Robbie's wanting—is forgotten now.

Robbie is very still, his face angled just slightly away so that the corners of their mouths barely meet. It's for Robbie to seal the kiss, but he hasn't moved yet.

Lance can imagine each possibility with equal clarity: Robbie kissing him, or Robbie gently pushing him away. Again.

CHAPTER FOURTEEN

Robbie

R obbie hasn't ever been in bed with a man—or held one, save the brief embraces of his brothers and a few friends. Holding Lance is nothing like that. It isn't just that his body is wondrously lean, yet hard and substantial, or the unmistakable strength held in check. His heart has been so open to Lance that the new physical response has an accelerated affect. Resistance seems as futile as trying to snatch back a beam of light or a note of music.

He's so close to kissing Lance, Robbie realizes in a daze, his hand wrapped around the shape of a lean hip which is frustratingly covered by the thick blanket. He wishes he could touch Lance's bare skin. Run his hands over him until he's memorized the texture and heat. He wants to see what was on display a few minutes ago when Lance only wore frayed boxers and one sock. He wants to see the rest of him, and with a desperation that leaves him dazed. He wants things he's never wanted, like to grasp Lance so hard that Robbie's fingerprints bloom against his skin.

Before he can act on any of these impulses, there's a knock on the door.

Robbie had forgotten she was coming, but as soon as he hears the knock, he knows exactly who's there. Swearing, he lets go of Lance and gets out of the bed.

How did he forget that Megan was coming by?

Robbie adjusts himself in his jeans with a grimace and looks down at Lance. Lance's expression is bereft for a moment, before it turns carefully blank. The transition sears Robbie. He bends back over the bed and touches Lance's cheek, which is still chilled even though there's a bright blush staining his skin. All he wants to do is get back down beside him, peel off those threadbare boxers, and...well, at that point, it gets a little fuzzy, either because Robbie doesn't have a parallel experience for source material or because trying to imagine it short-circuits his desperately turned-on brain.

Another knock sounds, and Robbie twists to look at the door, half-afraid it's going to open before he's had a chance to explain. Megan is waiting outside in the snow and won't think anything of letting herself in if she thinks he hasn't heard her. There's no way to emerge into friendship from a decade-plus relationship and still worry about privacy when you assume— with good reason—that the other person will be alone.

"Robbie!" she calls.

Robbie hears the little intake of breath from behind him and turns just as Lance scrambles out of the bed, untangling himself from the blanket as he moves. He looks at Robbie with an expression of pure betrayal.

"It's not what you're thinking," Robbie is quick to say, but Lance looks unconvinced—and also sinfully gorgeous with his damp hair and his flushed face and his heaving chest and his —goddamn, Robbie has been curious about men before, yes, but never before has the outline of someone's semi made his mouth water.

While he's staring, Megan finally loses patience and pushes open the door.

"Sorry," she says, stomping off her boots and obviously not yet having realized Robbie has other company, "but it's cold out there, and I figured you were—"

Robbie turns just in time to see Megan notice Lance, and her jaw drops. She almost trips over the boots she just shucked as she tries to backpedal out the door in her socks. "Sorry! Oh, my God, I'm so sorry, I—"

"Meg, it's not...." He *wasn't* going to say *"it's not what you think,"* was he? When did he become a liar? But at the same time, he does feel like he has something to explain. A drawer skids open behind him, and out of the corner of his eye, he sees Lance yank one of Johnny's old flannel shirts over his head.

"No, no, it's fine, I mean, of course, it is—*I'm* the one who just burst in, and...okay, yeah, sorry. I'll just be in the truck." She's managed to get her boots back on and escape back out the door. It closes with a thud that makes Robbie flinch.

He turns back to Lance. "I forgot she was coming."

Lance is halfway into a pair of jeans that are going to be an inch too short for him in the leg and will slide off of his hips. Despite everything, Robbie can't help but study his nimble fingers as they do up the buttons, and the flash of pale stomach above the waistline of his boxers that's briefly visible before the shirt falls back into place. Then, he rolls the top of the jeans over once so they'll stay up, and gives Robbie a look that can only be described as "cool"—it's one which Robbie has never before imagined seeing on Lance's face. He doesn't like it.

"It's fine." Lance rakes a hand through his hair in a gesture that would make more sense if it was still long. Robbie wants to know how long ago he cut it short, and why. He wants to see every photograph ever taken of him. He wants to rewind time and see what would happen if Megan hadn't come to the door. But more than anything else, he wants that soft, open expression back on Lance's face; the one finally coaxed out from the blank dismay that Robbie was first greeted with at the courthouse.

"I meant to tell you she was coming. But it slipped my mind, between you falling into the creek, and then...this." Robbie's gaze falls to the bed in silent explanation. Lance's face colors a little. He hugs the flannel shirt around him.

"I understand."

No, you don't, Robbie thinks desperately, but he isn't exactly sure what to say. "She's the only veterinarian I could get to make a farm call in this weather," he tries, "and I knew there were things we needed for the baby if we wanted her to have a chance."

There's a flicker of life in Lance's eyes that makes Robbie fall immediately silent. If he's said something right, he'll shut up before he gives himself a chance to say something wrong.

"I didn't think about that." Lance's tone is uncertain.

Robbie thinks of circling the bed and reaching for Lance. Pulling them both back into another moment like the one under the blankets, where everything felt so clear and easy. But he can't bring himself to move. He's always been good at reading animals, and decent at reading people. But usually he has the benefit of a clear head. Usually, he isn't just as emotional as the being he's trying to soothe. Here, he's paralyzed by all of the *newness*, as well as the stakes. He hasn't forgotten that he's the only person who can help Lance right now, much less the old habits of trying to protect Lance from his own feelings.

"I'd better go talk to her."

"Yeah. I'll just...wait here."

Robbie nods shortly, steps into his boots and coat, and goes outside to find Megan.

As promised, she's sitting in her truck. He sees her through the windshield, both hands on the wheel, staring down at it like the answers to the mysteries of the universe are in her steering column. He goes to the passenger side and gets in, which makes her jump.

Megan is one of the few people he's ever loved, and he loves her still. But there's always been just as much friction as harmony between the two of them.

When they broke up the final time, he knew they'd never get back together, and his predominant feeling was relief. Still, she's the only person in his heart who hasn't left him entirely alone, and none of the things about her which kept them from working out as a couple make her less of a good friend. He looks at her familiar, beautiful face, that strong jaw and long, sleek black hair, and bites the inside of his cheek.

"Are you freaking out?" he asks.

She rolls her eyes. "No. In case you forgot, I *do* know you like men, too." A sly smile glances over her lips. "*Danny* wasn't the first one to find your dirty magazines."

Robbie laughs, then groans, slouching against the seat. "Don't remind me." He rolls his head to the side, unable to control his surprise. "But I don't mean the...or, that he—"

"You mean, you're not asking me if I'm freaking out because you had a naked guy over?" Her smile grows wicked, and that's when Robbie realizes *why* she's not freaking out: She didn't recognize Lance.

He takes a deep breath. "I thought you might freak out because of *who* the guy is." When she looks confused, he exhales hard and comes right out with it. "Lance Taylor."

Her lips purse, her brows draw together, and she gives him a searching look that lasts several moments. She's surprised, he thinks, but not outraged. Uncertain, but not disgusted.

"Where's he been?"

It's a very reasonable question, but he feels himself narrowing his eyes. "That's what you're asking?"

She shrugs.

"Why aren't you yelling at me?"

She lifts a brow. "Did you expect to be yelled at?"

Robbie snorts, shifting restlessly in the seat. "I don't know where he's been. Well, he went to school. And now he's modeling."

"Tell me something I don't already know from the internet. I mean, why hasn't he been back here before now?"

Robbie frowns. "What does the internet have to do with anything?" Megan starts to look exasperated, and he lets go of that point of confusion and sighs. "I don't know why he hasn't been back."

"But, why now? How did he wind up here?"

"I don't know why he's *in town*. But he's *here* because I brought him here. He didn't have anywhere to go." He hesitates, has a brief but intense internal debate about whether or not to share the next detail, and then cautiously decides he has to. "I went and got him from the jail. He'd called Danny, and Danny called me. And before you ask, I don't know what he did."

She doesn't ask anything else. She's staring at the steering wheel again, which makes Robbie more nervous than he felt about being peppered with questions.

"Meg?" he asks when he can't stand it, sounding more plaintive than he means to. "Can you just yell at me and get it over with?"

She turns her head, looking genuinely perplexed. "Why? Because I would have yelled at you for it ten years ago?"

Six, six years ago, he doesn't say, because he's probably not supposed to be counting. So, he just shrugs.

"Jesus, Robbie. He was a kid back then." She shrugs uneasily. "It's not the same. He's an adult. It isn't like you're some kind of a predator." Her brows rise again. "Why do you have that look on your face? Do *you* think you're a predator?"

Robbie averts his eyes.

Now, Megan looks exasperated. At least he's used to her exasperation; it's almost comforting. "This is just like you, to morally police yourself into being miserable. It's just like this fucking ranch all over again. If you want something, it has to be wrong for you to want it."

"Don't start about the ranch, Megan, for God's sake." There's something new in what she's saying, but it's so interlaced with a hundred familiar arguments that Robbie's emotional reaction is instant.

Her hands flex on the steering wheel. "That's not even—" She seems to cut herself off, shaking her head. "It doesn't matter. I'm here on a call. The rest of it isn't my business anymore, is it?"

She's throwing words back at Robbie—words he shouldn't have said. "I didn't mean that. How many times do I have to tell you that?"

She waves a gloved hand at him. "Honestly, let's just not." She hesitates a moment, then twists to face him, grabbing his hand and squeezing it. "I just want you to be happy. Honestly." A smirk stirs the serious line of her mouth. "He sure grew up, huh?"

Robbie can't even look at her. "Megan. Jesus."

"I mean, I knew it abstractly, but in person, it's a different experience." She lets go of his wrist.

Her words connect with something she said earlier, and Robbie zeroes in on the thought as they climb out of the cab and she grabs a canvas bag out of the toolbox of her vet truck.

"What do you mean, you knew it? And earlier, what was that about the internet?"

She laughs incredulously. "You mean, you haven't seen pictures of him? He's, like, an actual model. Don't you look people up?"

Robbie is bewildered. "No? I don't think that's normal, Meg."

She rolls her eyes. "Please."

"Isn't it a violation of privacy? Maybe you shouldn't be doing it."

"Don't take the moral high ground with me. Now that I've planted the seed, you're totally going to start doing it."

Robbie glares at her, but he's pretty sure she's right. The idea that he could call up the images he's been wanting to see ever since Lance mentioned they existed, with just a few swipes of his thumbs—

His steps slow as his imagination runs away with him. Megan snorts and sweeps past. Robbie has to rush to catch up to her.

"So," she says crisply, slinging the strap of her bag over her shoulder as she mounts the deck stairs, all business. "Tell me about my patient."

CHAPTER FIFTEEN

Lance

After the door closes behind Robbie, Lance tries not to panic.

What just happened is eerily similar to a thousand dreams he had as a kid—Robbie gazing at him, touching him, wanting him, and then the dazzling, perfect fantasy was twisted suddenly into a nightmare where Megan, always Megan, descended from nowhere to come between them.

Lance hasn't needed a therapist to interpret those dreams for the childish and unfair flights of fancy they were. But still, standing in the hayloft alone in his too-big, borrowed clothes, looking down at the blankets where minutes ago he was lying naked in Robbie's arms, he has a hard time transcending the angry teenager who wants to smite Megan from the Earth for being the one Robbie touches and looks at and wants.

Rationally, he knows better. But his rational mind isn't functioning at the moment.

The bathroom would be the only place he could shut himself away and avoid them when they come back inside, except that Robbie said Megan, a veterinarian, is here to check out the calf. The calf that happens to be in the bathroom. He'd checked on her before and after his shower, but she just looked up at him, blinking those liquid eyes, and appearing not to have stirred from her towel nest the entire time they were gone.

But even if Lance *could* hide, he doesn't want to convince Robbie that he's just as immature now as he's ever been. He can face Megan—a perfectly nice woman who has never objectively wronged Lance or anyone else that he knows of—like an adult.

Through a monumental effort, he arranges himself into a casual lean against the kitchen counter facing the door, and waits.

When the door opens again, Megan smiles at him, calm and friendly. "Hi, Lance." She steps clear of the doorway so Robbie can enter behind her, and they both shed their coats. "I didn't recognize you at first. It's nice to see you."

Everything she says sounds perfectly sincere. Behind her, Robbie is looking at Lance with a careful expression. Lance wants desperately to know what was said while they were outside together, but at the same time, there's something in Robbie's expression that gives Lance comfort. He doesn't seem panicked or anxious or guilty.

Lance can even relax enough to smile back at Megan. "You, too. It's been a long time. How are you?" He doesn't look away from their eye contact, and yet he can clearly see Robbie, behind her, break into a small smile.

"Cold," she says with a wink. "And this weather is keeping me busy." She takes a bag off her shoulder that's lined with pockets and zippered compartments, presumably stuffed with her supplies. "So, I hear we have a little miracle on her hands?"

Robbie points to the bathroom, and Megan leads the way. Triplicats Two and Three are lurking in the doorway, peering at the calf in apparent fascination. Megan steps over Two, and Three hisses and tries to catch her with his claws as she passes. Robbie gently and carefully shoos them back toward their sofa.

Megan kneels on the floor by the calf. It's still warm and steamy in the room from the shower. She rakes her hand through the fur on the calf's hip. "What a pretty little girl," she croons to the calf, and then she takes a stethoscope from under her sweatshirt and listens at the calf's ribcage, belly, and chest. Lance crouches beside her. In the quiet, Robbie comes and stands over them.

After a minute or so, Megan leans back, sees their worried expressions, and smiles reassuringly. "So far, so good. No irregularities." She fills a needle and syringe with the contents of a tiny bottle and gives the calf a stick that makes Lance jump, but which the calf doesn't seem to notice. "Steroid," Megan explains as she preps a second syringe, this one without a needle. She puts it in the corner of the calf's mouth and tilts the animal's head back, emptying the contents more or less straight down her throat. "And a little extra colostrum."

"Colostrum?" The word is only vaguely familiar to Lance.

"First milk," Megan explains. "It's how newborn mammals get some important antibodies. Robbie says he milked the cow, which is good, but the colostrum isn't always there in the very beginning." She checks the calf's joints one at a time, pulls up her eyelids, and then smiles with a nod.

"I think she's in good shape. They're vulnerable at this age, and she definitely has had some stress, so we'll have to watch her closely for signs of virus or infection, but for now, the most important thing is to keep her fed. Isn't that right, baby?" She digs in her bag and produces a giant bottle, a plastic tube, and a sealed plastic bag of white powder. "If you'll let me mess up your kitchen, we can probably take care of that, at least. Hopefully, she's a quick study and will nurse the bottle, but if not, I'll show you what to do."

Half an hour later, the calf—who, thankfully, *was* a quick study, because just the thought of pushing a tube down her throat made Lance queasy—has sucked down the contents of a bottle like a vacuum and then immediately fallen asleep, the dampness of her bottle lingering on her upper lip like a mustache. Lance pats her mouth dry with the end of the towel.

"She should be up and moving around in the next eight hours. If she isn't, call me. Also, you're going to need milk replacer. I brought you everything I had, unfortunately."

"I can run into the farm store and get some," Robbie says. "I've got to get a few things at the grocery store, anyway." He slants a smile at Lance. "Considering we're down to one egg."

Lance hasn't even thought of food, for various reasons, but the cinnamon toast breakfast *was* a long time ago. Robbie's glance and offhand comment make Lance warm on the inside. He smiles back.

Megan looks between them and then quickly away. Lance's old fears rear up in his head, but then he sees the mystified little smile she can't quite hide and they vanish again.

Then, his whole mind blanks when she steps forward, slides her arms around him, and squeezes his waist. She's almost as tall as he is, maybe a half inch shy of his six feet. She smells like antiseptic and the calf's bottle, which isn't very pleasant, along with a whiff of the alcohol she used to clean the calf's neck before she poked her with the needle.

"Don't be a stranger," she tells Lance firmly, and then she lets him go, holding his eye a moment. "Not anymore."

He doesn't really know what to say, so he just smiles awkwardly and puts his hands in the pockets of the baggy jeans he wears.

Robbie follows Megan outside, and this time, Lance doesn't feel quite so agonized by what they might or might not be saying. He goes into the kitchen and washes the bottle that Megan left in the sink. When he's done, Robbie's walking back in.

"So, I'll run into town, then." He's still wearing his coat. The door is only cracked open behind him, but that's enough to let in a little thread of cold air that seems to snake around him and straight to Lance, where it nips at the back of his neck and his still-cold feet.

Lance shivers and nods. "Okay."

"You need anything?"

Lance's mouth twists into a wry smile. "Well, I have a Ziploc bag and a manila folder, so no, I'm all set." He wipes the dishwater off his hands and onto Johnny's jeans, then winks as Robbie laughs. "Actually, now that I'm thinking about it, one more egg. And a tablespoon of butter. Maybe a single water bottle?"

Robbie grins, rolling his eyes. And still he hesitates another moment, though there's nothing else to ask. It's more like he just doesn't want to go—or leave Lance.

Lance's chest feels warm again.

Robbie clears his throat. "I'd ask if you wanted to ride along, but you should stay here. Stay warm."

Lance would absolutely ride along. He was never that worried about how cold he got, frankly, though he took shameless pleasure in being fussed over. His body has always run warm, and though the cold had been horrible, he thinks he's shaken it off. But he doesn't really want to go into town, either, to see familiar faces, and think about what's waiting for him in a couple of days—that is, a return to the courthouse and the next step in the process of explaining why he was driving a car that Niall had reported stolen.

He grits his teeth just at the thought.

Better to stay cocooned here for as long as he can and pretend like it's not just a happy interlude, and rather that he'll never have to leave.

"Yeah, okay," he tells Robbie.

Robbie nods. "I'll be back in an hour and a half. Maybe less. Meg says the roads have been dozed, so the snow shouldn't slow me down much."

"Sounds good. Be safe."

There's another long hesitation that makes Lance want to laugh aloud in pure delight. Then, with a quick parting smile, Robbie finally goes.

Lance *does* remember the shock of the cold water, and the way it seemed to leach through his skin and muscle to fill his bones. He looks out the window at the snow-covered landscape and the memory makes him shudder. But he can't bring himself to just wander the hayloft, either.

He makes sure the calf is still asleep in the bathroom and the door is closed, warding off any triplicat attacks. He's already thinking of getting dressed and going outside when he sees a curl of smoke over the trees, coming from the direction of his old house.

Just like that, he's moving without having made up his mind to go. He's got his gear on in under a minute, and then he's walking fast through the snow toward his childhood home.

Unlike on his last trek, he doesn't wander aimlessly before he commits to crossing the creek and seeing his father's place. He takes the most direct route, which is as familiar to him as breathing even though he hasn't followed it in six years. Nonetheless, so many of the small landmarks are still in place. There's the barbed wire fence remnant, which is only a single old hedge-post, linked to the tree that grew over its wires and now wears it like an appendage. Then there are the three bulbous rocks in the rockshelf by the crossing—one yellow, one white, one brown. There are differences, too. Someone cut out hedge trees recently; their stumps are still sharp and ragged from the strokes of the saw, not yet softened and weathered by seasons of exposure. More, Lance sees it all from a shift in perspective. He's higher above the roots and underbrush, and he can close the distance in fewer strides.

As he begins to climb up the bank on the Taylor side, he sees a flash of lavender...an unnatural color amongst the dark foliage and silver snow. He pauses as a face swathed in the hood of a light purple snowsuit appears over the edge of the bank, looking at him sternly.

"Are you a trespasser?"

Her voice is surprisingly deep for someone of her size and apparent age. She has brown curls escaping from the confines of her hood, which is cinched tight around her face. Her cheeks are as red as apples in the light amber complexion of her face. She wears mittens with a rainbow pattern; they appear as she reaches for the edge of the bank and pulls herself forward. She's lying on her stomach in the snow.

"Mama doesn't like trespassers," she warns him when Lance doesn't answer her.

"Um," he says, too startled to think quickly, "I don't think I am? This is my father's property."

Her eyes widen. "The old son of a bitch is your dad?"

Lance doesn't know whether to laugh at her very accurate description or gape at the words coming out of the mouth of someone who looks to be about seven years old. "I don't know for sure that we're talking about the same person," he hedges, "but, probably, yes."

She wrinkles her nose. "My mama says we aren't trespassers, either. She says we're debt collecting."

"I don't mind that you're here. I just thought the house was empty, so I wondered who you were, that's all."

The little girl crosses her arms, stiff in the puffy sleeves of her snowsuit, her hands frozen into mitten-shapes. "I'm not supposed to talk to strangers." Then she pauses. "Well, I guess what mama said is not to talk to strangers in town, but she never said anything about strangers in the woods."

"Oh." Lance winces. "Um, yeah. I'm sure the same rules apply to strangers in the woods." They probably ought to apply *especially* to strangers in the woods.

She scowls at him. "That's a stupid thing to say when *you're* the stranger and *you're* the one talking to me. Are you a kidnapper?"

"No."

"So, what's even your point?"

"*I'm* not a kidnapper." He pauses, considering that's probably what a kidnapper would say, if asked. "But you shouldn't take my word for it."

She grumbles something that sounds like "*Grown-ups,*" obviously aggrieved.

There's a shout behind her. The girl turns that way. "That's Mama."

"You'd better go, then. And remember, don't talk to strangers in the woods."

She gives him a completely unimpressed look, then turns and runs, snow boots thumping.

When he imagines the little girl reporting a stranger in the woods to her mother, he supposes the adult thing to do would be to walk out to the house and introduce himself. Lance can see the old house in snatches through the trees. In the yard, the source of the smoke reveals itself: a metal barrel, the contents of which are burning. A young woman, maybe no older than Lance, stands beside it, dropping an armload of something into the climbing flames. The child in her purple snowsuit runs up to the figure of the woman, and as Lance watches, the woman's head jerks up and she stares toward the trees.

He should walk over and explain himself, but instead he hastens to hop back down the bank and walks fast toward the Chase side.

For some reason, the image of the little girl's face is lodged in his mind. There was something familiar about her, even though he also knows for certain that he's never seen her before.

CHAPTER SIXTEEN

Robbie

Nine years ago.

Every time Robbie has to speak to Lance's father, he gives himself a long lecture first. His inner voice alternates between sounding like his dad and sounding like Megan —the two voices of reason he's been lucky enough to have in his life. Obviously, he never had the opportunity to talk through the conundrum that is Lance Taylor with his dad, but Megan has listened to him rant time and again. He's never had any hard evidence that Lance's father is a complete waste of air, certainly never from Lance himself. But it's obvious Lance doesn't get everything that he needs at home.

Today is Danny's thirteenth birthday party, and Lance has been home sick for three days. Last year, Robbie finally convinced Lance to take a cell phone that he could keep for emergencies, and now he's used it to text Danny and tell him that he can't come to the party. An illness that would come between Lance Taylor and sugar in one of its purest forms— birthday cake—much less the chance to celebrate with

Danny, must be serious enough that he should be in a hospital.

Or, Robbie's other, more complicated fear is correct: Lance isn't sick at all.

He tried calling the Taylors' landline number first, but it only rang. And then, while he was finishing up the chore of picking up party supplies and debating driving out to the Taylors' house, he saw the familiar rusted-out Dodge that Paul Taylor, Lance's father, drives, parked in front of the roughest bar in town. That meant Lance was home alone, and if Robbie stopped in to check on him, no one would be there to get in his way.

He drives faster than he probably should, skidding out on the gravel in the turns. He's driving the pre-owned sedan he bought right after Danny outgrew his booster seat, and he can hardly believe it hasn't quit yet, though the engine complains every time he nudges the gas pedal. When he gets to the Taylors' and turns down the driveway, he checks his rearview mirror about a dozen times, half-expecting to see Paul's truck appear behind him. It doesn't.

One of the house's windows is boarded over, but strangely, it's boarded over from the inside. The other windows are dark. Robbie feels like he's approaching an abandoned place as he parks, jogs up to the door, and knocks. No one answers.

"Lance?" he calls.

Nothing.

Suddenly too frightened to hesitate, Robbie opens the front door. It isn't locked, which isn't a surprise; most people don't bother with locks in Trace County. The house is dark inside. A wave of fetid air greets Robbie, offering a gut-turning combination of stale beer, cigarette smoke, and old trash. He fights the urge to cover his nose as he steps past the threshold.

"Lance?"

There's a thud from his left, where he finds a closed door straight off the messy living room. It must lead to the room with the boarded-over window that he noticed from the outside. Robbie walks over and rests his hand against the door's surface.

"Lance? Are you in there?"

Another thud. Then, he hears a muffled voice. "Robbie?"

"Yeah," Robbie calls, struggling to keep his voice even. "I was just coming by to see if you're okay. You've been sick. You said you couldn't come to Danny's party." He's rambling a little, all in an unnaturally cheerful voice, standing in the dark interior of a house that feels haunted by past anger and raised voices. "Can you—can you come out?"

There's a very long pause, and then Lance speaks softly, almost whispering. "Is my dad here?"

"No," Robbie says, his voice threatening to break. He clears his throat. "He's in town. It's just me."

There are a few more thuds, and then the door opens. Robbie steps back, surprised and worried. His eyes skate over Lance, relieved to find him whole, not bleeding or bruised, and dismayed to find him looking paler than usual, his eyes wide and his lips dry.

There are various things on the floor. Books, a square nightstand, a few other items—all relatively heavy. The thudding sounds must have been Lance moving them. Robbie thinks uneasily that he was likely using them to form a barricade against the door. The plywood is fixed to the space over the window with at least two dozen nails, set in haphazard rows along each edge.

Lance is watching Robbie study the room with visible uneasiness. Robbie recalls a dozen brief exchanges they've had before—Robbie suggesting something might be wrong at home, Lance hurrying to assure him that everything is fine. Robbie feels like he's walking on the very thinnest ice when he looks at Lance and smiles. "You seem like you're better. Want to come to the party?"

The painfully thin shoulders go round with relieved tension as Lance exhales, and his grin, despite the stark paleness and gauntness of his face, is still sweet. "Yeah. Just let me change, okay?" He wets his dry lips and his smile turns strained. "And grab a drink of water."

Reluctant to leave him, Robbie nonetheless goes outside and sits on the front step. His head feels heavy suddenly; he can't help briefly resting it in his hands. When he hears Lance coming, though, he quickly stands up, smiles at him, and follows him back to the car.

When they get in, Robbie starts up the driveway before he dares to ask. He's *pretty* sure Lance won't jump out of a moving vehicle to escape this conversation, but he's not *absolutely* sure.

"So," he says as casually as possible, "I saw you've got a broken window. That happened at the house last winter. I still have some left-over caulk and window glass, if you want help fixing it. I could show you how."

Lance glances at him. "Sure, maybe."

"Lance." Robbie doesn't know how to ask, but indirect questions apparently aren't going to get him anywhere. He swallows. "Are you afraid of your dad?"

Lance goes utterly still.

Robbie, acting on pure instinct, lays his hand on his shoulder. For a moment, Lance's tension seems to double, tangible against Robbie's palm, and then it leaves him in a rush. Robbie gives him a gentle rub, like he would an uneasy animal, or Danny when he's crying. He doesn't usually offer Lance comfort; Lance doesn't seek it, not like the other boys do. Not from him. And Megan's warnings are ringing in his ears, but he thinks that in *this* moment, she'd understand why he can't help himself.

"You can tell me. I promise I won't do anything about it that you don't want me to." He regrets the words as soon as he says them, but at the same time, they seem to do the trick.

Lance swallows, and then answers slowly, each word sounding pried loose from his chest and flung past his mouth. "Sometimes I take things. Just little things." He wrings his hands in his lap between his spread thighs. "Dad doesn't like it."

Robbie swallows. "When he gets mad, you go in your room?" That was a very generous description of what Robbie guesses happened—Lance barricading himself in for three days—but he's still straining not to spook Lance so badly that this unprecedented moment of honesty will vanish.

Lance nods, like he's relieved Robbie figured it out so that he won't have to say it. Taking that cue, Robbie goes on, carefully choosing each word.

"And that's because you think if he gets angry enough, he might...?" But that's a sentence he doesn't know how to finish without breaking the fragile bubble they're in, or giving too much fuel to the coil of anger in his stomach that makes him glad he doesn't own a gun. He's afraid of what he might be capable of if he did.

Lance nods again with a heavy sigh. He leans slightly into Robbie's hand.

On the far side of the wooden bridge, when they're no longer at any risk of running into Paul on his way home, Robbie pulls over onto the shoulder of the road and pushes down the brake. He doesn't want to take his hand from Lance's shoulder to reach for the gear shift.

"Has he ever hurt you, Lance?"

Lance's eyes are wide as he turns and locks his gaze on Robbie's. "No. Never." He swallows and shakes his head. "He just yells a lot. Sometimes, I think—but...no. He never has."

Robbie nods, trying to plan the next question, but Lance speaks again before he can.

"Do you remember Caleb Parker?"

Robbie blinks. "Lance, that's not—that isn't what usually happens to kids in foster care." Caleb Parker was a local boy who'd gone into the system after his grandparents, who'd raised him, had suddenly died of a bad case of the flu. He'd been placed with a seemingly harmless couple in the next town to the east, and after he'd been checked into the hospital for a broken arm a year later, several healed fractures had been discovered in his legs, proving that he hadn't just fallen down the stairs and hurt his arm on accident, but that he'd been pushed. And not for the first time.

"Well, I've been on the internet. I know he's not the only one to end up like he did, or worse." Lance drags his sleeve over his nose, which is running. His eyes are glassy with unshed tears. "My dad's not that bad, okay, Robbie?" His shoulders quake. "And if I get sent away, I'll never see you anymore, or Danny or Johnny. Please, don't...please don't do anything, okay?"

His wide, unnaturally blue eyes are beseeching. So, Robbie gives him what he's asking for, knowing even as he says the words that he's going to wonder, one day, if his promise was a horrible mistake.

"I won't, if you swear you'll tell me if he ever lays a hand on you. Okay?"

Lance nods eagerly and wipes his nose again. "Thanks, Robbie. And I will, I will. But he won't. I just go in my room when he gets like that." A ghost of something passes over Lance's face and he swallows convulsively. "It's not so bad."

A minivan passes them on the road, honking. One of Danny's few friends smiles at them through the passenger window, waving excitedly at Robbie and Lance, oblivious to what he and his mother are interrupting.

"Can we go to the party now?"

"We'd better," Robbie says, "before the other kids raid the birthday cake and there's nothing left for you."

"That would be a nightmare," Lance agrees with exaggerated distress. "What kind did you get?"

"Yellow, with chocolate frosting."

Lance bounces in the seat, grinning. And just like that, he looks sincerely excited. His ability to cast aside the dark and seize the light leaves Robbie briefly awestruck, and then Robbie gives the slender shoulder under his hand a final squeeze, and smiles back, taking his foot off the brake.

It isn't as easy for Robbie as it was for Lance to shake off the shadows of the last hour. In fact, they never really leave him at all.

Today.

The seat of Trace County is Dell, population 2,833. Dell is as familiar to Robbie as the back of his hand. He could navigate its neat, rectangular blocks blindfolded.

Every house he passes calls to mind the names and faces of the people who have lived there from the time of his earliest childhood memories on until now, thirty-odd years later. He remembers taking Johnny to bible school at the Methodist church, which is a single-story brick box that squats at the first turn into a city street off the highway, over by the gas station. The only thing that clearly denotes its status as a place of worship is the plain metal cross bolted to its west-facing wall. He'd thought sending him was the right thing to do; their parents had sent Robbie. But Johnny had returned with so many unanswerable questions after the first day, Robbie had never taken him back.

The little white bungalow a block down used to be hunter

green, and it's where he attended his first sleepover when he was nine. Or, he attempted to. He had to ask his host's mom to call Robbie's mom around nine o'clock, after he panicked and shut himself in the bathroom for twenty minutes. He still remembers the bathroom very clearly—it had that old hex floor tile, but instead of in classic black and white, it was blue. There were several broken tiles next to the old iron tub. A single spider web clung to the upper cabinet above the sink.

At the edge of downtown is a big, ornately painted Victorian that belongs to Sadie Bannister, whose daughter, Chloe, Robbie once flirted with at a tailgate party to see if it was possible to make Megan jealous. His experiment had ended with Megan slugging him in the arm and kissing him silly, tasting like chocolate and rum. He'd been unable to look Chloe in the eye after that. She'd left for college and hadn't been back since. She was a university professor somewhere, now.

It isn't nostalgia that Robbie feels when he takes a good look around at Dell; it's stranger than that. More like all the years of his life overlap and time loses its meaning. Robbie'd rather just stay at the ranch.

The farm store, Cal's, takes up the space where there was once a Sears. Robbie can remember buying school clothes there, and a shiny propane grill that his dad used exactly once before giving it up as a lost cause. The farm store opened about a decade ago. It's named after the original owner, but his son and namesake runs it now. They charge twice as much as one of the chains would if anyone cared to drive another fifty miles. And luckily for Cal's, most people who live in and around Dell don't leave the area unless forced.

Megan said Cal's will have what he needs. He didn't bother questioning her or calling ahead. Where Megan is concerned, he's used to doing what he's told.

At least, he does when he understands what she's telling him, which isn't always. He thinks back to the lecture, or whatever that was, which she gave him in the cab of her truck earlier, and still isn't sure what his takeaway was supposed to be.

Mulling that over, he leaves the truck running in a parking stall close to the entrance and runs into Cal's, not bothering to button his coat, his bare hands shoved down in the pockets. He's only exposed to the cold for ten seconds or so, but it's long enough that he's shuddering as the door falls closed behind him in the vestibule at the entrance, where he scrapes the snow off his boots and passes through the second set of doors into the store's much warmer interior.

Cal Senior was an avid hunter in his youth, and when the store opened, it became a gallery for his moth-eaten trophies. As kids, Johnny and Danny had been torn between horror and fascination by all the taxidermy, and Robbie understood the feeling. Even now, he carefully avoids the stare of a coyote's slightly crooked glass eyes and the antelope that looks like its narrow lips are pulled into an eerie smirk.

The trophies are interspersed with actual, untidy inventory. The place looks like a hoarder's garage sale, but the Cals always magically know where everything is. So, Robbie heads toward the counter without bothering to try looking for himself.

Cal Junior is behind the counter on a tall stool, his feet propped up on the counter and a giant automotive parts magazine spread open across his thighs. He peers at Robbie from under the flat brim of a trucker-style ballcap and grins.

"Hey, there, Mr. Chase," he says, pulling his feet off the counter one by one, unhurriedly. "You need somethin' in particular?"

Being called *"Mr. Chase"* always makes Robbie feel old,

especially right now, speaking to someone who's probably a year or two older than Lance.

"Yeah," Robbie says, and tells him.

Cal nods, sauntering out from behind the counter. "I was just talking to Mel. He was in here a little bit ago. Mel Pryor?"

"I know Mel," Robbie says, following Cal around the end cap of the aisle adjacent to the counter and down the narrow gap between shelves. Mel was a couple years ahead of Robbie in school, and he's been a part-time police officer in town since he graduated, working more when things are slow at the family farm, less during harvest and calving season.

"He asked if I'd been past the cop lot. Guess they've got an impounded car. A *Mercedes*. Blue. You believe that?" He pauses and knocks back his hat so that he can read the labels on the various stacks of paper sacks filled with dehydrated milk, which he's found tucked between a plastic-wrapped block of mulch and a stack of garden hoses. "Here, this is what you want."

"A Mercedes, huh? Some out-of-towner?" Robbie asks casually.

"Well, it don't got snow tires on it, that's for sure." Cal winks.

Robbie heaves a bag of the milk replacer over his shoulder.

"I'm going to drive by after I close up. Bet it has to do with that al-ter-cation at the care home." He gives the ten-dollar word deliberate emphasis and slants a too-innocent glance over his shoulder as he leads Robbie on a zig-zagging path toward a row of big plastic bottles next to the birdseed. "Y'all still close with Lance Taylor?"

Robbie is spared answering that question because the landline phone rings.

"Be back in a sec," Cal says, and heads for the counter.

Robbie grabs an extra bottle, then follows and sets all of his supplies by the register.

"What was that? The twelve-footer? Let me just check." Cal has the phone tucked between his shoulder and his ear while he thumbs through a supplier catalogue.

Robbie settles in to wait, thinking about the gossip he just heard. An out-of-town Mercedes in impound, and a stranded Lance who Robbie retrieved from jail two days ago; an altercation at the care home, where Robbie knows Lance's father lives.

"Or there's a sixteen-foot panel, but that's not in stock," Cal is saying, and he looks like he isn't going to be done answering the caller's questions any time soon.

So, Robbie finds himself wandering from the counter to a few displays adjacent to the door that he didn't notice when he came in. He knows the farm store started selling some locally produced items a couple years ago, but he's rarely thought to browse them.

There's a table of honey, but not just the kind meant for eating—though that's there, in little jars adorned by hand with paper labels and ribbon. There's also small, vacuum-sealed chunks of raw honeycomb and a row of beeswax candles.

Next to the honey is a rack of hand-sewn purses in vivid prints and colors that make Robbie wrinkle his nose. Maybe he has an old-fashioned aesthetic, but he doesn't see the appeal.

His eyes linger on the shelves next to the purses, where raw wood bowls and boxes display artisan soaps. He reaches for a bar and holds it to his nose, smelling the rich odor of pine over the damp scent of his glove. Pleased, he puts it back and tries another.

This one smells familiar and unique at the same time, and so pleasant that he takes a second inhale. Then, he studies the label. Sandalwood. The soap was molded to look like a thistle flower. When he runs his fingertip over the dozens of narrow petals, he can feel its pleasant roughness even through his glove.

For no reason that he can explain, Robbie imagines the soap worked into a lather over Lance's white-gold skin, and his head swims. He's never had thoughts like this about anyone, but he can picture the scene vividly. Lance's hairless hands running all over his body, working the soap into his skin, leaving him bright-smelling and clean. And then, Robbie could put his face against the nape of Lance's neck and smell this scent on him, like Robbie himself had marked him.

"Hey, Mr. Chase. Sorry 'bout that. You ready?"

"Yeah," Robbie manages, and he clears his throat. He brings the soap back with him to the counter and feels illicit when he sets it down, like he's buying porn.

Of course, Cal doesn't blink at it. He scans the stuff, gives Robbie a total, and pops the box of soap into its own tiny plastic bag inside the bigger one that contains everything else.

Back in the parking lot, Robbie drops the plastic shopping bag into the passenger seat and slings the bigger sack of milk replacer into the back seat. Then, he gets back into the driver's seat and lets the blast of heated air warm his fingers after he unwraps his hands from his gloves and gets out his phone.

He has a browser. He can type names into a search engine. It just never occurred to him to do it, which, according to Megan, makes him the equivalent of an unenlightened octogenarian.

He types in Lance's name, and after about a half-second of processing, the phone lights up with a little grid of images above the text results.

All of the tiny pictures are of Lance.

Heat suffuses Robbie's face. He's had this feeling before—when he walked into a room and surprised someone, getting the distinct impression that he wasn't welcome there or that he was seeing something he shouldn't.

But he can't look away. More than mere curiosity has him bringing the screen closer to his face, swiping slowly to the right so that he can bring more images into view.

Lance with his hair a little longer than it is now, his curls falling over his eyes, his shirt half-unbuttoned, on one knee on a tile floor. Lance, mile-long legs encased in some kind of shiny fabric, with a matching jacket open so that his lean chest and whipcord stomach are displayed more enticingly than if he were nude. Lance lying on some sort of dark, furred surface, a strip of glossy black material wound around his arm and between his legs, barely hiding his cock and balls...and not concealing their outline in the least.

Robbie scrolls, his whole body turning feverish the more photographs he sees, until he consciously stops himself and carefully sets his phone in the console. He's in no state for the grocery store, abruptly, so he drives mindlessly, turning at random blocks. There's the laundromat, which he frequented for a time after the fire, before he got the facilities put into the hayloft. There's the drug store where he used to let Johnny and Danny get candy bars if they behaved during a Saturday afternoon spent running errands.

He isn't surprised when the seemingly random route he's taken to try to clear his head brings him to the police station and the vacant lot across the street, secured by rickety chain link. The cop lot usually doesn't offer much to see except an assortment of rusty bikes and a metal storage container with unknown contents. But today, in the midst of the rust and junk, draped in snow, is the elegant outline of a blue luxury sedan.

Robbie parks the truck on the street. He's staring at the

car even though there's not much to see. Its paint color is evident around the sides and the undercarriage, bright against the snow. But it's mostly covered by the snowfall. The shape of the car still draws the eye—a testament to its design, Robbie supposes.

He thinks of what it means that Lance drives something like this. That the pictures on his phone exist. That Lance's body is a honed work of art, and yet there was such a hollowness to his eyes when Robbie first picked him up. A hollowness that was banished by the warm expression on his flushed face when Robbie held him.

Take care of him.

Robbie pulls away from the curb, more confused than ever by what that means. But he can start by getting some kind of terribly unhealthy cereal with a cartoon character on the box, in addition to a dozen eggs.

CHAPTER SEVENTEEN

Lance

While Lance sits alone in the hayloft, he finds he's reached his limit for how long he can stop himself from thinking about his predicament.

He's good at fooling himself. Just like he avoided untangling himself from Niall, even when it became clear that he'd become too dependent. Niall had always made it clear that he expected Lance to do as Niall liked—and Niall liked to have Lance close, so he'd never even considered getting his own apartment. Niall covered all of the expenses of the business and their extravagant lifestyle, so it would have been ungrateful for Lance to ask to draw a salary. Niall hadn't even wanted him to have his own bank account, insisting that their lives were simplest and most pleasant when fully merged.

It had all built to an awful crescendo, where Lance felt like he couldn't breathe. He barely remembered getting in the car two nights ago...only that it had seemed imperative that he leave.

He'd assumed his father's house was empty. He'd figured he could stay there; it was the only place he'd been able to think of to go. Funny that he'd gone to the care home first, but a small, pathetic part of him had needed to see his father totally bedridden with his own eyes before going to the house. Otherwise, that part of him would have been sure that his father was inside, waiting for him, and he'd never bring himself to open the door.

But if he hadn't gone to the care home, maybe nosy cops wouldn't have noticed the Mercedes in the parking lot and decided to run the license plate. If he'd gone straight to the house and seen that it wasn't the empty hiding place he'd pictured, he would have turned around and driven back to Chicago. He wouldn't be facing criminal charges and he wouldn't have had to endure a night in jail.

But he wouldn't have had his time with Robbie, either.

That series of strange events led him here, where he still feels the pressure of Robbie's hand on his hip and the thrill of Robbie's hard, warm body against his.

Lance casts himself down on the bed because there's nowhere else to sit, and a distressed yowl alerts him too late to the presence of a cat. He still can't tell them apart, and even if he could, he wouldn't be willing to refer to them even internally by Robbie's ridiculous names. But as he quickly rolls away from the feline, whose hair is standing on end in fervent communication of its distress, he registers that there isn't a white hair anywhere on its body. Which is how he realizes he's officially meeting the cat that has been hiding from him since he arrived.

"Hello, One."

She glares at him, then streaks from the bed and out of sight beneath the horrible couch.

He makes a note to ask Robbie how he wound up with three vicious cat triplets. It's a question that he can ask without feeling like he's overstepping, unlike all of the others on his mind.

Lance rolls onto his back, thinking through those questions yet again.

What happened with your brothers?

It seems like more than just ordinary life events are separating the Chases. It's always been hard to imagine them being apart, but Lance knew that Danny would go to school eventually. He'd imagined constant phone calls, though, maybe with video. He can't be sure, but he gets the impression that all they really do is a bit of texting.

And Johnny—that Johnny has willingly been away from the ranch for so long is hard to reconcile with Lance's memories of him. His devotion to Riverside always seemed to surpass even Robbie's. Remembering him with his horses, Lance finds that his absence is especially hard to understand. Lance has never been a horseman, but even he was struck by the occasional, impromptu shows Johnny would put on for his brothers and Lance—riding one of his bays while the other followed like a shadow, or standing in the grass and sending them in loops and circles around him without halters or lines, like they were dancing together.

What happened with Megan?

Lance always thought Robbie and Megan would end up together. So had everyone else in Trace County and beyond who'd, over the years, dared to hope otherwise. The handsome, young, land-rich rancher and the knockout veterinarian each had long lists of admirers, but no matter how often they drifted apart, they always came back together. What finally stopped that cycle?

Lance knows what answer he'd like to hear: that all they ever were to one another was convenient. Not that either of them fell for someone else, and certainly not that Megan left Robbie and Robbie was still pining for her.

What do you want from me?

He remembers the almost tentative way Robbie touched

him at first, and thinks with unexpected excitement that he might be the first man Robbie has ever been with. The idea of being any kind of first for Robbie is almost unbearable—enough to make Lance want to slide his hand past the waistband of his borrowed jeans and moan.

Still, the question is dangerous. Lance isn't sure he knows what he wants the answer to be. Once, Lance wanted nothing more than Robbie's pure, nonromantic love.

Then, when he got it, he came to think it wasn't enough.

In the years since then, though, through the hardest and loneliest times when he's worried he'll never feel safety or joy again—in those moments, what he's wanted back wasn't a dream where Robbie wanted Lance the way Lance wanted Robbie.

No, he's wanted the reality, where Robbie loves Lance, and the way Robbie's love makes him feel warm and safe.

Lance buries his face in a pillow that smells just like Robbie, and fuck, maybe his heart doesn't know the answer it wants, but his body does. Just the idea of Robbie getting into bed with him again, and this time for more than just comfort, has him whimpering and thrusting into the rumpled blankets like the teenager he was just reminiscing about. The idea of Robbie fucking him makes his ass clench and his balls tighten. Lance has never found any particular joy in being on the receiving end of anal sex; it's something he thinks of as having learned to bear. But the idea of Robbie drilling into him...*Robbie's* finger-shaped bruises on his hips...*Robbie's* grunts and cries as he comes...*Robbie's* cum, painting him inside with a splash of heat....

Lance lifts his hips and gets his hand under his stomach and around his cock, suddenly desperate for any touch of skin, even if it's just his own. He folds his other arm and puts his face into the vee of his elbow, catching his own gasp as he works himself, hissing at the friction of his dry palm and then sighing as a surge of precum offers him a sweep of lubrication that makes everything more intense, driving him to a fever-pitch that has more to do with the fantasy in his mind than his own touch.

When he's about to come, he hastily rolls onto his back and cups his palm over his cock so he can catch all of his release on his stomach and in his hand. And then he lies gasping with his eyes trained on the capsized-ship ceiling of the hayloft, dazed.

Because Robbie will be back any time, he only gives himself to the count of ten to catch his breath, and then he scrambles out of bed to clean up. He worries that a telltale scent will still linger in the air, but then he realizes that a much stronger and less pleasant smell emanates from the calf's nest of towels.

Megan said that it would be a good sign when this happened. Still, he claps a hand over his nose and struggles not to gag as he peeks into the bathroom. The calf is looking at him with those big, innocent dark eyes.

"How can something so cute make such a terrible smell?" he asks her conversationally, and then he pulls on a pair of Johnny's jeans and carefully goes about the task of changing out the calf's towels and cleaning her up. He isn't sure where Robbie does laundry, and a hose might be the better first step for the towels, anyway, so he bundles everything into a trash bag and sets it on the deck, where he sees that Robbie happens to be coming up the steps.

"The baby took a shit," he tells Robbie proudly, holding up the bag. Then a gust of wind hits him and he steps back into the hayloft quickly, eyeing the bags in Robbie's hands and the sack of something over his shoulder. "Need help?"

Robbie smiles as he scales the deck stairs carefully. The snow he shoveled away earlier has already been replaced by a fresh, soft layer.

"I've got it," Robbie assures him. "But if you can take these sacks when I get up there?"

Lance nods, waiting in the doorway, shivering and peering at the silvery sky until Robbie is within reach. Lance is hurrying to take the sacks, which means he doesn't have a chance to figure out a way to take the bags without their hands touching. When he dips his crooked fingers through the handles, lifting the weight off of Robbie's hands in a silent signal to let go, he misses Robbie's cold fingers as soon as they're gone.

The intensity of these feelings is ridiculous, he thinks around his racing heart. Ridiculous even for Lance, who has never reacted proportionately to anything. Ridiculous even for feelings Lance has for *Robbie*, and the complex and tormented history of Robbie's place in Lance's heart.

Lance backs out of the doorway with the shopping bags, giving Robbie room to shake off the snow and shed his outer clothes. He busies himself putting milk, a dozen eggs, and a brick of cheese into the mostly empty fridge. In the second bag, he encounters the cereal, which makes him laugh. Robbie, now stripped down to jeans and a crewneck long-sleeved shirt in a navy blue so dark that it's almost inseparable from the spill of his hair and his beard, glances up from the calf he's knelt to pet with a smile. Lance can't meet his eye for more than a second before his stomach clenches and he remembers jerking off in Robbie's bed, to thoughts of Robbie, with a flash of guilt and shame. And excitement, too, that if Robbie knew, he might not mind. He might even....

Distracting himself by combing through another bag, Lance finds the box.

"What's this?"

The lid isn't taped down, so just Lance's handling has it tipping back and the smell of the contents wafting up at him.

Lance looks up to find Robbie on his feet where he was

kneeling a moment before, staring back. There's a splash of red on each of his cheeks. Lance feels that strange sense of being a second behind an important realization, and looks back down at the box. He pushes the lid out of the way altogether and a murmur of surprised pleasure escapes him as his thumb runs over the ridges of a cake of molded soap. It smells wonderful. He didn't see anything like this in the rows of economical bottles of shampoo, conditioner, and bodywash in Robbie's shower.

"What's this?" he asks, glancing at Robbie again.

"Um." Robbie lifts his right hand to rake it through his hair, pulling up the hem of his shirt. The resulting flash of smooth, hard abdomen grazed with a trail of black hair makes Lance's heart jump. "I guess it made me think of—I thought you might like it. It seemed nice." His smile eases toward teasing. "You know, fancy."

Lance can't remember when he last felt so breathless over a gift. He's always liked to have small and pretty things, so much so that he has a sordid history of taking them for himself. Some of the memories this feeling evokes are darker and uglier than others, but those threads of bad memory are quickly stifled by the thrill of the present.

Lance plucks the soap from its box and steps around the kitchen island countertop, and he rolls the edge of the soap against his opposite wrist, then lifts his arm toward his face and inhales the residual scent there, eyes half-closed.

Robbie looks like a feather could knock him over.

Lance continues to wander closer. "I do like it," he tells Robbie in a low murmur, stopping just within reach—if Robbie wanted to grab him. And he does; Lance can see with satisfaction that there's a fine tremor in his arms, the one still raised, his hand frozen on the back of his head, and the other, which dangles at his side, though his fingers have curled into a tight fist of restraint.

Dreamily, Lance recalls the first time he ever got in front of a camera. How the terror subsided and gave way to a pure sense of liberation. The wonder he felt at how he could lose himself in a performance. For Lance, it wasn't becoming someone else, as he'd heard others describe performing in the past. It was becoming a version of himself that was unbound by expectation.

He knows this dance with a man very well. It's been a performance, too, but one that he's grown to resent. This moment with Robbie, though, feels like being in front of the camera lens. That stripping away of restraint, that infusion of confidence that seems to have come from the ether and insists that he knows what he is doing; that if he gives in, he can't lose. He is a hawk on a thermal of air, lifted higher and higher. Nothing can reach him and bring him to Earth unless he agrees to return.

He lifts the bar of soap to his neck and rubs it there, looking at Robbie through hooded eyes, his eyelashes blurring the edges of Robbie's image. Somehow, that half-focus intensifies all the darkness of Robbie's beard and hair and eyes, which are snared by Lance like he's hypnotized.

"What do you think? Does it suit me?" Lance takes another step forward, head tilted, neck bared, and with a strangled sigh, Robbie leans forward to smell his neck. He isn't touching Lance, but there's a blooming heat from the proximity of their bodies, and Lance thinks Robbie must be aching just as Lance is, because the heat and energy he's radiating feels as tangible as a touch. Robbie's face hovers just over Lance's throat. His hair falls forward and brushes Lance's shoulder, but otherwise, they are bodies apart as Lance listens to the rasp of Robbie's inhale.

"It's—" Robbie begins to say, but the gust of his warm breath on Lance's neck as he speaks makes Lance gasp, which makes Robbie groan, and then, abruptly—

They go from being within a hair's breadth of touching to touching everywhere, bodies pressed tightly together as Robbie steps into Lance and closes his arms around him at the same moment, one arm an iron bar around Lance's waist, and his other hand splayed over his back. Robbie rubs his cheek against the line of Lance's neck, his nose against the crux of Lance's shoulder, and Lance isn't sure whether Robbie is kissing him so much as he's breathing him in. Overwhelmed, all Lance can do in return is anchor himself with both hands on Robbie's shoulders and whimper.

He studied these shoulders as a child, memorized their shape and carried the image with him every day of his life until today. Square, strong, able to bear anything. Lance has imagined being held like this, his hands just here on the warm curves of Robbie's shoulders, the biceps carved from ordinary hard work as beautifully taut and defined as anything honed in a gym.

But as soon as he has the feel of Robbie's shoulders under his palms, it's not enough. Robbie trails his mouth to map a new spot on the terrain of Lance's neck, his beard dragging over Lance's skin in a way that Lance wants to feel on his stomach, his thighs, and the back of his neck.

He leans back in Robbie's arms, because more than this, more than touch and heat and the circle of Robbie's arms, more than feeling the insistent press of Robbie's hard cock between their flush bodies and knowing it's hard because of Lance, Lance has wanted something else. Something simpler. Something much more complex.

"Robbie," he murmurs against Robbie's temple. "Robbie, Robbie," he says again, a murmured chant. Robbie lifts his head, his lips still parted from the charted path of hot laves he left on Lance's neck. The moment their eyes meet, by unspoken and instant agreement, Robbie's hand leaves Lance's back to cup his head, and they're kissing.

Despite the fervor of their grasping, straining touches, Robbie is so careful. So gentle. Even as he's insistent, he's responsive. He seems to interpret every yielding in Lance and every spot of tension, navigating the vocabulary of Lance's body like he's already fluent. He focuses on Lance's hypersensitive lower lip, stroking it with darts of his tongue and teasing it with his teeth, then sealing their lips together in a long, warm moment of pressure that's languorous and practically chaste.

They might have stayed like this forever, kissing, if Lance could have stopped himself from grinding against Robbie's pelvis, incredibly desperate for friction considering that he just had a decent orgasm only twenty minutes ago.

Robbie breaks their kiss and groans. "Lance. Sweetheart. I don't—" His hands fall to Lance's waist and he rolls his hips back against Lance's, which makes them both pant. "God. I have no idea what to do with you."

"Yes, you do," Lance says immediately. "You do."

"I don't—" Robbie interrupts himself with another gasp as Lance guides one of Robbie's hands lower so that his fingers are digging into the cleft of Lance's ass. "Oh, fuck. I mean—I've never done anything with a guy."

Lance feels incandescent at the admission, and also unspeakably tender. "It's okay," he says soothingly. The reality of taking Robbie somewhere unfamiliar is exponentially more intense than his earlier daydream. "Please, please, please. I want you so much."

Robbie doesn't protest as Lance separates them enough to drop his hands to Robbie's fly, then his. Lance thinks Robbie might startle if given the chance, so he doesn't bother getting himself out; he just reaches into Robbie's boxers and circles his hardness with his hand. He feels silky and thick, slightly curved. Lance strokes him slowly, feeling every bump and vein—another part of Robbie he wants to memorize.

"Oh my God," Robbie says hoarsely, clutching Lance's hips. With the jeans loosened, his hands are now closing around Lance's bare skin and the hem of the threadbare old boxers he fished out of Johnny's drawers. "You can't...I'm not going to last long," he warns.

Lance hums approvingly, and then, because he wants to be able to take his time and he's more or less assured that Robbie isn't going anywhere, he lets go of his cock, an exercise of sheer willpower, and nods toward the bed. "Lie down," he says, the word emerging as a low command.

CHAPTER EIGHTEEN

Robbie

Robbie crawls onto the bed and turns over to face Lance, finding him already on the bed and moving, walking on his knees into the space between Robbie's spread legs. Their eyes meet, and Robbie swallows.

His hands are already reaching for Lance; he makes them a cage around Lance's lean hips and his forefingers brush together low on Lance's waist, easily spanning his slender torso. Robbie's so hard that he hurts.

Lance's blue eyes are stormy, his skin flushed as his hands slide up Robbie's thighs. Lance's gaze drops to where the tip of Robbie's cock is protruding past the waistband of his briefs, desperate. He licks his lips, and Robbie's stomach clenches like he could come apart just from the way Lance is looking at him.

"Let me," Lance murmurs, slowly bending over until he's on his hands and knees over Robbie. He nudges Robbie's cheek, guiding Robbie into tilting his head, and then kisses him again. Robbie kissed Lance before and was kissed back; now, Lance is in the lead, and the act feels different. Fiercer, deeper. Lance presses their lips together before guiding

Robbie's apart, and then he touches the roof of his mouth with a clever tongue. Imagining that skilled mouth at work elsewhere on his body has Robbie's hips jerking, seeking contact.

Lance notices, of course, and with a satisfied purr, he lowers himself into the cradle of Robbie's thighs and rolls his narrow hips flush against Robbie's. What felt good when they were both standing up is excruciatingly perfect when Lance can bear half his body weight against Robbie, rocking into him with incredible pressure.

Robbie has to gasp, which breaks their kiss. Lance meets his eyes, smirks, and lowers his head again. This time, he skips Robbie's mouth and begins to kiss his way down Robbie's chest, then farther *down*, with unmistakable intent. Robbie's breath hitches, and he tenses. Lance freezes and looks up at him, a flash of fear in his expression. Fear of what, Robbie can only guess—but still, he thinks his guess is pretty good.

"I want you to," he rushes to say; in fact, his cock is objecting intensely to the fact that he's interrupted Lance on what was obviously a path toward putting his mouth around Robbie's throbbing cock. "But first, I want to look at you," Robbie says. "Please." He takes two handfuls of Lance's borrowed shirt and tugs communicatively.

Lance's expression eases somewhat, but he still looks nervous. He flashes a tense smile, kneeling up and stripping off his shirt—revealing all of that long, narrow, beautifully angular body to Robbie. The last time Robbie got a glimpse was torture—this time, it's a revelation, because Robbie is allowed to touch. Or at least, he thinks so? He finds his hands hovering an inch away from Lance's waist until Lance smiles again in silent permission. Then, Robbie strokes him from his ribs to his underarms, which makes Lance squirm and laugh, and then he trails his hands down the planes of Lance's pectorals and abs, which makes him shiver. Below that, Robbie cups the rigid bulge of his cock and then the softer heft of his balls, and his head spins. He knows that he's discovering something in this moment that, now, he'll always crave.

"Off," Robbie murmurs, meaning the boxers, and Lance seems to agree that they need to go. He gets out of them with impressive coordination for someone on his knees in the middle of a soft mattress, balancing himself on Robbie's thigh, and just like that, his long, pink, erect cock is in view, the skin of his sack a darker shade, liberally dusted in light gold hair. His thighs are so long and lean, if Robbie saw them in a photograph, he'd suspect they were digitally enhanced.

"You're stunning," Robbie breathes. "You are so beautiful."

Lance inhales like he might argue. Robbie sits up, takes him by the back of his neck, and kisses him quiet. Lance's cock slides against Robbie's stomach, and he sighs against Robbie's mouth.

"I want to take care of you," Robbie says when they break apart. He holds Lance's face and kisses his jaw, his chin. "Will you tell me what you like?"

"Anything," Lance says at once. "Anything you—anything you want to do, I'll like it." He makes a noise like a plea when Robbie slips his hand between them and takes hold of his shaft. The feel of him in Robbie's hand is heady...something both like and nothing like holding himself. Robbie does know the mechanics of cocks, though, he reasons, and tries a twist and pressure that he would appreciate if he took himself in hand, closely observing Lance's reaction.

Lance bucks against him and says, "Fuck!"

Encouraged, Robbie does it again, with similar results.

But he wants to do more than just give Lance a handjob fifteen seconds after he's undressed. So, he reluctantly lets go of that incredible, hot length that he intends to get to know much better and takes Lance by the waist, flipping him onto his back and reversing their positions. Lance peering up at him in surprise from the pillows is a sinful sight. But Robbie is unrepentant, bending his head to Lance's long, pale throat and wondering what it is about Lance's neck that makes him want to lick and bite every inch. He's never had this kind of fetish before. At first, it was about smelling the lingering residue of the soap on Lance's skin, and while that is still making him more than a little wild, he also has an almost primal urge to bite and claim.

Lance, apparently noticing, laughs lowly. "You're such a—ahhh—vampire."

Robbie rakes his teeth over Lance's pulse point and pauses. "Do you mind?" He's not particularly worried about how Lance might answer, based on the needy noises he's been making every time Robbie's tongue or teeth or beard touch him between his chin and his sternum.

"No," Lance assures him. "Just be careful. I have to go to court in a couple of days, remember?"

Robbie pushes himself up, his hands on either side of Lance's shoulders, and they look at each other. The charge between them is still there, but it's momentarily suspended by the reminder of everything beyond this hayloft. Into that brief but heavy silence, Robbie says slowly, "There's a lot we should talk about."

Lance's pupils are so blown that they've chased the blue of his irises to nothing but a rim of color, itself dark as a midnight sky. "We should talk," he agrees weakly.

Robbie looks down at him, those questions he's been pushing back feeling too far away to concern himself with. He knows this is a trick of his body, his speeding pulse; he knows he's not thinking clearly.

And still, he thinks clearly, *Fuck talking*, and lowers his mouth down again, this time just skimming the reddened skin of Lance's tantalizing throat before he's pressing his open mouth over Lance's left nipple instead.

Lance jerks and twists, his hand suddenly buried in Robbie's hair, holding him in place with surprising strength. It only lasts a moment, and then Lance swears and loosens his hold.

"Sorry, fuck, but...*fuck*."

Robbie interrupts his apologies by circling the bit of soft skin until it forms a tiny, hard peak, until Lance is clutching his head again in the same way, which Robbie is happy to encourage.

It takes him a minute of shifting his weight to arrange himself so that he can accomplish it, teasing Lance's nipple all the while, but he angles his arm and grips Lance's cock again, rubbing his thumb over the precum-slicked head, mimicking the movements and rhythm of his tongue until Lance is leaking copiously and pulling Robbie's hair, making his eyes sting. Robbie loves it. He loves the abandon in Lance, loves the helpless way he's toppled over by pleasure. Pleasure Robbie is giving him. *Care* Robbie is giving him. He stretches his legs further out behind him so that he can grind his own desperate hardness against the rumpled bedclothes, and then, summoning his courage and hoping he isn't about to become Lance's most disappointing lover ever, he lifts his head from Lance's chest, pushes himself the crucial foot further south, holds Lance firmly by the base of his cock, and adds his mouth.

Lance's cock is long, but Robbie's hands are big. Big enough that he can take Lance in until his lips meet his hand, enveloping Lance from root to tip. Robbie is so eager that the urge to gag at the feeling of a cock at the entrance to his throat doesn't stop him. He keeps going, having received enough blowjobs in his life, and fantasized about twice that many, to have a list of things he's always wanted to try on someone else. Lance is delightfully responsive the entire time, shaking and writhing. And when he's gotten Lance thoroughly wet, Robbie pauses to stroke him a few times.

"Robbie," Lance says in a strained voice, pushing Robbie's hair back as he lifts his head. The smell of male arousal and warm, intimate male skin—that should be familiar, but it's heady, new when it's not just Robbie, but Lance. The two of them together.

"What, sweetheart?" Robbie asks, the endearment slipping out. He hears it, and a thread of worry that Lance might not like it stabs at him, but Lance smiles down the line of his body, tucks his lower lip over his bottom teeth, and bites down. Robbie wants to kiss him again, but he stays between his legs for now, well-aware that that's where he's needed most at the moment.

"If you keep going," Lance begins, and then cuts himself off with a gasp as Robbie licks down his shaft and nuzzles in fascination at his balls, wondering if getting both of them in his mouth would be as easy as it looks in porn, "you're going to make me come."

Robbie smiles up at him. "Isn't that the point?" he asks, and puts his mouth on Lance's cock again, this time trying to take him a little deeper.

True to his word, Lance comes about thirty seconds after Robbie resumes his fast rhythm of stroking and suction. He pulls back so that the cum lands on his tongue instead of his throat, which isn't as distasteful as he'd expected—especially when it's accompanied by Lance's hoarse cry. Robbie feels his heart swell in his chest like he's just done something worthy of the highest praise, and he slips a hand past his own stomach and finishes himself off in a matter of moments, his forehead against Lance's thigh.

As Robbie drifts down from his orgasm, Lance strokes his

hair. There's a fleck of cum that must have escaped Robbie's mouth on Lance's hip bone, and a cooling, sticky mess in the cup of Robbie's hand, still tucked under his body. Lance's thigh is also just as lean and hard as it looks. The position isn't exactly comfortable, and at the same time, Robbie doesn't ever want to move.

But.

"Stay right there," he tells Lance, and then he kisses his knee and gets out of the bed before he can change his mind. The hayloft feels horribly cold after leaving that sex-heated nest, even though Robbie is somehow still wearing his shirt *and* jeans *and* boxers, and even his socks. He washes his hands in the bathroom, then runs warm water over an old washcloth that doesn't have any obvious stains. Still, while he's never noticed before, it practically has bristles, the pile is so rough. He makes a mental note—*new towels*—and buttons his jeans and hurries back.

Lance is sitting up, but he hasn't pulled the blanket around himself. He's looking out the window at the snow coming down. Robbie's steps slow, because if someone were here with a camera right now, he knows this image would wind up at the top of those search results he couldn't stop himself from pulling up earlier.

He slides back into the bed and, suddenly shy, hesitates for a moment before putting his hand on Lance's shoulder.

Lance turns to him with an uncertain smile that Robbie instantly wants to banish, so he leans in and kisses him. He never wants Lance to have to doubt how grateful, how eager, Robbie is to have the gift of touching him, kissing him. He gently dabs the spot of cum off Lance's hip, then eases closer, his arm going around him.

"You're still wearing all your clothes," Lance says.

"Yes," Robbie agrees.

"And I didn't even get to suck you off," Lance adds, this

time with what can only be called a pout.

Robbie laughs. "I wanted to." He clears his throat. "I wanted to do it, for *you*, and then I couldn't wait to come." He meets Lance's steady blue stare. "You were so sexy. I loved doing it. I hope it was…?"

Lance's grin is immediate, the warmth in his eyes unmistakably sincere. "It was perfect."

Robbie smiles, kisses his shoulder, and then arranges himself against the headboard behind Lance, pulling him back between his legs before arranging the blankets over him. Lance's hard back against his chest and Lance's ass between his thighs is giving him all kinds of ideas, but somehow even more distracting is the easy access he now has to Lance's neck, and how he can brush his nose through his hair, and how Lance's arms lie over his, their fingers threading together upon Robbie's knees.

"I need to tell you something," Robbie murmurs against Lance's shoulder. "I looked up your name on my phone," he confesses in a rush.

But Lance just twists around to look at him and grins. "Finally. I'm kind of offended you hadn't done it already."

Robbie snorts. "Why? Have *you* searched for *me?*" The idea of anyone thinking there's anything about Robbie to be found on the internet seems comical. But to his dismay, Lance is nodding shyly.

"Yeah. I never found anything. Well, one time I saw your name on some approval list of BLM subcontractors. I didn't really know what I was seeing at the time. I guess I do now." He shifts against Robbie, leaning back so his head rests on Robbie's shoulder. "It wasn't what I wanted, though."

Thinking of the pictures has made Robbie hot all over. Especially now that he's holding in his arms their untouchable, forbidden subject. He can't help sliding his hand down the center of Lance's chest toward his navel.

"What *did* you want? Did you think you'd find a picture of me?"

Lance nods his head.

Robbie smiles. "I couldn't compete with yours. Did you really want to see *me* standing naked by a lighthouse?"

Lance laughs. "That one? Ugh, that one is so cliche."

"You look amazing in it," Robbie says earnestly. "I didn't look at it for long enough. I'll have to study it more later."

Lance laughs again, but more breathily. Possibly, he's affected by the fact that Robbie's hand has drifted lower, between his legs.

"Maybe you wanted to see me tied up with a bolt of lace."

Lance's response is just a sigh. Robbie smiles at the feeling of his cock filling in his hand as he gently massages the shaft, thick even in repose, and tugs on his heavy balls. Definitely a mouthful, but he's sure, now, that he could manage both. The idea makes him salivate more than a steak dinner ever could.

"I liked that one." He pushes his nose against the spot where Lance marked himself with the soap, but the scent is lost for now. He only smells salt and Lance, and maybe an undercurrent of cum, which is undeniably in the air.

"You like me when I'm pretty?" Lance asks, sounding breathless, and Robbie's cock is quickly hardening again, pressed against the perfect ass that's nestled against him.

"Yes," he admits.

Lance leans his head far to the side, presenting his neck again, like an offering, and Robbie is helpless to do anything but bend and suck on the white skin there, tonguing a fine blue vein as he, unbelievably, starts getting hard again—something that hasn't happened to him in such close succession since...ever.

"That's why you brought me that nice soap. You want me to smell pretty. You want me in lace. Maybe panties. What about stockings, would you—fuck, fuck, fuck," Lance interrupts himself with a string of hissed curses as Robbie, acting purely on instinct, pushes his hand past his balls and probes the hot, lightly-furred skin around his asshole. Lance groans like it's his cock there and not just his fingertip, and Robbie, head full of a reel of fantasies, contains himself to just stroking, pressing. Knowing he is miserably lacking required knowledge to do more than that.

Then, Lance's hand covers his and guides him. Lance's fingertip pushes Robbie's deftly against Lance's incredibly tight hole, the tiny ridges of skin strange and tantalizing, until the muscle yields and Robbie's forefinger is inside him, just to the first knuckle, and dry, but it's still an overwhelming heat and pressure, especially because Robbie is already thinking about what it would be like to have his cock where his finger is.

He makes a ragged sound against Lance's neck. Lance has hooked his own arm around the back of his own thigh, holding himself within Robbie's reach, holding himself *open*. Robbie is overcome, somewhere between tears and laughter, feeling some kind of shocked joy. He's also perilously close to having a second orgasm in his jeans, which might be further into martyrdom than he's willing to travel.

But before that thought can complete itself, Lance, perfect Lance, is guiding Robbie's hand again, this time drawing it away from Lance's body. Then, Lance turns over between Robbie's legs like a panther, and in a show of strength that reminds Robbie that he's earned all of those ridges of lean muscle on practically every inch of his body, he jerks back the sheets and lifts Robbie's hips easily, divesting him quickly of his jeans and boxers, and he swallows Robbie to the root with the same kind of anticipatory noise that someone makes when they're very hungry and presented with a meal.

CHAPTER NINETEEN

Lance

Lance has always enjoyed sex. The basic act, yes, but almost more so, he's enjoyed the sense of honing a skill that he has an aptitude for. Maybe it's competitiveness—or a fundamental need to please—but even when he isn't particularly attracted to a partner, he can still take pleasure in pleasing someone.

With Robbie, though...obviously, with Robbie, it's different. But not in the way Lance would have expected. Giving Robbie pleasure makes Lance want to smile, to laugh, and to stop and tease not as a strategic delay of gratification, but because it gives him a visceral thrill to hear Robbie curse and beg. And because he *must* occasionally stop what he's doing to kiss Robbie's mouth, rub his cheek against Robbie's soft beard, and nuzzle the fascinating, thick curls in the center of Robbie's hard chest. Every time he gets distracted, Lance is sure to keep lazily stroking Robbie's length, which is wet and warm from Lance's mouth.

His entire body feels warm and bright from happiness, like he inhaled sunlight along with every breath of air perfumed by Robbie's skin. In short, there's a joy in being with Robbie that Lance hasn't felt before.

Maybe everything is made more intense by the ticking clock. Lance knows that whatever they're doing together won't last past Tuesday night, the deadline that Lance has given himself to tell Robbie everything. When Lance does that, he harbors no illusions that Robbie will continue to look at him like he's some kind of magical creature who could never do wrong.

This stolen time will end soon, which is all the more reason Lance is determined to enjoy it right now.

He pulls his head up again. He's had Robbie deep in his throat, and his voice is a rasp as a consequence. Robbie's cock isn't the biggest one he's ever sucked, but it's the biggest one he's had the privilege of swallowing in a while, and he's so greedy for it.

But he's greedier for something else. He meets Robbie's eye.

"Will you touch me?"

"Yeah, yeah," Robbie breathes, stroking Lance's hair.

Lance smiles at his touch. But that isn't what he meant. He rearranges himself in silent explanation, straddling Robbie's chest backward, tugging Robbie's hand back to his cleft. Lance almost lost it at the idea of Robbie there— Robbie fucking him, even with a dry fingertip. He thinks briefly of lube, but dismisses it. He can't wait. So, he just spits into his own hand, reaches back, and smears it over his hole.

"Jesus, Lance," Robbie pants. Lance leans down and takes Robbie's cock back in his mouth again, this time burying his nose in Robbie's balls instead of his pubic bone, tilting back his hips in a silent quest for Robbie's hand, and Robbie—

Robbie puts his *mouth* to Lance's hole instead.

Lance almost comes from the shock of it, the intense rush of pleasure an afterthought to the euphoria of his thoughts.

Robbie. Robbie's mouth on him. Robbie's tongue pushing against him, oh, God—

He moans around Robbie's cock, which makes Robbie's hips jerk, and his mouth more insistent, which makes Lance moan again. They keep feeding off of each other in a fast and brutal cycle that quickly ends with Robbie pulsing and coming straight down Lance's throat, so Lance only notices that Robbie is coming because of the undulations in his shaft. And when Robbie in turn closes his hand around Lance's cock, he comes at that first touch, though after two orgasms in close succession, it almost hurts.

Even after he's come, Robbie is tonguing his hole, laving it, and Lance can do nothing but fall onto his forehead and elbows between Robbie's knees while Robbie holds him up by the waist and thigh. He worships Lance until Lance is whimpering with the feeling of a trail of saliva dripping down his balls and his over-sensitized shaft.

Lance collapses, rolls onto his back, and stares at the ceiling, panting. Robbie lays back against the pillows so they're lying next to each other, but head to toe. Robbie takes Lance gently by the ankle and Lance bats at his calf, warding him off.

"You can't. You'll break me."

Robbie chuckles and guides Lance's reluctant foot into the center of his body, where he cradles it between both hands, then slowly and gently rolls his thumbs into the arch.

"Oh, my God. I take it back. Do that. Keep doing that." Lance's eyes drift closed, and he says nothing else except the occasional murmur of approval for what Robbie's hands are doing, offering a whimper of protest when Robbie stops and then a happy sigh when he discovers he's only switching to Lance's other foot. He throws his arm over Robbie's leg and strokes small circles into the skin of his thigh, just above his knee, until he falls asleep.

The next thing he knows, he's lying on his side, neatly tucked under the top sheet and blanket that smell exactly like what they were doing earlier, and he can hear Robbie speaking to the calf.

"Look at you, you big, strong girl," Robbie coos. "Up on your feet. Lance is going to be sorry he missed this."

Lance props himself on an elbow, blinking sleepily. "Sorry he missed what?"

Robbie looks up from where he's crouched. The calf is back in front of the wood stove, but instead of in her blanket nest, she's standing. She's definitely wobbly, and looks skeptical about the wisdom of the act, but she's upright and balanced on her tiny, sharp hooves like they're four spindles and she's a trainee acrobat.

Her empty bottle rests on Robbie's knee. He rubs the calf's chest and beams at her.

Lance has the absurd urge to ask, "*Can we keep her?*", and then to demand that he himself get to name her, considering Robbie's track record with animal names.

He manages to stop himself.

Regardless of the bliss of the past day, he and Robbie aren't *together*. They don't get to build a picket fence around a new farmhouse and pen in a frolicking pet calf. Soon, Lance will have his court date, and the best-case scenario after that is for him to get to Chicago and take back the small parts of his life that aren't irretrievably entangled with Niall. Robbie hasn't invited him to stay forever, and even if he did—

"Hey, what is it?" Robbie rises to his feet, frowning in concern. He's incredibly beautiful when he's sleep- and sex-rumpled. His dark eyes are soft and focused on Lance in just the way Lance has always craved, but all of the old intensity is magnified by the fact that Lance still has the taste of him in his mouth, the feel of him on his skin.

He forces a smile and gets out of bed so that he'll have an

excuse to avert his eyes. "I'm just worried she won't be all right."

Robbie's speculative glance lingers, suggesting he isn't buying Lance's diversionary tactic, but he plays along, looking back at the calf and giving her a fond rub on the back of the neck. "Megan seemed optimistic." The calf cranes her head up and sticks out an absurdly long, curled tongue to try to lick Robbie's wrist. They both laugh.

Lance pulls on Johnny's jeans and surrenders himself to the welcome distraction of the calf, petting her wonderingly, careful not to let his touch throw her off balance. After a minute or two, she grows tired, anyway, and after taking a few triumphant steps that garner further praise from Lance and Robbie, she collapses back into her towel nest.

"We should set her up downstairs in one of the stalls," Robbie says. "She's cute, but she's going to seem a lot less cute when she starts making regular, um...outputs."

Lance wrinkles his nose. "You don't have to convince me. I learned firsthand, remember?"

Robbie grins and nods. "I guess you did."

"But isn't it too cold for her?"

"I don't think so, not now that she's dry. And it's a lot warmer down there than it is outside. I also have an overhead heater that I can turn on...provided it still works."

While Robbie goes about dealing with the logistics of moving the calf to more appropriate quarters, Lance pets her, stroking her from the soft whiskers around her wet nose to the tips of her fluttering ears. It's been a long time since he's allowed himself to draw an alternate reality around himself. He knows firsthand what the fallout is like when one of those crumbles around him. But he lets himself indulge, just for a minute. If Robbie were his, and his home were with Robbie, he'd convince Robbie to keep the calf. It probably wouldn't be hard; she's much more endearing than the triplicats. And then he'd choose a name for her. He knows exactly what it would be, and the thought makes him grin. Robbie happens to come in while his smile is still lingering, and he smiles in turn.

"The heater fired up just fine. Want to give me a hand with the door?"

Lance dons a coat and boots, and opens and closes the doors so that Robbie can navigate them with both arms full of the calf. When they reach the lower story of the barn, Lance looks around curiously.

"It's weird, seeing it without the horses," he says while Robbie places the calf in a nest of fresh straw in the first stall. A wide, flat infrared heater that's affixed to the ceiling glows red, giving off enough heat that Lance is too warm in his coat.

Robbie looks wistful and nods. "Yeah, to me, too."

Lance dares to ask a question that he's had on his mind since Robbie brought him to the ranch on Saturday morning. "What made you stop training?"

Robbie tucks a strand of hair behind his ear, his expression faraway.

"There were a lot of signs that it wasn't for me. It was hard for me when people took a horse home and didn't get along with it like I had. Which happened a lot of the time, you know? Every rider feels different to a horse, so they never work exactly the same for two different people. Especially if the second rider doesn't put the time in with them. It made me anxious, always wondering if a customer would be happy or not. And even though forty-nine out of fifty people were happy, it was always the unhappy one who I couldn't forget about."

He steps out of the stall and Lance follows.

Robbie keeps talking. "But I could have dealt with the unhappy people. It was the unhappy horses I couldn't stomach in the end." He shoots Lance a sad, strained smile.

"The last straw was this nice red mare named Sienna. The young couple who owned her bought her as a foal, and they loved her, even though they were beginners and she was pretty high-strung. I had a lot of fun with her, but I told them all along that I wasn't sure she'd turn into something they'd get along with. They were inexperienced, and she was a lot of horse for someone without a quiet hand and a lot of confidence. But she and I—well, I like any horse. But every once in a while, I just click with one on another level, and Sienna was like that.

"She went home after about four months, and it took a good six months after that before I got over not seeing her looking over the stall door at me every morning. I never heard a word from her owners. Usually, I considered no news to be good news, but I had this feeling about all of it...and, I really couldn't get her off my mind. So, one day, I called to see how they were doing with her, and maybe ask if they'd consider selling her to me."

Lance leans against the stall wall, not taking his eyes off of Robbie, his heart speeding up like his body has already sensed what's coming even though his imagination hasn't quite put together how the pieces of this story end in disaster.

"The guy answered, and he was real short with me. I knew right away something was off. But he said he'd be happy to sell her. Rattled off a price that I was sure I heard wrong; seemed like it was missing a zero. He said I was just in time because they'd been planning to pack her off to the auction house, but if I could come that day, I could have her. He told me that, a few days after they brought her home from here, they took her out on a trail ride. His wife was riding, and she had some trouble and got thrown. She wasn't hurt, but they were upset and scared. So, they sent Sienna to a trainer who some friend of theirs said would get her 'good and broke.'" He pauses to roll his eyes. "But that didn't work out, either, he said. She was hopeless, he told me, and they just wanted her gone."

Robbie swallows and continues in a softer voice. "I went that same day to get her. I wouldn't have recognized her if she hadn't heard my voice and looked at me just the way I remembered she would when she was here at the ranch. It seemed like they'd decided to stop feeding her while they waited for the auction date to come. And she had a big swollen joint in her hind leg that no one could explain. I gave him his price, which was about twice what he would have gotten at the sale, without saying a word, and I brought her here."

He rubs his wrist against his cheek, which is when Lance realizes he's crying. Not much, just a tear or two, but Lance aches. Still, he stays glued where he is, with his hands trapped between his back and the wall. He senses that he shouldn't touch Robbie right now, or in any way disrupt the story.

"She didn't make it," Robbie says a few seconds later, almost whispering. "I don't know how she got injured, but we tried everything and couldn't make her right. She had an infection that got into the bone, then into the joint. Megan helped me find a specialist to look at her who confirmed the worst." He shrugs. "We couldn't help her, but at least she had a little peace at the end.

"And after that, I felt like I couldn't trust anyone who called. I'd thought that was such a well-meaning couple, you know? So, I worried every time that people who seemed decent were actually monsters. And the horses I already had here, I could hardly look in the eye. Here I was teaching them to trust me so that they'd go on to trust other people, and *I* didn't trust anyone further than I could goddamn throw them.

"It was all worse for Johnny. He was having a hard time, anyway, and the whole deal with Sienna about broke him. But if training horses is hard on the heart, raising livestock someone is going to eat one day is even harder." He looks at the calf with an absent, pained smile. "So, I didn't know what the fuck to do."

Lance can't help wishing he'd been there; not that he could have been any help. He imagines the pain all three of them must have felt, and the worry. But of course, they had each other.

"But you figured out the thing with the BLM. The mustangs," Lance supplies hesitantly, hoping to coax Robbie out of the darkest part of the memory.

Robbie turns a small smile on him, giving his eyes a last brush with his sleeve. "Well, I can't take any credit for that. That was the brains of the outfit—Danny."

Lance gives his own small smile back. "Yeah, you said that. But anyway, I already would have known."

"That's right, you should have. Anyway, he holed up for a couple of days doing whatever he does to come up with brilliant solutions, and came out with what we should do and how we should do it. I think a timeline, a chart, and a business plan were all involved, but it's kind of a blur."

Shaking his head, Lance smiles ruefully, a little bowled over in the moment by how much he misses Danny. "When did all this happen?"

"About five years ago. Not long after you...well." Robbie's eyes flick to Lance's as he trails off.

Lance bites his lip, filling in that blank without difficulty. *Not long after you stormed in here, humiliated yourself, and ran off, never to be heard from again.*

"Want to help me with this bale of straw? I'm going to break it up for her. It'll be better bedding than those old towels, won't it, little girl?"

Lance carries one end of a bale of straw that looks like it's been collecting dust in a corner of the barn for more than one season, but when Robbie cuts the twine with his pocket knife, the interior is bright gold and smells fresh. They spread it in the stall in silence.

It's strangely therapeutic, the quiet work of breaking the packed straw into a fluffy carpet. The strain in the air from the telling of Robbie's story seems to have eased by the time they finish.

"Let's get upstairs," Robbie says gently. "I think she's pretty cozy down here, but you and I don't have fur coats."

"*I* don't," Lance allows, glancing at Robbie to gauge his reaction. When Robbie arches a brow, he continues, stepping forward and running a hand down Robbie's chest. "But you, on the other hand."

Robbie laughs. "Are you saying I'm *hairy?*" He puts his hands around Lance's waist like it's automatic, an impulse. The thought chases any suggestion of chill from the cold space straight out of Lance's fingers and toes, leaving them tingling.

"That's exactly what I'm saying," Lance admits, and then he leans in and lowers his voice to a murmur against Robbie's ear. "And I love it."

"Upstairs," Robbie orders, his voice rough. "There's a few more things I want you to show me."

CHAPTER TWENTY

Robbie

"There's so much I want to ask you," Lance murmurs when the sky is getting dark, and the hayloft with it, since they haven't bothered to turn on the lights. Lance's cheek is pressed against Robbie's chest. Robbie has been teasing one of the short curls at Lance's temple. For several minutes, it's been silent between them as they've watched the snow and the darkness lying two silent blankets down over the trees, like the whole world is being tucked in.

"Me, too," Robbie says quietly.

Lance's parted fingers slide through his chest hair, absently, and Robbie, now convinced Lance wasn't teasing about having a thing for the dark body hair that has always made Robbie self-conscious, feels his already compromised heart turn over yet again.

"Maybe," Lance says, almost whispering, "we could trade. You answer a question, and then I'll answer one."

"Okay," Robbie agrees, hoping he doesn't sound too eager. Then, Lance is quiet for so long that Robbie almost thinks he's fallen asleep.

But he hasn't. Finally, Lance asks, "Why are you still here?"

It hadn't occurred to Robbie that Lance could ask questions Robbie wouldn't want to answer. He'd only been thinking, eagerly, of being invited to ask *Lance* some of the questions that he's been holding back for days.

But this question. *This* question. Robbie takes a deep breath, remembering there's a somewhat easy answer, even if it's incomplete. "Because someone has to be," he says. "There's a really weird provision in my grandfather's will. It says that my dad's kids get the ranch *if* at least one of us lives here, continuously, for twenty-one years after my dad's death."

Lance twists around under Robbie's hand to blink up at him. "Seriously?"

Robbie smiles wryly. "Yeah."

"That's like something out of a movie."

"Yeah." Robbie smiles grimly and leans his head back. "A *bad* movie. A bad *TV* movie."

He laughs. "No argument here. My dad told me about it in vague terms. He didn't really think it would be relevant, I guess. He was like you; he thought it was too absurd to hold up in court. He had a lawyer working on it off and on for a couple of years. But then, he died, and it—it didn't turn out the way he'd thought it would. So, we'd lose the ranch if I ever moved."

"It has to be you? It couldn't be Johnny or Danny?"

Robbie shrugs, his gaze skating away from Lance. "They have lives somewhere else. I don't want them to be tied here." He darts a quick look at Lance and finds that his expression is a little pinched.

"That's not fair to you, though."

Robbie pushes back the tightness in his chest and strokes Lance's hair off his temple. "Where else would I go, anyway?"

Lance looks like he was about to say something, then changed his mind. He settles back down with his head on Robbie's chest. "There's no way out of the twenty-one-year thing? I mean, no loopholes?"

Robbie just shakes his head, exhausted at the thought of summarizing all of the various research trails his father's old, talkative lawyer got excited about over the years, all of which came to nothing. "No. It's technically the property of my grandfather's trust, and if we don't meet the condition, it all goes to my uncle instead."

"That's crazy."

"It is."

"But what about your uncle? Does he...?"

"That wasn't the deal," Robbie interrupts hastily. "I answered your question, and now it's my turn." He strikes a compromise between what he most wants to know and what he thinks might not send Lance running. "Why did you come back here?"

Lance sighs. "My dad's dying. For real, this time. I already needed an excuse to get out of Chicago. So, when the hospice people called, I just drove." Before Robbie can comment, he says briskly, "My turn. What happened with Megan?"

"I think me and her both just realized something we should have figured out a lot earlier. We're friends, you know? That's all it ever really was between us. What do you like better—taking pictures or being in them?"

Lance rolls over so his head is on Robbie's thigh and grins up at him. "Will it make me vain if I say 'both'?"

Robbie pulls a shocked face. "Lance Taylor, are you admitting that you know how pretty you are?"

Still grinning, Lance bats his lashes, which should be ridiculous, but instead makes Robbie feel a tingle of interest between his legs. "I don't know," Lance says then, laughing. "But I love self-portraits. I guess because I can make all the decisions. The light, the angle, the expression on my face. Maybe it wouldn't be so appealing if I was better at telling other models what to do while I shoot them. I even did a whole series of self-portraits, and it's probably the closest thing I have to a success. My turn." His smile fades. "Why isn't Johnny here with you?"

Robbie feels his smile slip away, too. He shrugs. "He's off having adventures. Can't blame him, can I?"

Lance's eyes narrow. "I don't know. Can you?"

Puzzled, Robbie just looks at him, uncomprehending.

"Does he know about the whole inheritance thing?"

Technically, it's a second question, but Robbie rubs his jaw and nods.

Lance presses his lips together. "Then you definitely *can* blame him." He looks at Robbie cautiously from under his lashes. "That makes it your turn."

The moment feels too heavy already. All of the questions Robbie still has, he doesn't think the link between him and Lance could bear without breaking. So, he pushes Lance into the blankets and kisses him until they're both smiling again.

"I'll save my turn for later," Robbie says.

———

The two days since their ride in the woods have passed in a blur of talking and sex, with brief pauses for food and longer ones for sleep. They trade questions, but Robbie is too afraid of breaking the soap bubble they seem to be inside, spinning and afloat, to ask anything too serious. So, instead, he now knows that Lance doesn't like tea, except when he's sick, and that the gym he's a member of in Chicago is called Fit Place, and his favorite kind of cookie is a ginger snap.

And he knows more serious things, too—like the story of the first photograph Lance sold, and that Lance has a penchant for stealing things, little things. He gives them back, sometimes. Of course, Robbie already knew something about that.

"Danny used to call you a magpie."

Lance, who's been sprawled over Robbie's chest with his face next to his heart, in what seems to be one of his favorite positions, pushes himself up, giving Robbie a fairly solid blow to the solar plexus in the process. While Robbie gasps, Lance looks down at him with narrowed eyes, apparently unrepentant. "You remember that?"

Robbie's grin turns into a softer smile. "I remember everything, sweetheart."

They look at each other, Lance's expression changing so fast, like it can't settle between worry and affection and happiness and uncertainty. After a moment, he slowly lowers himself back to Robbie's chest. "Magpie. Well, that's a nicer word than other people have used." Then, after a few long moments pass, he adds, "You haven't asked me when I have to go to court."

Of all the things about "court" that Robbie would have thought to ask, somehow that—something so purely logistical—hasn't crossed his mind. He carefully traces a line up and down Lance's back with his palm.

"I have to go tomorrow," Lance continues. "I'm scheduled for one o'clock, at the courthouse."

"Do you want me to help you call lawyers?"

Lance just shakes his head. He's going tense, which is easy to feel when he's draped all over Robbie, but he puts his head back down and doesn't roll away, so Robbie dares to push.

"I know a few. All that stuff with my grandfather's will, remember? I could...?"

"Not yet," Lance says forcefully. Robbie isn't exactly sure what he means, but he pretends that Lance distracts him by kissing his neck, and lets it go. And a few minutes after that, gasping while Lance pushes aside the blankets and sits up to straddle him, rocking so their cocks slide together, he isn't just pretending to be distracted anymore.

But he remembers later, in the dark. And Lance must, too, because he turns to Robbie so they lie facing each other on their sides, and he laces their fingers together.

"I've done some stuff I'm not very proud of," he tells Robbie.

So have I. So have we all, Robbie wants to assure him, but he knows how fragile the moments are where Lance will share things like this, so he doesn't dare interrupt.

"I promised myself I'd tell you, before tomorrow. I have— I was—seeing someone, I guess. In Chicago. His name's Niall."

Robbie tells himself he shouldn't be surprised. And he definitely shouldn't be hurt. He definitely shouldn't be panicking. He just holds still and listens over the noise of his own pulse, a thudding in his ears like a drum signal of impending doom.

"I lived with him. He's older. A photographer. And he took care of everything, so when we had a fight, and I left—" Lance breaks their handhold and rubs his head; Robbie feels the movement of his body—can even hear the soft rasp of his hair on his palm. "Well, he turned off my phone and reported the car stolen. When I walked out of the care home after I saw my dad, there was a patrol car pulled up behind me in the parking lot and they were running the plate."

Of all the things Robbie wants to say, he settles for, "Is he an idiot? Didn't he know what would happen after he reported the car stolen?"

He feels Lance flinch before he answers, "He was mad. I don't know what exactly he thought would happen. Actually —he probably did know. And he probably thought I'd call him after I was picked up and beg for forgiveness." Lance rolls onto his back and a small, bitter laugh escapes him. "He wasn't completely wrong. I *did* think about calling him. But I couldn't bring myself to actually do it. Niall is...I don't know. We had some pretty good times, I guess. But the bad times got to be too much for me. I told you I got that call about Dad, being in hospice, at just the right moment for me to get in the car and drive, didn't I? Well, they called when Niall had just thrown my favorite camera out the window."

His tone is so matter-of-fact. The tone of someone accustomed to abuse; raised with it. Robbie knows he shouldn't reach for him, but he can't stop himself. "Lance." His fingers brush Lance's arm, and just like that, Lance is darting away from him like a bird out of a thicket. He sits up and swings his legs over the side of the bed so that his back is to Robbie, lit with a silver glow from the moonlight in the window, and Robbie can see the knobs of his spine.

"I didn't love Niall or anything. I was there for the stuff. The money." His voice is hard, like he's challenging Robbie to —what? Judge him for having been in a transactional relationship?

Just as he sensed he shouldn't reach for Lance before, he knows he should wait, and let him talk, rather than speak up himself right now. But he can't stop himself. "I don't care about any of that. I just care about you."

Lance wraps his arms around himself and doesn't turn. "I thought it was worth it. And for a long time, it was. Niall knew people. He helped me get work. And I love working. I love my friends. I really thought I belonged in Chicago."

"You need to talk to a lawyer."

Lance glares over his shoulder. "That's not—aren't you listening to me?"

"I'm going to give you a few names you should call. And you can use my phone. You can use my phone for whatever you need it for. And—"

"Robbie," Lance interrupts again, his voice sharper now. "Are you *listening?*"

Robbie sits up slowly, the sheets pooling in his lap. His expression will be almost invisible to Lance; the room is dark and all of the feeble moonlight is on Lance, highlighting the impatient gleam in his narrowed eyes, the sweep of the bridge of his nose, and the curve of his back and shoulders. "I'm listening. But what needs dealing with is tomorrow. The rest of it—"

"Don't you think I deserve this, at least a little? I was basically—I told you I was only with Niall because he *kept* me."

Robbie thinks about it. "I only care that you don't go back to him."

"You should hate me," Lance insists.

"Lance. I'm never going to hate you." An image of Lance as a wide-eyed, scrawny boy running through the woods flashes in his mind, and he smiles. "I've known you since you were nine years old. You're *family*."

It's the wrong thing to say. He realizes this at once, but he can't grasp the reason why. Lance's expression shutters, and he's off the bed and six feet away, still hugging himself, naked and barefoot and suddenly as untouchable and unreachable as if he were back in Chicago already.

"I don't want to talk about this. I'm tired, and tomorrow is going to be a long day."

"I'll drive you," Robbie says immediately, even while, in the back of his head, he's panicking at the broader implications of this moment. "One o'clock, you said. I'll have you there at twelve-thirty."

Lance nods stiffly. "Thanks."

"You're not sleeping on that couch," Robbie says. "Come on, Lance."

Lance doesn't move, and Robbie feels a flare of desperation. Maybe he's always sensed this was a stolen time between them, but he didn't realize he'd have no more than a few minutes to prepare to lose it.

"Get back in this bed," he says quietly, defeated, and climbs out of the place where they've passed so many perfect hours, the memories suddenly leaving him cold. "I'll sleep on the air mattress."

CHAPTER TWENTY-ONE

Lance

Six years ago.

His father found Lance's new hiding spot.

It's been a long time since he's used floorboards, as his father has long since learned all of the small signs that lead him to those underfoot spaces. So, Lance has found other spots, most of them outside. But those are dangerous, too, because he has to mark them somehow. He can't exactly draw himself a map—then, he'd have to hide that. That means he's ended up using little stone towers, like cairns, marking each place. A part of him knew it was only a matter of time before his father found one of them, and apparently that time has come.

There's a broken glass jar on the kitchen table, a crumpled piece of black fabric amidst the shards. There's only one thing it could be: the lace panties Lance took last spring from the department store downtown. Sure enough, as he looks for another moment, a ridge of lace catches the light and Lance can even see the shiny pink tag, still attached.

When Lance takes things from stores, he always leaves

the tags on. In his mind, that means that he could still return the items, one day. That makes it *taking*, not stealing. Certainly not *shoplifting*.

It's not the first time his father has gotten angry at Lance for taking. But Lance knows that, this time, *what* Lance took is the detail that has thrown his father completely out of orbit. He's yelling at Lance so loudly, and his words are all slurring together. That's partially because Lance's ears are ringing and partially because his father has already emptied a bottle of whiskey. It's lying on its side next to the kitchen sink.

He's still steady enough to cross the kitchen, pick up the bottle by the neck, and raise it in Lance's direction. That's when Lance runs.

He runs out into the summer starlight. And he runs to the only place he ever runs, really—the Chases' farmhouse. The porch light motion sensor comes on as he crosses the yard, and a relieved breath rushes out of him. He quiets his steps out of habit, though he knows that even if he wakes them all, they won't ask him why he's there or turn him away. Still, it's better to sneak in. It's better to reach the empty side of Danny's bed without having to talk to anyone, not until morning. Everything always seems more bearable in the mornings.

Lance avoids all of the creaky places in the floors of this house he loves and knows so well, until he's upstairs and halfway down the hall to Danny's door.

But he doesn't make it there in the end, because Robbie's light is on and his door is half-open. He calls out as Lance passes.

"Lance, is that you?"

Today.

Lance doesn't sleep. He stares out the window at the piling snow and the moonlight, until the marbled silver wall of clouds passes over the moon and there's only darkness.

Robbie wasn't kidding about how noisy the air compressor is. He scared all three cats into hiding under the sofa while he ran it. Under any other circumstances, Lance would have laughed until his stomach ached. But in the aftermath of his conversation with Robbie, he found no humor in the situation. He just lay still with his back to Robbie and pretended the noise was nothing, watching the window.

Before he laid down himself, Robbie explained he was leaving his phone where Lance could use it if he needed it. He wrote down the password on a slip of paper in case Lance forgot. Then, he got down on the air mattress, in the dark near the bathroom door outside the span of the moonlight. Even when Lance snuck glances over his shoulder, he couldn't see Robbie. He could hear the blankets rustling, though, for a while—quite a while. He wondered if either of them would sleep at all. But then, eventually, Robbie's breaths grew deep and even, leaving Lance alone as if he were the only person awake in the world.

He thinks of his father's house across the creek. He thinks of his younger self in his room, facing the window framed by curtains laced by a mother he can't remember. So many years have been spent thinking of his inability to sleep the way he's imagined everyone else in the world does, slipping under and out with the lights...another thing that's made him different. Another aspect of himself that's separated him from other people. It wasn't until he was almost through college that he got his sleeping pills. He thinks of the little bottle tucked into his luggage in the trunk of his—or rather, Niall's—car, which would solve his sleeping problem in just fifteen to twenty minutes. Then, he thinks about those dreamless nights on the pills, veiling a deeper problem with a surface remedy, but not letting himself consider it too carefully. Focusing instead on the way he could lie down next to Niall and not have to spend the whole night staring at him and hearing his snores.

He tries not to think about how soundly he slept, unmedicated and nestled in Robbie's arms. He fails.

To torture himself a little more, he thinks about how he chased Robbie out of the bed they were sharing and across the hayloft, for reasons he can't even untangle in his own mind, let alone hope to explain to Robbie. Shouldn't he have been relieved when Robbie heard the truth about Niall and wasn't angry or disgusted?

Maybe he was angry and disgusted, and just didn't say so.

Yet, Lance doesn't think Robbie could have hidden his real feelings so well. There'd been no trace of condemnation on his face.

Maybe I'm the one who's angry and disgusted.

That thought is the one that lingers in Lance's head until sunup.

When the sun rises, Robbie wakes. He doesn't say anything to Lance; maybe he thinks Lance is sleeping. He runs water in the sink; Lance hears the now-familiar sounds of the pat of a scoop of powdered milk against the surface of the warm water, and then the tinny call of the swirling whisk against the thick plastic mixing bowl. When he's finished, Robbie opens and closes the door, and for a few minutes at least, Lance is really alone.

Lance slides out of bed immediately, gets the clothes he dug out of the odds and ends of Johnny's old wardrobe just for the occasion of today, and walks fast for the bathroom, trying not to look at the air mattress and its single pillow and blanket as he dodges it. He shuts the door and turns on the shower, getting cleaned up as fast as possible and hoping the steam might take a few of the wrinkles out of Johnny's khakis and button-down.

Under the stream of water, Lance remembers running from his father's house to Riverside for the last time six years ago, and offering his heart to Robbie, knowing Robbie would never take it. For some reason, there's an echo of that same feeling in the visceral reaction he had last night when Robbie calmly reminded him that there was nothing Lance could do which would change the way Robbie feels about him.

You're family. It's all Lance ever wanted, until he began to want more.

Lance can't quite puzzle through the feelings, as there's too much white noise. And he knows that if he says anything to Robbie, Lance will break down. He'll sob. He'll act like the broken child he was at sixteen.

Maybe he already ruined everything last night, but maybe, if he can get through the next few days…if the case could somehow just *go away*—

There's an audible click in his mind.

That's it.

If he's going to have a shot with Robbie, he has to get rid of the criminal case. He'll fix things with Niall for long enough to make it all go away. It's a half-formed idea, but he knows immediately that it's the course he has to take. Pulling on yet another ill-fitting set of Johnny's clothes, he dares to emerge from the bathroom, pretty sure Robbie isn't back yet, and he's right. Lance lopes across the hayloft to the dresser where he's been rummaging for all of his borrowed clothes, but this time, he opens the top drawer, where he put the plastic bag of stuff from the jail. He hasn't bothered with the phone since he realized it was disconnected, but if it still has enough battery to turn on, he can pull up Niall's number and call him from Robbie's cell.

He worries that the battery might be dead even as he

reaches for the slim leather case at the bottom of the bag, but the screen lights with a touch. And then, to his surprise, he realizes the phone not only has a third of its battery left, but it's been reactivated. He has three missed calls from Niall himself, all dated the night before.

Six years ago.

"Lance, is that you?" Robbie's voice is soft but clear. Not like the voice of someone who's just woken, but the voice of someone who hasn't been to bed. He appears in the shred of lamplight that fills the part of the doorway that's cracked open. Lance just sees a slice of him, a vertical line—the center of his face, his mussed dark hair, and a soft t-shirt so large and with its collar so stretched that Lance can see a glimpse of Robbie's bare chest and its covering of dark hair.

Lance's throat is suddenly dry. He swallows, but doesn't answer Robbie. After all, it's a rhetorical question, especially now that Robbie is looking at him, with his smile of cautious welcome fading to one of concern. Cautious—that's how Robbie always is with him. He takes care in their every inter-action, and Lance usually doesn't know if he likes it or hates it. Right now, though, he hates it.

"My dad knows I'm queer," he says, his voice ragged with the effort of keeping it quiet, as well as the strain of running here. And all of the other strains on top of that, which feel far greater than the burn of exertion in his legs and his chest.

"Did he hurt you?" It's not the first time Robbie has asked this question, but it's the first time that there's been a sense of—danger, almost, in his voice. Like he could do violence against someone who was violent toward Lance.

"No." It's not exactly the right answer. Lance thinks of the bottle, the words. All of the nights when his father wasn't there, and the nights when he was. He's never been sure which are worse.

"If you don't feel safe there, then you shouldn't go back. You know you're welcome here." Robbie pulls open the door. "Do you want to sit down?"

Lance's gaze flicks past Robbie and into his room. He's only been in Robbie's room the few times he's snuck in over the years, looking at all of Robbie's things in their places with greedy fascination. He's never been in Robbie's room with Robbie in it.

Robbie hesitates, as though he means to close the door. "Why don't we go down—"

"No," Lance interrupts. "I mean, yes, I want to sit down." He walks toward Robbie and Robbie moves out of his way, still looking like he might protest, might send Lance down to the kitchen table instead. But it's too late; Lance is in the room with him, and Robbie is slowly closing the door behind them.

Today.

Lance calls Niall back, heart pounding with worry that Robbie will return and overhear. So, he sits on the toilet in the bathroom, the door closed, and keeps his voice quiet. He can make this quick. He may have miscalculated the extent to which Niall could overreact to Lance leaving him, but at least that means he knows exactly how badly Niall wants him back. He can use that.

The phone only rings once before Niall answers. *"Lance? Is that you, Angel?"*

The endearment has always grated, but it's nauseating now, in Robbie's home that smells of Robbie; looking at Robbie's toothbrush on the bathroom counter, next to the one he took out of a new box for Lance.

For a moment, Lance isn't sure he can do it. A couple of days ago, Lance's whole sense of self rearranged; the man who knew how to play Niall like an instrument stepped aside for the guileless, artless boy who ran barefoot in these meadows and waded in this creek.

But he can shift back, and he will. It's the only way he can give whatever is beginning with Robbie a real chance.

"Yeah, it's me."

"I've been calling and calling. I was worried sick. What were you thinking?"

Lance makes his voice low and apologetic, or maybe even afraid. It's not hard to feign those feelings when they're all part of the tumult of conflict in his head. "I didn't realize the phone was working. When I looked at it a few days ago, it was disconnected." He tries to tamp down the accusation in his tone when he adds, "And then I got arrested—for *stealing* your car."

"Well, I had to get your attention somehow, didn't I?" Niall sounds put out, like Lance is a petulant child and Niall's a reasonable adult. *"If I just let you have your tantrum without consequences, how would you ever learn?"*

Lance closes his eyes. "You're right. I messed up. I was being...immature." He swallows and tastes acid. "But, honey," he adds, his voice low and wavering, "I'm in really big trouble now. They put me in *jail*. And today I'm supposed to go back to court."

"Let's not get ahead of ourselves," Niall says with calm conde-scension. *"If you'll behave yourself, we can work everything out."*

"You mean you'll call the police here and explain?"

"I won't have to call them. I can speak to them in person. I arrived last night."

· · ·

Six years ago.

Lance stares at Robbie's throat as he turns away from the door and faces Lance, right arm crossing his chest to hold his left elbow in a posture Lance recognizes from years of observation: Robbie's flustered.

Lance sits on the edge of Robbie's bed, which is neatly made, as though Robbie hasn't slept in it. The room is built into a curved sort of turret of the house, creating a small, semicircular area that Robbie uses as an office. The desk lamp is on. There's an open book on the surface, as well as a notepad.

"Were you busy?"

Robbie walks slowly toward him, following the direction of his glance into the office space. "No. Just reading." Their eyes meet and Robbie smiles. "Sometimes, I can't sleep."

The thought that he's not the only person along the creek who lies awake at night makes Lance uncharacteristically bold. "I love you, Robbie," he murmurs, and the admission seems to open the dam on his tears. His cheeks are wet in a flash, his vision blurred.

Robbie unfolds his arms and quickly sits next to him on the edge of the bed. A warm arm encircles him. "I love you, too, buddy."

Lance winces and hunches his shoulders even as he helplessly leans into the strong, warm presence of Robbie next to him.

"That's not what I mean. I *love* you."

Robbie's hand was making circles on his bicep, but now it freezes. "Lance," he whispers.

What was I thinking?

He jerks away from Robbie and dashes at his tears. "I know you don't want me back."

"Lance, I care about you so much. I *love* you, so much."
Robbie's voice is pleading, but he's clenched his hands on his
lap like he thinks he'll infect himself with something if he
touches Lance.

Suddenly furious, Lance leaps to his feet and spins around.
"I don't want you to love me!" Robbie stands, too, and steps
toward him, but Lance shoves him back with all his strength.
Robbie staggers, eyes wide with alarm, and then a sound from
the hallway makes him turn away from Lance for just a
moment. In that moment, Lance backpedals and collides
with Robbie's nightstand. He catches himself on it, knocking
a paperback to the floor as his hand lands on top of something else. Something soft and cool.

There's bunched silk against his palm. Lance knows at
once what he's touching without even looking; he closes his
hand instinctively over the prize before Robbie turns back to
him. It's like muscle memory, instinct, the same impulse that
has seized him so many times before, and yet this feels so
much more forbidden than taking something with a price tag.

He puts the faded paisley scarf in his pocket, and then he
runs.

Johnny is in the hallway, shirtless and squinting, obviously
waking up to their shouts. And past him, standing in his dark-
ened doorway and draped in a full set of pajamas, Danny is
putting on his glasses.

"Lance?" Johnny asks, blinking.

"Lance!" Robbie calls from behind him.

But Lance is already down the stairs, and then he's out
the door, what he took weighing like lead in his pocket, and
what he said like lead in his chest. He's set fire to the only
place of refuge he's ever had with those words—he knows it.
And he can't go back to his father's house. So, when he
reaches the woods, instead of crossing the creek, he walks
down the bank and sits on a stone at the mouth of the

stream, where it pours its muddy heart into the river. And when the sun rises, he digs his cell phone from his pocket and calls his aunt.

Today.

Lance is dressed when Robbie comes back.

The look on Robbie's face is hard for Lance to meet. It's questioning, uncertain...maybe even afraid. Lance wants to wipe the look away—and he will. But first he has to clear the path between them. That's more important than ever now that he knows Niall is *here*, in Trace County. If Lance isn't careful, his worlds will collide and implode. He has to convince Niall to get rid of the criminal charges—and then, somehow, get rid of Niall, as well—before the fragile thing he has with Robbie crumbles.

"I know you said you could take me to town, but I got a ride," he says, not quite meeting Robbie's eye, and then he tugs on the lapel of the heavy corduroy shirt he chose from Johnny's cast-offs because it looked like the warmest option. "Is it okay if I borrow this stuff? I'll give it all back as soon as I have my things."

There's a long moment of silence, which forces Lance to meet Robbie's stare. He looks miserable. Lance's resolve almost falters, but he hangs on by a thread.

"You can take whatever you want to. I already told you, whatever you need is yours." He grasps his right elbow with his left hand.

Lance blinks and looks at the floor. "I'll give it all back," he repeats.

"Who's—" Robbie clears his throat. "Who's giving you a ride?"

Lance shrugs. "I still know people around here." It's not

exactly a lie, he thinks, while at the same time knowing that Robbie wouldn't appreciate the technicality.

"Yeah, of course."

"I said I'd meet him out at the road. I don't want him to get stuck halfway down the driveway."

"I'll drive you up there. The snow's deep."

"I'd rather walk."

"Lance—"

Lance forces his feet still against the urge to run. He's not a child now. "I'll walk," he says firmly, still without looking at Robbie, and goes for the door.

CHAPTER TWENTY-TWO

Robbie

Robbie watches Lance go in a daze. He's still holding the calf's empty bottle; he's unzipped his coat, but hasn't shrugged out of it. His boots are still on. And the door is closing behind Lance, whose departure feels like a strange inversion of an ambush. A sudden abandonment instead of a sudden setting-upon.

He's just unstuck his feet to follow him, without being precisely sure what he's going to do—stalk after him up the driveway? Plead to know if he's coming back?—when his cell rings.

It's his neighbor, Ed. Robbie answers, if only because Ed's been so impossible to get on the phone. He'll make it quick.

"Robert Chase!"

"Hi, Ed, listen, could I call you back...?" Robbie steps toward the door, dropping the bottle on the bench. He can see Lance through the glass, walking fast through the snow, both swallowed by the bulk of Johnny's coat and yet almost too tall for it; it just reaches his waist. Robbie can see the tail of the corduroy shirt clearly, extending past the fall of the coat.

Ed, typically, doesn't seem to hear Robbie suggest that now might not be the best time, and barrels on. *"Oh, I'll just take up a few minutes of your time, I swear. Sorry I missed your calls. When can I come by and gather up those strays? The weather isn't ideal, but I'd like to do it while I still have my nephew here to help."*

Robbie freezes with his hand on the door handle. What's he going to do? Sprint down the stairs after Lance, calling after him? What entitles him to stop Lance if Lance wants to go? He thinks of their few, shared days together, and even though, the day before, he was sure they'd brought to life something vivid, real, and lasting, now he has to wonder if he imagined it. It *was* dreamlike, those passionate, languorous hours with Lance, learning Lance's body and feeling like he was rediscovering his own. Standing here alone feels much more like reality as Robbie knows it, the figure of Lance getting smaller and smaller with each step he takes, hurrying away from the place where Robbie kissed him and touched him, and came for him and made him come.

Robbie's hand falls to his side. He leans forward until his forehead is pressed against the glass panel in the door. The wind must be picking up; he sees Lance duck his head like he's bracing against a gust. He's almost to the first bend in the driveway, which will take him out of sight.

"Sure, come whenever," Robbie tells Ed, resignedly. "I'll be here." As always.

"Great, great. We'll go ahead and head your way now, before there's any more snow down."

Robbie says that's fine, ends the call, and sets down the calf's bottle on the counter to wash it. And it isn't until that moment that it sinks in that, when Ed comes for the cows, he'll be taking the calf, too.

Robbie doesn't think about Sienna if he can help it. The reasons for that are myriad, and hard for him to unpack. In some ways, the bad memories are interspersed with just as many that are good, which makes it all the harder to reflect on. The complicated things always are.

He loved that horse, and he likes remembering how smart she was, how quickly she caught on to new things, and how bright her eyes got when she saw him coming. That's rare in a horse. Even a good, fair horseman who can convince most horses to enjoy their work will still find that, to the horse, it's work nonetheless. The ones who are sincerely glad to see you coming with their bridle are rare. Poco is one of them; Sienna was another.

And in the months after those terrible days of trying and failing to save Sienna's life, he and his brothers were working together in the best way. He remembers the mustangs coming off the truck with a clarity with which he can recall few other moments in his life. How the ground shook as they came spilling out of the dark rectangle at the back of the trailer, and how the grass parted for them, like the land itself had been waiting for them.

Maybe it was inevitable; maybe if tragedy hadn't struck with Sienna, something else would have pushed the Chases and Riverside over a new horizon. But he isn't sure; the timing was all so critical. It had to happen before Danny went to school, before Johnny went on adventures; it took the three of them, together, to make it happen. So, maybe without Sienna—without her terrible sacrifice—it wouldn't have happened at all.

It's easier, somehow, to believe that. He likes to think that something good came out of her suffering...something that wouldn't have happened otherwise.

But maybe he's just taught himself to look for every silver lining, even if he has to make them up. It's a habit born from necessity.

He can't see Lance now. What if his ride doesn't show up? Or what if it does, and Robbie misses a chance to know who he's with? That last thought makes him feel a moment's shame, but knowing he has no right to every detail of Lance's life doesn't lessen the desire. He pushes open the door, rushes down the stairs, and jogs down the driveway toward the road.

He imagines Lance waiting alone. He had his hood lowered; the glare off the snow made his dark curls silver-tipped, like they'd been touched by the same frost as the bare branches of the trees. Robbie isn't a runner, but he speeds up anyway, until his breath comes short.

When the point where the driveway meets the road comes into view, there's no tall, boyish young man shivering on the roadside. Just fresh tire tracks carved through the thin layer of snow that accumulated since the last pass by the snowplow, and still winter air.

Robbie pushes his hands down into his coat pockets and starts back the way he just came. He ran out without stopping for gloves. Still, he doesn't hurry as he treks back to the house. Sometimes, he likes the cold; it can feel cleansing. Or like a justified punishment.

He's always liked to take a long ride when he has decisions to make, but with Ed heading over now, he doesn't have time for that. So, he turns over the questions he has to solve sooner rather than later, starting with the most pressing one. The calf in the barn—the one he and Lance brought back from the brink of a snowy death together. He tries to recall the value of the average orphaned calf, and imagines it doesn't much exceed the cost of the vet call that Megan made—not that she'll bill him for that, no matter how many times he asks. Robbie can make Ed an offer he won't refuse, and that'll be that.

Or will it? Ed is a strange guy. Maybe he'll decide he isn't selling. There's only a very small chance of that, and yet, the possibility makes Robbie uneasy. He's still mulling it over when Ed's familiar pickup appears down the driveway, towing a small, rusty stock trailer, its gates rattling like gunfire as it lurches over the banked snow on the curve. The noise flushes the horses out of the run-in shed, even Dusty. They dance around excitedly, tails flagged high, snorting out visible clouds of steam. Despite his anxiousness, Robbie finds himself smiling at their antics. Riverside has become a pretty sleepy place if an unfamiliar trailer can rile them up this much. Back when he was training, they were used to people—and other horses—coming and going almost daily. They'd barely raise their heads at the sight of a rig. Now, it's a novelty.

Ed's nephew is with him, Robbie sees as they climb out of the truck. Or at least, Robbie assumes that's who he's seeing. They're a study in contrasts, to a comical degree. Ed has a body type Robbie's dad would have described as a "beanpole" —taller than Robbie, arms and legs like sticks, his coveralls so loose that they're practically flapping. He's wearing a camo hat with earflaps.

His nephew is short, soft, with pink cheeks that don't look like they've ever needed a razor. He looks like he just stepped out of a catalogue for the Gap, dressed in a wool coat, flannel-lined jeans with the cuffs turned up to flash their red plaid lining, and a navy hat with a red pom that matches the scarf expertly swathed around his neck.

Robbie is so surprised, he finds himself staring. But he shakes himself out of it when he realizes that not only has the kid noticed, but he's starting to blush.

"Robert!" Ed calls in his booming voice, which is completely incongruous with his scrawny frame. "Where should I back in?"

Robbie considers mentioning the calf, and then, instead, he says, "Right there," and points to the gates to the pen the cows are observing from, almost as intently as the horses.

Ed nods and hops back into the driver's seat of the pickup, pulls through the circle drive, and then starts to back toward the gate. Only, the angle is all wrong, Robbie can see at once, and the trailer veers left—whereas the gate is to the right—so Ed puts the truck back in drive and pulls forward to try again.

What is Robbie going to do with a calf? He's not running a petting zoo. He should probably just tell Ed everything that Megan told him, hand him the bottle, and wish him luck. He'll probably do fine.

But Robbie thinks of the special attention and monitoring it takes to care for any fragile animal, and worry spikes in his chest at the thought of sending her off with his careless neighbor.

This time, Ed's efforts to back the trailer result in it going right, but so fast and so sharply that Ed nearly jack-knifes the rig before pulling forward again. Robbie imagines, based on the way the pickup's rear tires spin in the snow for a moment before getting traction, that Ed is getting frustrated and therefore a little aggressive with the gas pedal.

So, Robbie will just offer to buy the calf. Maybe he'll overpay, but he has all the money from the house's insurance sitting in an account, untouched. Even spending a grand would barely make a dent.

Finally, Ed has gotten himself backed up to the gate. His nephew waves him on until he's six or eight inches from the fence-line, and then Ed hops out and walks back to open the trailer gates.

The cows are pretty docile and seem to know the score. They back up into a corner of the old shed and act like they're going to be stubborn, but there's nowhere for them to go and they've been hauled around enough to know that the three humans can out-maneuver them and do intend for them to go into the waiting trailer. So, after circling the pen, dodging Ed and his nephew's half-hearted efforts at herding them, and twice being turned back by Robbie where he stands close to the gate, the cow with the white band around her belly gives them a long, assessing look, then turns and trots toward the waiting trailer of her own volition.

Robbie takes a deep breath. There's not always an obvious difference between a pregnant cow and one who's just calved. He can tell a difference in the belted cow himself, but is it only because he's studying her so closely?

He watches Ed, who's watching the cows as they hop on the trailer. The belted cow jumps in first, her two companions behind her as close as shadows. Robbie holds his breath, but Ed just closes the trailer door behind them and latches it.

Some of the tension in Robbie's chest eases. Ed obviously doesn't realize anything is materially different about the belted cow that left his property and the one he's taking back home. But, now, Robbie has nothing to distract himself from the fact that Ed is taking three animals off the ranch, animals Robbie doesn't trust him to care for. He thinks of the belted cow's stubbornness, the bewildered expression she had when he pried her newborn calf from the ice, and how many times she kicked him when he got her squeezed behind a gate and milked her. Still, he'd rather she stayed in the pen where he could take care of her, and now, instead, she's back at the mercy of an untrustworthy man.

Ed turns to him, and Robbie half-expects him to ask what he owes Robbie for the hay and the trouble of having the cattle, but then again, he isn't surprised at all when Ed just grins and salutes.

"Thanks, neighbor. Hope I can return the favor some time."

He turns to head toward the cab of the truck. Robbie knows this is the moment he should mention the calf and make his offer to buy. There's no way Ed will refuse to sell him an animal he doesn't even know exists at this moment.

And even if he'd been anxiously awaiting the calf's birth, all livestock has a price.

But sometimes people are irrational. Sometimes people tell you no, just out of spite. Robbie can't bring himself to interrupt the silence as Ed and his nephew open and close the truck doors and pull away. Ed waves out the window. Robbie waves back.

The horses lost interest in the truck and trailer when they realized it didn't have any horses as passengers. But while the others have gone back into the shed, Poco is standing at the gate, gazing hopefully at Robbie.

Robbie looks at him and blinks. "I'm a thief," he confesses, abashed.

Poco flicks his tail; his right ear swivels back, then forward again.

"I don't know. Don't *you* think that's worth feeling bad about?"

Quickly losing interest in human moral dilemmas, Poco turns and makes his way toward the hay bale, leaving Robbie alone, staring down his driveway for the second time in an hour, wondering how well he really knows himself.

CHAPTER TWENTY-THREE

Lance

A t least twice as he walks down the driveway, Lance considers turning back.

But as tempted as he is to run back to the hayloft, into Robbie's arms—his bed—and pretend that there's no world outside Riverside Ranch, he also knows that isn't a reality for him.

In reality, he's made a mess of things, and it's a mess he has to set right before he and Robbie can possibly have their impossible chance.

So, he puts one foot ahead of the other and doesn't turn back. Not even when, moments after he reaches the road, he sees a dark car that can only be whatever Niall rented at the airport in Omaha, going far too fast for the conditions, which results in a wild fishtail as he brakes at the sight of Lance.

When the car is stopped, haphazard in the middle of the slick road, Niall throws open the door and steps out cautiously, but his face lights up at the sight of Lance. His square white teeth flash in the steel-grey frame of his always-impeccable beard, and the corners of his eyes crinkle into those deep crow's feet that caused Lance, early in their acquaintance, to mistake Niall for a happy person.

"Thank God you called," he says, stirring as though he means to walk toward Lance, but the foot he's moved slips and he clings to the car door instead, and his smile quickly contorts into a frown. "Well, get in, won't you? I'm parked in the middle of the road." As always, his voice is so soft that it shouldn't carry like it does, but his every quiet word rings in Lance's ears as clear as a shout.

Lance has had a lot of practice behaving a certain way around Niall, and people like him. Right now, though, clothing himself in the disguise he's worn so much during his years since leaving home, where he's a sweet, docile young man grateful for the guidance of someone older and wiser, takes more focus than it used to. He still feels like he's out of character as he offers a sheepish smile and steps toward the passenger door. Though it hasn't been even a week since he donned this ruse daily without a thought or a care, now it feels like it's woven from nettles, prickly and wrong.

"My poor angel," Niall says, scanning him with a frown as he settles into the passenger seat of the sedan. "What on Earth are you wearing?"

Lance pushes back his hair—an old habit he can't shake, even though it's too short now to get in his face. "All of my clothes were in the car. They didn't let me take anything out of it." He tries to sound subdued and repentant. "R—my friend loaned me these."

If Niall notices his slip, and how just the suggestion of speaking Robbie's name in Niall's presence makes Lance freeze, he doesn't show it. He's probably preoccupied with navigating the road, which he's not doing with any skill, but he's going slowly enough that if the worst happens and they careen into the trees, they're at least unlikely to die. Lance hastily buckles his seatbelt, though, just in case.

"Well, we'll have to take an inventory and make sure none of the local law enforcement had sticky fingers when they were handling our property." He glances askance. "Is there anything you'd like to tell me, Angel?"

Lance is still thinking bemusedly about the suggestion that someone might steal his used, wrinkled clothes. He blinks at Niall. "I'm sure they didn't take anything." But then he remembers that he did have a camera and a laptop in his luggage, and frowns. Not because he thinks they were stolen, but because he hates to imagine those expensive electronics subjected to freezing temperatures.

"I'm sure there's something more important that you mean to say to me," Niall says, his voice almost a whisper, the timbre that always makes the hair stand up on Lance's arms. Niall takes excellent care of his hands, and they look like they could belong to a much younger man's. Right now they're gripping the steering wheel so tightly that his knuckles are white.

Lance swallows. "Thank you for coming all the way here."

Niall relaxes, but not entirely. "That's a start. Anything else?"

"Yes. I'm sorry that you had to come."

"Nonsense, Angel," Niall says, taking one hand briefly from the steering wheel to reach out and pet Lance's hair. "My goodness," he says, with a faint giggle, "but do you look a fright. I have some things you can use at the hotel to clean up."

The urge to lean away from Niall's touch is on the edge of irresistible. "Before my hearing? I'm not sure we have time...?"

"Oh, my love, there won't be any hearing!" Niall scoffs. He puts both of his hands back on the wheel to keep it steady. "Didn't you trust me when I said I'd take care of all of that?"

They follow a curve in the road, and Lance tries not to

hold his breath as the car skates sideways. Niall curses. But then their course straightens out and assumes a slight decline for the rest of the distance to the pavement, where the salted and plowed surface will be much easier to navigate. Lance exhales in relief, then tenses again as he reconsiders Niall's last words.

"Of course I trust you," he says carefully, "but I didn't think you could get it handled so fast."

"Oh yes. It was no trouble at all. I spoke to the prosecutor on Monday, just before I booked my flight."

Lance feels a flare of anger; nothing new, but this time, it takes him a few seconds to quell. When he trusts himself to speak, his voice is still tight. "Why didn't you tell me?"

Niall smiles at him with such fond patronization that Lance wants to scream. They hit the pavement, and now that the car isn't drifting on the ice, Niall takes his right hand off the wheel again, puts it on Lance's knee, and squeezes.

"Don't ask silly questions. If I'd told you, you might have gotten stubborn. You can be so dramatic." He chuckles. "Everyone says I'm insane to put up with your moods, but what we have is so much more special than they realize. I admire your passion, even if it can be vexing when you get carried away."

Lance forces a smile, but because he isn't completely sure what it looks like, he aims his stare out the window to be safe. He hopes the averted look can pass as embarrassment or shyness, and that Niall won't feel the tension that's filling Lance through the hand on his leg. He doesn't think Niall will. Niall has had his hands all over Lance when Lance's body was rigid with discomfort of various kinds, and it's never seemed to faze him.

"I still don't understand, though," Lance says as evenly as he can manage. "No one told me I don't have to come to court. Should we still go to my hearing, just in case?"

Niall snatches his hand back from Lance's leg, his voice laced with frustration when he answers, "Haven't you been listening? I told you it's taken care of."

"But, how—?"

"I added your name to the title a few months ago. It's something Lindsay suggested, for tax reasons. All I had to do was send them the documents and they no longer had a case, you see."

Lance's skin is crawling. There have been worse moments than this, he knows. Much worse. But the contrast of how he feels right now, so small and twisted, compared to how he felt at this time yesterday, makes the familiar feeling even harder to bear.

But he bears it anyway. Summoning all of his composure derived from years of practice and grim determination, he swallows and turns from the window to Niall with the most earnest face he can put on, and looks up at him through his lashes, reaching slowly for his hand.

"Thank you, Niall."

Niall's stormy expression clears at once, and his benevolent smile is back in place. He takes Lance's outstretched hand and laces their fingers together.

"You're welcome, Angel," he says approvingly, and kisses Lance's knuckles. His carefully conditioned beard is objectively softer than Robbie's, and yet it feels like thorns raking Lance's skin. "Now, we'll go pick up the car, and then you can follow me back to the hotel, and we'll have a long talk." He squeezes Lance's hand and lets go of it, voice lowering again. "I may have forgiven you, but that doesn't mean there aren't a few things I expect you to learn from this experience."

"Yes, Niall," Lance says, with a faint smile that he hopes looks abashed instead of nauseated. He should be relieved that everything has been dealt with, but he can't help feeling the strange depression of an anticlimax, instead. He'd thought he would untangle the mess Niall had gotten him into through his wits and ingenuity; instead, Niall made it go away as easily as he created it.

Or did he? Niall has a bad habit of overestimating his own understanding of a situation—a symptom of his arrogance. Lance worries the inside of his lip, which is a mostly invisible tic when he's nervous, and then swallows and dares to ask, "Did they give you any papers that I should have? About the case being dismissed?"

He braces himself for Niall's temper, but just gets another pat on the knee, and then Niall points to the dashboard, where a yellow mailing envelope rests. Lance doesn't let himself snatch it; he takes it calmly, shooting Niall a sidelong, rueful smile, and shakes out the contents into his lap.

The life-changing declaration is just one page of straight-forward black-and-white with the prosecutor's and judge's signatures at the bottom. Lance looks at it for a long time. A part of him wants to give Niall a piece of his mind, jump out of the car, and walk the six-or-so miles back to Robbie's drive-way. But he still needs the car. Not because he cares about the car at all, though it'll be convenient to have. But because he desperately needs a particular item from his luggage in the trunk.

The police station is so nondescript, they circle the block once before they see the sign on the low brick building that confirms that they're in the right place. There's a small, unfurnished vestibule inside, and a woman behind a plate glass window wearing red acrylic glasses. She looks up from a cell phone in a fuzzy yellow case, and then leans in to speak into a slim microphone mounted in front of her face. "Can I help you?" Her voice comes out distorted and from the wrong direction—from a cheap speaker somewhere behind Lance. He ignores the urge to look reflexively in that direction and smiles at her, about to approach her when Niall does, instead.

"We're here to pick up a vehicle in your impound," he explains with one of his smiles, but it doesn't seem to have its usual effect on the woman. She pushes up her glasses and blinks at him.

"Name?"

"Lance Taylor."

Something registers briefly in the woman's face, and she stares at Lance over Niall's shoulder. She must know who Lance is. For a moment, he thinks her frown has something to do with his past or his father, even though *he* has no idea who *she* is.

But then she says, flatly, "Mr. Taylor, if you could step up here?" and he realizes that she was just discomfited by Niall behaving like Lance's personal agent—and, well, that makes two of them. He edges past Niall to the window and gives her a strained smile.

"I.D.," she says, stretching out each letter into its own word, *eye dee,* "please." To Lance's relief, she's back to being businesslike. He fishes his wallet out of Johnny's pocket and shows her his driver's license.

Then, she stamps a few things and slides a sheet of paper to him through a tiny, plastic flap that's almost invisible between the bottom of the plate glass window and the top of the shallow, chipped counter.

"That's an inventory of everything we found in the vehicle. If you agree with the list, sign at the bottom. If you believe there is something missing from the list, I'll give you another form to fill out to register the dispute."

Lance looks at the list, skimming. Two parcels of luggage, and that's all he remembers. He has no idea if there were, in fact, twelve socks and two pairs of shoes, et cetera, inside. Then, at the bottom of the column listing clothing, he sees it —*"one (1) handkerchief, flowered"*—and his shoulders sag in relief, to a degree he wasn't fully anticipating.

"It looks fine," he murmurs, and signs his name at the bottom. She nods and picks up a landline phone to call someone to unlock the gates.

Niall, predictably surly after the uncomfortable moment, isn't smiling when Lance turns to him. *This will be delicate*, Lance thinks, as he switches to worrying his lip from the outside and gives Niall an apologetic smile.

"I need to go by and see my dad," he says in a low voice. "He's really sick. He's in hospice care now."

Niall's face is completely blank, but his soft voice sounds properly apologetic. "Oh, dear. I didn't realize."

Lance nods. "He's in a care home across town. I don't...if you don't mind, I'm really not sure I want you to see him." He lowers his voice, as though ashamed. It's surprisingly easy to act ashamed of himself; he has a store of that feeling, and it's close to the surface, even if its origin has nothing to do with worrying what Niall will think of him. "Maybe you can go back to your hotel, and I'll meet you there, after. It's the Holiday Inn, right?" There are only two options in Dell, and Lance already knows Niall would never choose the Midnight Motel.

Lance tries not to hold his breath while Niall considers. Niall's face is completely still, but his eyes, an ordinary medium-brown, somehow betray the volume of his thoughts. Lance knows how Niall feels about being around elderly people, and Lance has framed it so he doesn't even have to betray a principle by not going with Lance for emotional support. The plan should be air-tight.

Still, he's inordinately relieved when Niall nods slowly, his smile simpering. "I'll text you my room number." He makes a move toward Lance, and Lance braces himself for an embrace or a kiss. But then Niall's look slides toward the woman watching them steadily from behind the plate glass, her phone apparently forgotten for the moment, and he aborts the movement. "I'll see you soon," he adds—very, very quietly.

CHAPTER TWENTY-FOUR

Robbie

Eighteen years ago.

His dad has been dead for six months, and despite the pastor's and everyone else's promises that things will get easier—that they'll *be easier*, any minute now—Robbie still feels either numb or terrified, all the time.

In the numb moments, he's susceptible to his uncle's claim that Robbie's too young to take care of two kids. That he has his whole life ahead of him. That he should follow his girlfriend to college like he's planned, and leave the raising of his brothers to a man who his parents hated so much that they barely spoke his name in the house, despite he and Robbie's dad being one another's only living relatives.

In the terrified moments, he wonders how he can handle the task he's been given. How can he possibly be the parent to the boys that his father would have been? And how is he so selfish that he can't set aside his own grief to share anyone else's?

In the numb moments, he sometimes looks at the boys and feels almost nothing, like all of his other emotions are eclipsed by his sadness, and he'll never get any of the good ones back.

At least Johnny will be back in school soon, and Danny is old enough for preschool. Robbie's tired of seeing them drifting around the house like ghosts while Robbie tries to sanitize the rooms of all of their small reminders of their father. He keeps everything he picks up—pictures, old cowboy paperbacks, handfuls of flint arrowheads—in shoe boxes filed in the basement. One day, he plans to bring them back and spread them out. But he has to wait until things get easier.

Because they will get easier. Everyone says so. And if he lets himself doubt that promise, then the hollow moments are going to swallow him, and that's all he'll be.

He's thinking about washing the pile of dishes in the sink that's been there almost a week when he hears a noise from outside and glances out the window above the faucet. Johnny is charging by on a horse, bent over its neck, galloping head-long through the grass. It's Johnny's horse, a gentle old gelding who's a former mount of their dad's, so seeing Johnny riding it wouldn't ordinarily bother him. Johnny's been coaxing the gelding up next to the fence so he can crawl on bareback to avoid asking anyone to help him with the saddle that's still too heavy for him. Today, though, eight-year-old Johnny isn't just bareback—there's not a halter or bridle on the horse, either.

"Robbie, Robbie!" cries four-year-old Danny from the porch. "Johnny's on the horse and he didn't tell nobody!"

"Stay there!" Robbie orders, not pausing as he brushes past his younger brother and races into the yard, toward the meadow where Johnny's mount is thundering by. But he breaks stride halfway to the fence when he realizes that, rather than grimacing in terror, Johnny is grinning hugely. And rather than running blind, the horse has one ear cocked back toward Johnny, and each stride is measured, controlled. Johnny sees Robbie watching and throws up his hands, that cocky smile broader than it's been since the funeral. He guides the horse into a circle using just his seat and legs, like a pint-sized circus performer.

Danny appears at Robbie's side, because of course he wouldn't do a thing Robbie tells him, including staying on the porch in the presence of what Robbie had thought to be a runaway horse.

"He's in trouble, isn't he, Robbie?" Danny demands, scowling. "He's supposed to tell somebody if he's getting on the horse."

Robbie can't help it. He laughs. He laughs so hard that he has to bend over and brace his hands against his legs.

Danny pats him on the back, his little face solemn. "It's okay if you forget the rules sometimes. I remember. I can tell you."

Robbie, still laughing, grabs Danny around the waist and picks him up, upside down, until he's giggling.

"Don't be so serious," Robbie says, mock-sternly, and kisses him. "That's my job."

Danny's little arms go around his neck, and Johnny rides the horse, and the sunlight comes down. Their dad always loved the fall. Robbie remembers how he pointed out all of the colors to Robbie when Robbie was about Danny's size. So, he puts Danny on his hip and they call out the shades of gold and auburn and russet together.

Even those moments are still backlit by enormous grief. But all of the people who made that same promise to Robbie were right, after all—it's suddenly just a little bit easier.

Today.

When you need to make up your mind about something, go for a long ride.

Another piece of advice that Robbie hears in his head, in his father's voice, just as it sounded more than twenty years ago. Like all the rest, this bit of his dad's wisdom has always held true.

He goes to the gate, but for once, Poco isn't waiting for him. He's deep in a mutual grooming session with one of Johnny's bays, his head twisted around so that he can nibble delicately at the sensitive skin of the other gelding's flank. The other bay looks on, a hind leg cocked, dozing despite the brisk wind that combs through his dense coat. The snow is trampled down to grey slush in their pen.

Robbie hears the whisper and crunch of hooves dragging through the snow, and looks askance to find Dusty approaching him. She meets his gaze with calm willingness, and he feels a rush of gratitude as he steps up to her and slips the halter meant for Poco onto her head instead. It seems fitting to ponder these strange, yet somehow inevitable circumstances he finds himself in on the back of his oldest living friend.

He remembers Dusty from when she was a foal, sunshine-yellow and full of energy at the side of her dam, a horse his father had bred and raised himself. He remembers the first few rides his father put on her. Robbie watched every second of those sessions, dangling from the round pen fence with his arms hooked over the top rail, fascinated. He remembers the day from a couple years later when his father suggested, *"Why don't you ride Dusty today?"* and how his grin felt like it took up his whole face, but was nothing compared to the radiance of his dad's warm, answering smile.

In the barn, Robbie snaps a loose crosstie to either side of Dusty's halter. She seems no worse for the wear after her dip in the icy creek, but Robbie gives each of her legs a careful once-over, just to be sure. Then, he runs his hands firmly down her back and shoulders, looking for soreness. She doesn't stir, except to stretch her head down as far as the ties will allow and inspect one of the barn cats who's rolling enthusiastically in the bits of straw scattering the barn aisle.

"Such a strong old girl," he tells her as he strokes her neck. Her eyes fall half-closed, but that's as close as she'll get to showing appreciation. Dusty has always had this dignified air about her, like she's just allowing people the privilege of petting her out of the graciousness of her noble heart, but Robbie knows better. She has tells. He digs his fingers in at the base of her neck, the spot she likes best, and smiles when she curls her upper lip with pleasure before she can stop herself.

He saddles her up and they head up the trail. It's evident before they've gone far that the wild ones are back in the trees. He and Dusty come upon the bachelors first, which means that they make the rest of their way with Kyle and his band filing after them on the trail like a string of pack horses. Kyle keeps daring to get close enough to sniff at Dusty's tail, which makes her give a guttural squeal and tense in the hindquarters, ready to aim a kick. Kyle hastily backs off every time but can't contain himself for long before he edges nearer again.

A couple times over the past few days, Robbie has rolled over in the darkness beside a sleepy Lance, and thought with a rush of adrenaline that he could just go. He could find someone to mind the ranch and follow Lance to Chicago. Maybe he'd enroll in college. In this little fantasy, Lance wants to be followed and wants Robbie to stick around. In the same fantasy, Robbie gets to see Lance in his element, the brightest-shining facet of a shining city, a precious stone in the setting it deserves—one honed from gold, not of rough wood and wire. Robbie gets to chase one of the degrees on his list of interests, a list he built without ever expecting to actually pursue any of them. He could leave for a weekend and visit one of the places on his list of dream destinations, places he only ever expected to read about, because you can't leave a ranch full of horses and responsibilities even for a weekend vacation.

In his fantasy, his uncle doesn't find out; there are no consequences. In his fantasy, he has someone he can trust who's actually capable of fulfilling such a massive favor as minding the entire ranch, and for however long Robbie wants to be gone.

It was easier to shake off the allure of the impossible when the boys were here. Caring for them rooted him more strongly to the ranch. Caring for the horses does that, too, but only to an extent. It hasn't been the same since both Johnny and Danny left.

Dusty comes down a slick place in the slope with careful steps. Robbie adjusts his balance so that he won't throw her weight. He's focused on the snowy way just ahead of them until they reach the bottom, and level ground, where they're ready to cross the frozen creek in a shallow place that's as much rocks and fallen branches as it is frozen water. He looks up and finds himself practically face to face with the elusive Bandit, who's standing a dozen feet in the direction that would be upstream, if the water were still flowing instead of stuck in winter's lock.

More of his father's words drift into his head. *"People will tell you they're 'just horses.' People are damn idiots, sometimes."*

Bandit's winter coat is such a thick, luxurious black, she could be a streak of midnight sky left over from the evening before. It always surprises Robbie to remember that she's one of the smallest of the mustangs, but standing there, facing him with her head raised and her dark eyes locked on his, she has the presence of a much larger horse. Her band seethes behind her uneasily. It's been some time since Robbie has seen them, and he can't think of when he was last so close. He's relieved to see they all look fat, healthy, and well.

He doesn't know why Bandit chose this moment to show herself to him. But she watches him for several long moments, steam trailing from her nostrils, which are frosted by her breath. Then, she turns and trots off, pushing her band down the bending path of ice and out of sight.

Robbie's heart is full, and heavy. Maybe those two things are the same. What he knows is that he's not going anywhere. And he suspects that Lance *is* going somewhere, and soon.

———

Robbie's back at the house making the calf's bottle when Danny calls. He turns off the water, dries his hands, and answers. "Hey, kid."

"Hey. I just wanted to see how everything is going. Is he doing okay? It's been a few days. Do you know anything about what happened?"

Robbie does his best to answer, but his tone is clipped. Danny must notice, because instead of firing off another string of questions, he's uncharacteristically quiet. Robbie does nothing to fill the silence and make it easier. He doesn't feel quite himself; it's like he's still drifting up the trail to the meadow, a part of him carried by each of the wild horses he walked amongst an hour ago.

"Is everything okay?"

Robbie doesn't mean for his laugh to be quite so bitter, or to let the petulant words escape him. "Do you really want to know?"

"Of course."

Robbie rubs between his eyes. "I don't think I'm okay. I don't know."

Everything had been okay the day before. No, everything had been *perfect*. He doesn't know how to talk to Danny about yesterday. It isn't shame that makes him reluctant to confess what happened with Lance. He just doesn't want to do it on the phone. Maybe he'll never tell Danny at all. Maybe it will be a secret he keeps to himself. When Lance goes, maybe he'll want to shelter the memories of that stolen time together, rather than sharing them with someone whose reaction might tarnish something he intends to cherish.

"Is it Lance?"

Trust Danny to be astute, but for some reason, his very valid question fuels Robbie's bad temper. "What if I say no? If it doesn't have anything to do with Lance, are you still going to care?"

"What? Rob—"

Rob, Dan, John. They've only ever called each other that. Robbie dashes at the tears gathering under his eyes and fights to keep his voice steady. "It's hard sometimes, out here all alone." With that enormous, shameful sentiment out of him, he deflates, most of the anger leaving him in the same rush. "I don't mean I don't love it. But it can be...hard." He swallows.

There's silence on the line again, but this feels different than before.

"I didn't know you felt that way."

"I don't—it's not always." He's kept any thoughts of this kind to himself, always. His brothers have gone, and he never wanted them to feel like they had to stay. But the words come out of him, a tumble he can't stop, like rocks knocked loose from a cliff face. "I'm just lonely, I guess."

"Oh." Danny's voice is so small, almost a whisper. There's a flash of static, like he's cleared his throat but with his phone a little too close to his mouth. Then he breathes, *"Me, too, sometimes."*

Robbie stands up straight, pushing himself upright from the countertop. "I didn't know that."

A huff comes—one of Danny's humorless laughs. *"I didn't want you to think I was ungrateful. For all you did, and for what you didn't get to do because you were taking care of us. But even though all I ever wanted when I was growing up was to get off the ranch...as soon as I got out here, all I wanted was to come home."*

Robbie is floored. He doesn't know what to say except, "I wish you'd felt like you could tell me."

"Well, likewise."

"You know I love you?"

"Yeah. I do. And me, too. You know that, right?"

"Yeah." Robbie rubs a hand over his faint smile, heart a little fuller, and the strain of the pressure causes him a faint pain. "Yeah. I know that."

There's an almost comical irony when he figures it out— that burst of strange adrenaline that makes a body want to laugh even though something's not exactly funny. How has it taken him this long, he wonders, to realize that it wasn't *only* taking care of the boys that made him content here on the ranch? It was caring for them and being cared for in return.

He misses having someone to take care of. But what he misses as much, and maybe yearns to have on a level he hasn't in the past, is to be taken care of himself.

———

He considers his father's advice about solving problems on a long ride, but he thinks it might have less to do with being on the back of a horse and more to do with moving, preferably through trees and grass. Somewhere you can hear water running. He thinks of playing by the creek as a child with only his imagination and the quiet trees for company. He used to wish his parents would have another kid—someone he could play with. Part of the reason he was so glad when Lance first showed up in their lives was because it meant that Danny wasn't so alone.

That memory leads to thoughts of Lance; not as he is now, but as he was then. It leads to Lance at sixteen, recklessly and bravely asking Robbie for something Robbie didn't have to give, and then fleeing the farmhouse, disappearing into the dark.

Robbie has never been sure whether he made a mistake by not following Lance that night. It seems like anything he could have done or said would have hurt more than it could have helped. But he's pretty fucking sure he made a mistake by not following Lance this morning.

Maybe it should be no surprise that his feet are carrying him toward that point in the tree line where he got so accustomed to seeing Lance appear as a slip of a kid with a head of messy curls, clear blue eyes, and a wide, shy smile. Robbie only ever wanted the ranch to be a safe place for Lance, and that hasn't changed. But the role that Robbie has to play in that safe harbor has.

He thinks it should feel more strange than it does, his shift in feeling. Maybe some people wouldn't understand, but in his own head and heart, it feels clear. Right.

Robbie has almost reached the shallow part of the creek where he knows the boys liked to cross when he hears the high, lilting voice of a child, and freezes, wondering briefly if he's stepped back in time. But, no, it's not one of the three boys whose shouts and cries kept him worried for a decade— and still, to an extent, do; it's an unfamiliar little girl in a pastel snowsuit.

In the same instant he spies her, she seems to see him, and after a half-second's stare, she bolts like a rabbit, leaving Robbie on his side of the creek while she flees from hers.

Lance must have been right about someone staying in the

house. Robbie pauses at the edge of the ice and looks down. Then, seized by some strange impulse, he steps onto the slippery surface. He holds his balance with a careful reorganization of his weight, keeping one toe skimming a piece of fallen wood that's half-buried in the ice.

It feels symbolic, standing upon the creek like this. If he looks ahead, he can trace the winding path in his mind that leads all the way to the river.

He's still thinking of that, of the way tributaries find their way, and all the little drops of water that feed and flow to them, when a familiar voice calls his name like he's been conjured by the magic of ice and land and sheer force of will.

CHAPTER TWENTY-FIVE

Lance

Lance throws open the trunk of the blue Mercedes without even waiting for the guy who showed him onto the lot to walk away. He fishes through his smaller piece of hand luggage, knocking aside bottles of lotion and shampoo that have frozen solid...until he finds the scarf. The silk is cold when he clutches it.

He'd known it would be there, but having it in his hand is an enormous relief.

He closes the trunk, gives the man an awkward nod, and then gets into the driver's seat, the scarf wrapped around his hand when he sets it on the wheel. The sight of the familiar pattern gives him a rush of much-needed comfort as he starts the engine and pulls past the uneven asphalt on the edge of the parking lot and into the street.

When he'd told Niall he was going to go see his dad, he'd been inventing the story he thought was most likely to get him away from Niall *with* the car. For some reason, though, he finds himself driving there anyway. Maybe it's because he still feels that invisible nettle shirt all over him, like he's tainted himself by handling Niall, and he needs to shake it off before returning to Robbie. He doesn't dwell on his reasons as he makes the few turns down increasingly narrow streets, then finds himself on the one-way lane through the care center's parking lot. He stops close to the door; the lot isn't large, but apparently he's the only guest.

Lance looks through the glass-paned doors. He has no intention of walking inside, but he can remember going through the entrance on Friday. He may never forget the smells of antiseptic and wet paper, and the sight of his father, drugged to unconsciousness, with his wrinkled face slack and half-covered by the oxygen mask. He'd been glad that his dad hadn't known Lance was there, then guilty for being glad. If he could talk to his father, in a coherent state, what would he say?

There should be some satisfying confrontation he can imagine. Maybe his father would cry and apologize, beg for forgiveness, or somehow redeem himself. But all Lance really wants, now, is the luxury of not having to see him anymore. If that makes him terrible, well, he'll add it to the list. After several long minutes, a woman's face appears in the door. She's wearing scrubs with purple puppy faces all over them and looking at him curiously. Lance smiles awkwardly and backs out of the parking space; he winds through the parking lot to the exit side and doesn't so much as glance in the rearview as he points the car out of town.

While he drives toward Riverside, he tries to plan what he'll say and do with Robbie, like he's always planned conversations when he wants a specific outcome. But all of the tactics he's used before to cement a relationship, earn an invite to stay, or secure a declaration of attachment, he can't envision with Robbie standing in the place of past boyfriends. Robbie is something else. Robbie transcends those people and those arrangements to an impossible degree.

Robbie told Lance he didn't know what to do with him; the memory makes Lance laugh, his eyes pricking with tears. Lance doesn't know what to do with Robbie, either.

When he reaches the driveway to the ranch, he feels an odd panic and keeps driving. That's his excuse for going on, over the wooden bridge, and turning down the driveway to the old house instead.

He has no idea what he intends to do here, either. No more of a plan than he's come up with for the moment when he faces Robbie and has to explain where he's been and the outcome of the theft charges in a way that won't make Robbie look at him like a lost little boy, forever ruining their chances of being more.

But the stakes are manageable out here, with these strangers who've settled into the husk of a place that carries so many of Lance's most conflicted feelings.

He has the wild fear and hope that they won't be home, and the idea of standing alone outside the little house fills him with a dread which is similar to the feeling of standing at his father's bedside. But he's spared having to walk to the door and knock, at least. The woman and the little girl are outside, apparently as immune as all Nebraskans tend to be to the biting cold under a midday sun. The little girl is back in that lavender snowsuit, packing snow together into the lumpy semblance of a snowman, and the woman is watching her from the front steps, where she's sitting wrapped in a blanket. The moment Lance comes around the bend in the drive and sees them, though, the girl spins around and the woman jumps to her feet.

Lance feels another moment of unease, but the young woman doesn't pull out a rifle and point it at him; she just trots down the steps in her slippered feet and takes the little girl's hand. Her face reminds Lance of someone, but he can't figure out who. He stops a careful distance from the house, and then, because he's backed himself into a corner and left himself with no other choice, he gets out of the car and walks over to talk to them.

The little girl's eyes widen as she gets a good look at him, and she tugs on her mother's hand. Lance easily overhears her loud whisper. "Mama, *that's* the man from the woods!"

Lance winces and stops, rounding his shoulders in a way that he hopes makes him seem less intimidating. "I told her she probably shouldn't talk to strangers in the woods," he says helpfully.

The woman is even younger-looking up close than she was from a distance. She's definitely no older than Lance. He still hasn't figured out where he's seen her before, though he's increasingly sure he has. He thinks through the names of people close to his age while he was growing up, but her face doesn't match any of them.

"You told her your dad owned this place," the young woman says, her voice a little stiff. Her eyes are intent on his face, though, like she's seeing something that surprises her— and not in a good way.

Lance just nods, and hurries to add, "But I didn't come to bother you. I don't mind that you're here, if you want to be here. Maybe you worked something out with my dad and maybe you didn't. It's not my business either way. I haven't lived here in a long time."

That little speech comes pretty easily, considering it's mostly bullshit. Sure, he doesn't mind that they're here, but his casual tone belies the fact that he's been oddly drawn here ever since he realized the house was lived in. He can't say why, but it's true. He didn't wind up standing in front of them solely out of a desire to put off facing Robbie.

The woman keeps searching his face. Finally, she seems to come to a decision. She rakes her upper teeth over her lower lip and then says, "I'm Nora, and this is Alice." She lifts her chin a little, like she's bracing herself for a challenge, and in that moment, seeing that stubborn little tilt to her head— Lance understands why he recognizes her.

He's practiced the same look in the mirror, and it doesn't look much different on his very similar face.

Still, it's kind of a shock when she says it out loud.

"I'm your sister."

———

The inside of the house looks almost exactly like Lance remembers, but it bears some signs of turmoil from the past six years. The old wallpaper is curling here and there from leaks; there's a patch in one of the windows, made of cardboard and duct tape, where a pane was broken. There are new stains on the old floorboards.

Lance wonders how long the house was empty. Or maybe it wasn't empty; maybe his father just stayed here, alone, for far longer than he should have, not much different than a feral animal building a nest.

Some of the unfamiliar details have nothing to do with abandonment, though. In mason jars around the room are dried flowers. Drawings, probably by Alice, plaster the refrigerator, which has its door cracked to keep air from being trapped inside—it's unplugged, along with the other appliances. A small generator is in the living room, serving as the hub at the center of a space heater, a lamp, and an old laptop computer, all of their cords stretched toward the generator. Lance sees a neat stack of DVDs of kids' movies next to the computer. Blankets curtain the living room windows, the sun stronger in the spots that are most threadbare so that the whole room looks dappled.

Nora watches Lance take it all in. She's still wrapped in a blanket and wearing that expression that dares him to say something rude or sympathetic. He thinks the latter would be the worst received.

Alice, on the other hand, is enthusiastically guiding the tour. "This is my bed," she says, pointing to one half of the pile of blankets, "and this is Mama's. In the summertime, I sleep in my own room, but it's cold right now. Do you want to see my room?"

Heart stuttering at the thought of which room that's likely to be, Lance smiles and hesitates. He's grateful when Nora chooses that moment to break in.

"So, you're not going to call the sheriff?"

Alice looks interested. "The sheriff? Why?"

Nora gives her a stern look. "Don't interrupt."

"I'm not calling the sheriff."

"Why would he call the sheriff?" Alice insists.

Nora puts her hands on her hips, which causes the blanket to slide to the floor. She's wearing a sweatshirt and sweatpants that are obviously covering at least two other layers of clothes; she would probably be as lean as Lance if she weren't artificially padded. Leaner, actually—there's a hollowness in her cheeks and a frailness in her wrists that suggests it's been a difficult winter. Lance feels a pang at that, especially because there are no signs that Alice is anything but well-fed. In the lean winters Lance spent in this house, his father wasn't the one who bore the signs.

"He'd call the sheriff because the old asshole doesn't know we're here, and some people would say that makes us trespassers," Nora tells Alice. Hearing her matter-of-factly call his father—fuck, *their father*—an asshole, to Alice—his niece—makes Lance smile. He feels somewhere between amused and incredulous. He ducks his head to hide it, but Nora notices.

At first, her eyes narrow. Then, slowly, she smiles back.

"We're not hurting anything," Alice says, her hands on her hips as she faces Lance. "So, you shouldn't call anybody."

"I'm not going to," he assures them both. This time, Nora nods, seeming to accept his answer. She sits on the edge of a sofa that Lance only recognizes because of the remnants of upholstery on its threadbare arms. Some kind of nesting animal gutted the cushions, apparently, but she's replaced them with folded blankets. Lance sits in the matching armchair and discovers it's more comfortable than he remembers, like exposure to the wilderness softened it somehow, cleansing it. Then, he shifts his weight and an errant spring digs into his ass, making him rethink the judgment.

"So, how long have you been here?" he asks Nora, but Alice is the one to answer.

"One school year," she tells him. Then she looks at Nora, and back at Lance with a shy smile. "I'm in second grade."

"That's really cool."

"I'm the best reader in my class," she adds.

Lance grins at her. "I bet. You seem like you're really smart."

She preens a little, playing with the ends of the flyaway hairs pulled out of her braid by the winter hat she shed at the door. "I am."

"It's not polite to brag," Nora reminds her daughter, but her eyes are soft and fond despite the correction.

Alice sighs. "Sorry." She looks at Lance again. "I'm actually not that good at some stuff," she admits. "I'm pretty bad in art. I get tired of going slow, and when I go fast, everything kind of turns into a mess."

"Oh, yeah. I know the feeling." And the funny thing is, he really does.

Nora is smiling at him again. When she smiles, it's like she's trying to keep it secret. There are dimples in her cheeks, and that's all; her mouth stays in a straight line. He realizes with a pang that some people wouldn't even know she's smiling, it's so subtle. He notices because he sometimes wears the same expression.

"Alice, go get some of your books to show Lance," says Nora, and when Alice runs for her room, their eyes meet again.

Lance swallows. "How long have you known about me?"

She shrugs. "I don't know. Always? My mama used to say that my daddy had a wife and another kid. But I always imagined you as a girl. Prettier than me, better. Someone he preferred." She wrinkles her nose and flashes a quick smile that stretches her lips and reveals a glint of straight white teeth, but it's gone as soon as it appeared. "Obviously, you aren't a girl, but I think you might be prettier than me."

Lance laughs and plucks self-consciously at his borrowed flannel shirt. "Not a chance." He sobers. "I don't think he preferred me, either. He really didn't like me at all. If that...helps."

Another shrug is her only answer.

"And he's dying," Lance adds.

"That helps a little bit more," she says flatly. Then, she frowns. "I knew he was sick." She hesitates, glancing in the direction Alice disappeared, and when there isn't a sign she's returning just yet, Nora goes on. "My ex threw us out, me and Alice. I had no one to ask for help. No one at all. So, I came here to ask *him*." She makes a face like there's a bad taste in her mouth. "But he wasn't here. No one was. The door was standing open, and there was a hole in the roof. I had to chase racoons out of the furniture." She looks at Lance, daring him to question her choice with her uptilted chin. "I thought he owed me this much. A shack with a hole in the roof."

Lance swallows and nods, unable to think of a word to say.

He's spared the effort by the return of Alice, who has the promised books—an armload of them.

"These are the best ones," she says, staggering under the combined weight of her collection, which she unloads onto the sofa next to her mother, and then she chooses just one to present to him first. "And this is my most favorite. Do you like rabbits?" She pulls the blanket back from the window so they have light enough to read by.

———

Lance knows the afternoon is wearing on because the sun that's been pouring through the window shifts, casting the room in sudden dimness and throwing the book that Alice has been reading to him into shadow. They blink at each other, and Alice makes a face.

"Mama, can we turn on the lamp?"

"We aren't wasting fuel while there's daylight. About time you went outside to play, anyway."

Alice is reluctant, obviously caught up in the excitement of Lance's presence, but after another nudge, she jumps to her feet, seized by the perpetual energy of childhood, and races out the door. Lance stands up from the chair, cautiously avoiding that invasive spring, and regards Nora uncertainly.

"Do you think we can keep in touch?" he asks.

He sees her dimples for a moment before she casts down her eyes. "Sure. I wouldn't mind that. I don't have a phone right now, though."

"That's okay. I'm...." He was going to say *"I'm staying nearby,"* but now he wonders if that's still true. He looks impulsively toward the ranch, even though at present there's a wall coated in peeling paper blocking his view. Still, he feels its draw as strongly now as he did the last time he stood in this house—itching, as always, to get across the creek.

"You're living at the Chase place," Nora says matter-of-factly. "Alice saw you come from there."

Lance's breath hitches. "I was staying there. But, now—I'm not sure."

"Well," she says with a shrug, and under the tough exterior, he sees a glimpse of a generosity of spirit that's totally humbling, "you're always welcome here. S'not much, but we stay warm enough."

"Thank you for offering that. Maybe I'll take you up on it." He smiles at her, choosing his words carefully. "But either way, I'd like to come back and see you two."

She nods. "Okay. I hope you do that."

They step outside, just as Alice shrieks, "Mama!"

She's streaking up from the creek, and Nora whips in her direction. Alice looks unhurt, still bundled tight in her snowsuit and running easily, but she's breathless when she reaches them. "There's another man down there!" she gasps. "A tall one with black hair."

Lance finds himself moving toward the creek. He saw the spot from which Alice emerged, and it's just the same tiny thinning in the trees where he used to make his own way, day in and day out in his treks over the creek. "I bet I know who it is," he tells Nora. "I'm sure I do," he adds with growing certainty, and then he breaks into a run for the tree line.

He reaches the trees and slows enough to navigate the branches, and the brambly new growth that tripped him up the last time he came this way, too, and then he reaches the decline toward the frozen stream. From there, he sees him: Robbie, standing on the center of the ice, one arm outstretched like he's just come close to losing his balance. He looks up at Lance, red-faced above his beard, with the tips of his ears dark red from cold. He isn't wearing a hat or a hood, and his eyes are cautious but hopeful when they meet Lance's.

Some tide carries Lance the rest of the way down, over the treacherous ice and under Robbie's outstretched arm. For a moment, he thinks they're both going to lose traction and fall in a heap, but then as Robbie's arms settle around his waist, and Lance's around Robbie's shoulders, they're pressed together in perfect balance.

"I just saw a kid back here," Robbie says. "I think you must be right about someone living there."

Lance breathes out a laugh against Robbie's neck, then smiles when the gust of his breath makes Robbie shudder and hold him tighter.

"I'll tell you about them," Lance promises, "but first there are some other things I have to say."

"Okay," Robbie says, his voice uncharacteristically quiet, soft and tentative. "I'm really glad to see you." He moves his head, pushing his bearded cheek against Lance's.

Lance closes his eyes. "It's all done. They dropped the charges."

"Oh," Robbie says, with clear surprise. His arms flex like he's prepared to pull back, maybe to look Lance in the eye, but Lance doesn't loosen his grip, and after a moment, Robbie relaxes back into their embrace again. "That's good," Robbie says, rubbing his back. "But what—are you okay, or—?"

"I'm okay," Lance says, and in this moment, it's true. "I'm good." He makes himself let go, but only retreats enough that he can tilt his head back and meet Robbie's eye. "Last night, when you said I was family, it made me think about—" He has to force the rest of the words out, and they run together under the pressure. "—all the times you said you loved me."

Robbie's hands bunch in the back of Johnny's jacket. Lance slides his hands from Robbie's shoulders and uses them to frame his face.

"Do you remember that last night, before I left?"

Robbie nods, pressing his lips together like he's having to make an effort not to speak.

"I didn't want you to love me. I wanted you to *want* me."

Robbie nods again, this time so shallowly that it's almost imperceptible.

"Well, I was wrong. I always thought that it had to be one or the other, and that if I could choose—I'd choose you wanting me, even though a part of me knew that you never would. But then, these past few days, I had what I always thought I wanted. You wanted me back. And it was amazing. But I don't know if it's enough, because—because I'm really fucking selfish, as it turns out, and—"

"I love you," Robbie interrupts him.

Lance falls silent, heart pounding with a desperate, painful hope.

Robbie's dark eyes are so intent, the color of the bare-branched trees where they show wet and walnut-dark between the patches of snow. "I love you, and I want you," Robbie says fervently. His grip on Lance's waist has turned bruising. "It scares me how much."

Lance manages another breath, somewhere between a gasp and a sob, and then anything else he might have said is precluded by Robbie kissing him. He's still holding Robbie's face, his fingers curling slightly so that his fingertips rest on his cheeks, his palms curved against his bearded jaw.

With a moan, Lance tries to push himself closer, lifting himself onto his toes without thinking, and that small shift in their weight, and Robbie's adjustment to compensate, results in a fantastic loss of that temporary, careful balance they'd found on the patch of ice under their feet.

They land in a heap on the creekbank, and Lance registers that the wind has been totally knocked out of him—judging by the gasp he heard from Robbie, he's not alone. Robbie regains his breath first, though, and he uses it to laugh.

Lance lifts himself onto his elbows and glares to his right, where Robbie lies flat on his back beside him, though their legs are still tangled together.

"At least the ice didn't break this time," Lance observes with a smile, and Robbie laughs some more.

CHAPTER TWENTY-SIX

Robbie

They walk hand in hand into the clearing that surrounds the old Taylor place. Robbie is struck by the sight of it.

The house was always shabby, but it's in rougher condition than ever now. He can see where broken windows have been papered over with cardboard and plastic, and a sheet of water-stained plywood looks to be screwed to the roof, probably to patch a hole.

Lance is beaming. "I don't know why, but I felt like I had to come out here," he murmurs. A young woman stands beside the child in the snowsuit who Robbie saw in the woods. Both of them are watching Robbie and Lance with cautious expressions. "And I *still* don't know why I felt it, but this is Nora, and her daughter Alice. And, Robbie, Nora's my *sister*."

Robbie might not have believed him so easily, but Nora is the spitting image of Lance. In fact, she's the spitting image of a younger Lance; manhood made him taller and stronger than he was as a child, but she's small and slight like he used to be. She's painfully slender, too, like he was back then.

Robbie is bit in the heart by the familiar impulse to feed her and give her something warm to wear.

Alice, on the other hand, looks snug in her snowsuit, and her plump cheeks are still flushed with color from the excitement of spying a stranger in the trees. She's been watching warily, but when she notices that he and Lance's hands are linked, she instantly relaxes and wriggles out from under her mother's arm.

"I'm Alice," she says. "Lance is my uncle."

———

An hour later, Robbie isn't sure how he feels about walking away.

"But it's so cold," he tells Lance, not for the first time. He's following Lance toward the blue car he last saw in the impound lot. He has mixed feelings about seeing it again now. He knows Lance has plenty to tell him, and he has a feeling some of it will be hard to hear.

"They've got a generator and a heater. They've been making it just fine, and there have been colder nights." Lance glances past Robbie at the house, where they've left Nora and Alice behind a closed door as night falls; the temperatures have already begun to drop. "I want to help them, too, but if I do too much too soon, I don't think Nora will like it."

Robbie opens his mouth to argue, but the quelling look on Lance's face stops him. In fact, Robbie *doesn't* know how someone in Nora's situation would feel about being offered help. And Lance, unfortunately, does. So, Robbie just nods and spares the house a final glance before he gets into the passenger side of Lance's sleek car.

The engine starts with a purr which is so subtle, it's almost silent, and Robbie is pretty sure the seats are grain leather.

Lance looks uneasy as he pulls off his gloves and then takes the wheel in his bare hands. "Niall is here."

Robbie stiffens. Lance doesn't look at him except out of the corner of his eye, putting the car in drive and easing it slowly through the gathered snow on the driveway.

After a few seconds, Robbie works through the shock enough to put the pieces together. The charges went away. Lance has the car back. Niall is here. So, Niall is the reason that Lance's case was dropped and the car was released. Robbie wrestles with his reaction. He remembers how dismissive Lance was of Niall and their relationship. But— Niall has been in Lance's life for a long time. Lance *lives* with Niall in Chicago. Their careers are intertwined. Robbie rubs his jaw and struggles to keep his voice even. "He dropped the charges, then?"

Lance nods, focused on the road as he pulls away from the end of the driveway. The layer of snow is just enough to lend the car traction; there's a crunch under the tires, but the vehicle doesn't slip an inch, instead navigating the white-drenched road smoothly.

"He thinks I'm visiting my dad. He thinks that after I do that, I'll go to his hotel." Lance looks at Robbie, then quickly away. "I let him think all of that."

"Good," Robbie says roughly. "If it got him to drop those bullshit charges, then I'm glad you told him whatever you had to." He hesitates. "At least, I assume that you just *told* him... that you didn't...well." He trails off, hating himself a little for saying anything at all.

Lance gives him a desperate look. "I didn't do anything," he promises. "I didn't—we didn't—" He reaches his right hand toward Robbie, swallowing. Robbie catches it in his, Lance's bare fingers held tight in his gloved ones.

"Okay," he says. "Okay. That's good."

Lance's eyelashes are fluttering, like he could cry.

"It's okay," Robbie says, low and soothing. "It's okay, sweetheart. Just drive."

When they've reached the snowy yard at the ranch and Lance has the car in park, Robbie leans over and kisses his cheek, then his shoulder, feeling him tremble. "It's okay," he says again. "You don't have to see him again if you don't want to."

Lance presses a knuckle into his left eye, then his right. "I do, though," he says on a breath. "He has most of my stuff back at our—*his* place. Everything except what I threw in a bag when I left." He turns his face toward Robbie's and their lips graze. It's not quite a kiss, but Lance makes a low, needy sound that Robbie feels in his gut, and lower.

"But right now, I—Robbie, right now, can we just—?"

"Yes," Robbie says, divining his meaning despite the jumbled words. He tilts his head and brings their lips ghosting together again. "Yes."

The cold is the only thing that keeps them from grappling against one another over the gear shift, or against the hood of the car. Instead, they lope up the steps to the hayloft and make it past the door before Lance grabs Robbie and pulls them together. Lance is rough and uncharacteristically grace-less, the solid, lean weight of him forcing Robbie back against the door, his hard thigh prying Robbie's legs apart; his long-fingered hands are everywhere, quickly divesting Robbie of his coat, then dropping nimbly to his fly. All the while, their mouths are pressed together, inhaling each other's exhales until Robbie is dizzy and burning and aching, feeling Lance everywhere.

"Could you...?" Lance says, and interrupts himself to kiss Robbie again, his teeth raking Robbie's lower lip. "Will you?" he murmurs against Robbie's neck, and then kisses him there, too, this time with his tongue.

Robbie arches his head back and gasps, bucking into

Lance's hand as it slides up and down between Robbie's jeans and his briefs, rubbing the cotton against his aching cock. All he's managed to do in response to Lance's assault is to dig both of his hands, hard, into the lean curves of Lance's ass. He adjusts so that the next time he squeezes, his fingertips are deeper in Lance's cleft, and they both gasp.

"Tell me what you want," Robbie begs. "Fuck," he moans when Lance's nimble fingers find their way past his boxers and grip him, skin to skin. "Lance, sweetheart. Please, tell me. I wanna give you what you want."

Lance tilts his head back, his lips swollen and parted, his eyes bright with the fever of their bodies bucking against one another, seeking each other in quick, desperate thrusts. "Would you fuck me?"

Robbie freezes, but he imagines Lance can feel his answer in the way his cock jumps in Lance's hand. Still, he hesitates, slowly kissing Lance, gentle against his bottom lip, then tracing a path to the corner of his mouth, and he kisses him there, too.

"Yeah. God, yes." He rests their foreheads together and his breath hitches. "But I don't know what to do."

Lance is the one to kiss him, this time. "I know," he says when they part. "I'll tell you what to do. If you—if you're sure you want—?"

"To be inside you?" Robbie breathes. "Fuck, yes. I do."

Lance shivers. "Then," he says, sounding just as breathless, "I'm really hoping you have a condom and lube around here somewhere."

Robbie chuckles. "Another thing we're going to be borrowing from Johnny," he admits with a wince. "Second drawer in the nightstand."

They break apart and Lance practically sprints to the nightstand, which makes Robbie laugh. He follows just as eagerly, though. Lance opens the second drawer, fishes out a condom, and holds it aloft triumphantly. He gives the small bottle in his other hand an experimental shake near his ear, and flashes a grin that fades to something hungrier as their eyes meet.

"I can get myself ready," he starts, but Robbie interrupts him by shaking his head, taking him by the waist and turning him so his back is to the bed.

"Lie down," Robbie commands softly, and Lance obeys.

The fever pitch of earlier slows to the careful steps of a new dance. Robbie sheds his boots and jeans, holding Lance's eyes as he does the same. He helps Lance with the second part, getting two handfuls of the calves of the khakis and pulling after Lance finishes with the button and fly. The sight of his cock, outlined by the cotton briefs, makes Robbie's mouth water on sight, like it's a conditioned response. He's almost sorry that his mouth isn't what Lance asked for. He's gotten a taste for sucking off Lance, and he's pretty sure he'd be content if they never did anything else.

Lance tugs his briefs down and rolls onto his stomach, revealing his perfect ass, and Robbie swallows convulsively, hastily withdrawing the errant thought. He definitely wants to fuck Lance. He's never wanted anything quite so much, though his hands are shaking with uncertainty.

Maybe sensing Robbie's unease, Lance looks over his shoulder and smiles reassuringly. "Put some lube on your fingers, and touch me," he instructs softly, and Robbie fumbles with the cap of the lube in his eagerness to obey. He gets a liberal amount of slick on the pads of his fingers, rubbing them together, testing the lube's viscosity. He's barely used lube, but he instantly appreciates the feel of it on his skin, the promise of how it will feel elsewhere. He crawls onto the bed behind Lance and trails the fingertips of his left hand over the curve of his body, wonderingly, then reaches in with the slicked fingers of his right and draws a line through the shadow between his cheeks, toward his hole.

"God," Lance breathes, falling forward onto his elbows, face buried in the sheets and ass raised obscenely. Robbie swallows, wondering if he could come just from seeing him like this, from feeling the wrinkled skin around Lance's hole beneath his fingertips. When Lance guided his hand before, everything felt different, and he wasn't able to see exactly what he was doing. Even when Lance straddled his face, he only got a glimpse before he closed his eyes and used his mouth. The change in perspective, and the addition of the lube, hypnotizes him. He can see Lance's balls suspended in the shadows of his thighs, and he's filled again with the urge to try to get them in his mouth.

Before he's consciously decided to do it, Robbie turns his head sideways, leans in, and pulls one of Lance's testicles past his lips, his right hand still gently fingering Lance's rim. Lance gasps and swears and pushes back, just enough that Robbie's fingertip breaches him and is suddenly squeezed between the tight, smooth muscles, made slippery with just a pinch of lube.

It's overwhelming, having Lance's smooth-skinned sack on his tongue, the weight of his testicle in his mouth, the smell of the clean sweat between his legs filling his nose, and Robbie's finger inside him, offering a tiny pantomime of what he intends to do with his cock. He could come from this eventually, if Lance would just touch him, just a little. But that's not what either of them wants, so instead he pushes his finger in deeper, to the next knuckle, and opening his mouth wider and using his tongue, he pulls both Lance's balls past his teeth, caressing them one at a time with his tongue, moaning at the sensation of having his mouth so full in a way that makes Lance shake and moan above him.

"Robbie, fuck me now, okay? Just, fuck. I'm ready. Do it."

Robbie pulls his head back, wiping a string of saliva off his mouth onto his shoulder. He's made a wet mess of Lance's perfect balls, and it's a satisfying sight.

"I don't—" he starts to say, but Lance growls an interruption.

"Put some lube on the condom, and fuck me."

Robbie's finger is still deep inside Lance's body. He crooks the finger experimentally, shuddering at the bracket of tightness around the base of his finger, and the wider passage beyond that is so smooth to the touch.

Lance bucks back on his hand. "Please, please, please," Lance is babbling. "I need you, right now."

Those prove to be the exact words Robbie needs to hear to roll on the condom and kneel behind Lance. His hole still looks impossibly tight, but after having his finger inside, and having seen plenty of porn, Robbie knows Lance can take him. Still, he hooks his teeth over his lower lip and strokes Lance's flanks, hesitating.

"Are you sure? Do you want me to put in another finger first?"

Lance shakes his head. "No. Please. Do it. I'm ready, I'm so ready."

So, Robbie lines himself up and then presses himself forward, one tiny increment at a time, almost dizzy with the effort of restraint. But after about five seconds of this, slowly breaching Lance with the head of his cock, Lance makes a frustrated noise and pushes himself back against Robbie, and Robbie's dick slides in a few inches until it's half-sheathed.

"Holy—*God*," Robbie gasps, gripping Lance's hips. Instinct overcomes his hesitation, and he eases himself forward the rest of the way, panting by the time he bottoms out. Lance's spit-wet balls are pressed warmly against his, and even through the condom, he can feel the smooth sleeve of Lance's ass like velvet.

"God," he murmurs again, bending his head so he can nuzzle the sweat-damp curls at Lance's nape, "you feel amazing."

"So do you," Lance whispers back, and then he rocks back against Robbie—just an inch of range in his motions, but the friction is bliss. "But I said to *fuck* me," he reminds Robbie. "So, do it, for fuck's sake."

Robbie laughs against the back of his neck. "So bossy." But then he straightens his back, and does as he's told.

He's never been inside this part of someone's body, but the act isn't unfamiliar in every way, and Robbie experiments with things past partners have liked—rolling his hips, shifting the angle, keeping his hand busy on Lance's chest, then between his legs. But there are differences, too. He doesn't think he's ever wanted to touch anyone quite so much. He doesn't think he's ever been so constantly inundated with his own pleasure. He isn't chasing an orgasm; it's always a hair's breadth away, and it's just Robbie's will that's holding it back.

When he finds a slow rhythm and a certain angle that make Lance wail, he doesn't stop or slow. Sweat breaks out on Robbie's shoulders and rolls down his back. The pressure in his balls builds to a point where it's so intense that, for a moment, Robbie thinks he won't be able to bring Lance over the edge before he comes himself.

"You feel so amazing," Robbie pants. "I can't last much longer."

Lance starts jerking himself, the movement making his muscles seem to glow as they move under a layer of glistening sweat. "You're—perfect. I'm close, too, Robbie," he gasps. "Robbie, please."

Robbie doesn't know what Lance is begging for, but he drags Lance up off the bed so they're both kneeling, Lance's back flush to Robbie's chest, Robbie still deep in Lance's body. Lance moans, and Robbie can't help thrusting again, shallower and harder than before. Lance twists his head toward Robbie's and gasps, then whimpers against Robbie's mouth when Robbie plays with his nipples, pinching and pulling.

"Gonna—fuck—" Lance starts jerking his cock again, so fast that his arm feels like it's vibrating. Robbie bites his shoulder as Lance convulses.

Robbie lets go, feeling like more than just his cum is spilling into Lance; his hips jerk against Lance's ass, stunned by the force of his release. For a half-moment, Robbie thinks he's lost the battle much too soon, but then, Lance cries out and splashes his stomach and Robbie's forearms as he comes, too. They rock against each other, gasping for breath while they both shudder through the long moments of aftershock.

When Robbie thinks he can't stay upright another moment without collapsing, he pulls out carefully, helping ease Lance's sweaty, perfect, limp body down onto the bed on his side. He leans in and kisses him; Lance's mouth moves under his, curving into a smile.

The condom is incredibly uncomfortable, so Robbie rolls over and disposes of it as quickly as he can, then slides back into place behind Lance, their bodies fitting together in a gentler reprisal of what they were doing minutes ago.

Robbie touches a bite mark on Lance's shoulder and frowns. "Sorry."

"Mmm. Don't be."

He strokes Lance's thigh. "Thank you."

Lance huffs a quiet laugh. "For what?"

Robbie pushes his face into Lance's curls. "Letting me."

"*Letting you*, what?" Lance sounds incredulous, and a little amused. "Fuck me?"

"No!" Robbie pushes himself up on his elbow and frowns down at Lance, who turns his head so their eyes can meet. Robbie swallows, all his vehemence leaving him. He touches

Lance's bottom lip. "For letting me take care of you." He trails his thumb down to the curve of Lance's chin and brushes the ridge of bone, following its elegant curve to his jaw. Lance's lakewater eyes are deep enough for Robbie to drown in, and he'll go happily. "And for taking care of me, too."

CHAPTER TWENTY-SEVEN
Lance

There are two places to get a room in Dell. One is the Midnight Motel, a half-circle of shabby but painstakingly well-kept one-room units; it was built in the fifties with a moon-and-stars theme and an excellent, if slightly chaotic, rose garden where there used to be a small swimming pool in the middle of the parking lot.

The other place to pass a night is the Holiday Inn, a place just as large, rectangular, and sanitized as most of its chain. It sits out by the highway, ringed in anemic-looking juvenile trees.

Danny used to say that where someone decided to get a motel room in Dell told you all you needed to know about them.

At least the establishment takes snow removal seriously. Through a combination of plowing and spreading what must have been a square ton of rock salt, they've kept their parking lot completely clear. Lance doesn't have to dodge a single patch of ice as he walks from the lot inside the building, past an early-twenties clerk who doesn't look up from her phone, and straight to the stairwell.

When he gets the phone from his pocket to confirm the room number from Niall's text, he sees that Niall has sent a few impatient messages since that one. Lance only skims them, grimacing, before he drops the phone back into the pocket of his pea coat. It's his own coat, rescued from the backseat of the Mercedes. Actually, everything he has on now is his own—an undeniable pleasure, though he'll probably always have oddly fond memories of wearing Johnny's clothes. Lance is a little ashamed of how important clothes are to him; he knows it's shallow, but he feels so much better when he's wearing his own, carefully chosen things.

Right now, that just means dark jeans, leather ankle boots, and a sky-blue cashmere sweater under his coat. He brushes his fingertips over the styled curls at his temple, absently; clothing wasn't the only thing that he was reunited with in his luggage. The citrus pomade was frozen solid, and thawed to a grainy kind of texture, but a conservative application has still given his curls just the right amount of separation and a subtle sheen.

Niall is on the third floor, in a room close to the stairs. So, Lance is at the door to his room less than a minute later, still unprepared for what he's about to do. But determination, and a reminder of Robbie's hands cradling him back against his chest while he was lost in Lance's body, steels Lance's resolve. He knocks.

Niall answers the door immediately, his hair flat on one side, his reading glasses on and slightly askew. His ears are a little crooked, which means glasses need constant fine-tuning —a fact that Lance used to find charming.

"Good God," Niall says shortly, "it took you long enough." He pauses as he looks Lance up and down, and then his scowl softens to a wry smile. "Oh, Angel, did you stop somewhere so that you could get cleaned up for me? I appreciate the gesture, but you could have done it here."

"That's not—" Lance's words don't quite get past his mouth. Startled, he swallows. It's been so long since he's had something to say and couldn't get it out.

Or has it? Yes, he's had an easier time with words since he was a child, a child who used to feel the truth roaring at him to be spoken, but was so afraid to speak it that he didn't say much at all. In the years since, he's learned to talk, sure; too well, he thinks, sometimes. He's had no problem charming people—guiding them to think of his ideas as their own. But that's not the same as what he wants now, which is to give Niall a piece of his mind straight-out, no games.

And he's not sure he can do it.

Niall's bemused smile has faded fast, and he's quickly turned impatient. "Won't you come in here?" he says tersely. "We don't know who might be prowling these halls. Honestly, this place makes my skin crawl."

The sound of Niall's voice alone triggers Lance's anger, which seems to help loosen his tongue, too. "I'm just here to give you your keys." He reaches into his pocket. "And the phone, too. I don't think you could have me arrested for keeping a *phone*—I just don't want it." He holds out the phone in its sleek case, and the keys, in one hand extended toward Niall.

Niall stares back at him, his mouth unbecomingly slack and his eyes wide behind his crooked glasses. It's almost time for him to have another Botox appointment, Lance thinks with cruel satisfaction. The skin beneath his eyes is starting to part and sag again. He's never looked less impressive to Lance than he does in this moment, all of his affectation stripped back by shock.

Then, Niall gets himself under control and gives Lance a pitying smile, ignoring the phone and keys held toward him.

"Now, now, Angel," he says, the words hardly more than a gust of breath. Lance's heart instantly kicks into overdrive, his pulse an audible pounding in his ears. "Think about what you're doing. Your life is with me."

"I *am* thinking," Lance says. His voice rises as he goes on. "For the first time in a *long* time, I'm thinking *clearly* about my life. And I know, without a *doubt*, that the best thing I could possibly do is to get away from you."

Niall's cool smile has slipped from his face. Lance realizes that the other man has never heard Lance raise his voice— hardly anyone has.

Seeing that Niall is not, apparently, going to take the phone and keys from him, Lance just tosses them on the floor at his feet.

Niall's eyes drop to the floor where the keys and cell phone landed. Then he slowly raises them again. "Very well." He straightens up from his graceful lean in the doorway. "A fussy, self-important whore I could tolerate. But ingratitude— that is not a flaw I can stomach."

Lance blinks; Niall's words skate close to the profanity he so abhors, which is almost as shocking as the words themselves.

Niall seems pleased to have struck Lance speechless. "You think you can just walk away?" When he's truly emotional, truly furious, it's easier to remember that wealthy, cultured Niall was once a roughneck growing up on the south side of Chicago. "I'll ruin you. Don't think you can just walk back into the business. And you can forget about the series. It's mine; my lawyers will make sure of that."

Lance's eyes narrow, his fingers curling into the end of the wooden railing in the stairwell, his foot half-raised for the first step. He knows he shouldn't take Niall's bait, but somehow he can't help himself. "You're bluffing."

Niall's smile is serene. Then, he bends down with the ease and grace that Lance used to admire in him, and plucks the keys off the carpet. He tosses them in the air and catches them jauntily before giving Lance a mirthless wink.

"I suppose you'll find out whether that's the case. Take care, Angel." The door to his hotel room closes with a snap. The phone remains discarded on the floor in the hallway where Lance left it.

Lance looks at the phone lying on the carpet for a few long moments, focused on breathing in and out. Niall didn't have to specify which series he meant. There's only one that Lance could claim any ownership of; it's the one he modeled for and shot himself, the one that he pitched to a gallery himself. He's been waiting to hear back, but the curator had all but promised their answer would be yes.

He's not sure what he's going to do yet, but there's no way he'll let Niall strip him of his rights to work Niall had nothing to do with.

He hunches his shoulders and rushes down the stairs, past the hypnotized young woman still fused to her phone and out into the parking lot.

Robbie gets out of the Chevy at the sight of Lance and meets him by the hood, his big, warm hands encircling Lance's wrists, his eyes pinched with worry.

"You okay?"

Lance nods mutely, trying to shake off the uncertainty he feels over Niall's parting shot and focus on the jubilation he felt when he was yelling at him. "I'm okay." He shivers. "Let's just go home."

He catches his slip a second too late, but when he freezes and stares up at Robbie, Robbie is grinning.

"Home. Yeah. Let's go there." He squeezes Lance's hands, his touch lingering, before another gust of wind nudges them apart. When they're in the cab of the truck, though, Lance doesn't buckle himself in on the passenger side. He wedges himself into the bucket seat, which is much trickier now than it was when he was younger and smaller, but he manages. And once he's there, the awkward position is worth it; he can feel Robbie's chuckle through his ribs where they're pressed together, side-to-side, and Robbie's arm is the perfect headrest after he snakes it over the back of the seat behind Lance's shoulders.

They don't speak until they get back to Riverside. Lance is lulled halfway into a doze by the sunshine coming through the windshield to warm his hair, and Robbie's arm and body warming him everywhere else. When Robbie puts the truck in park, neither one of them stir at first. Robbie had to pull his arm from around Lance's shoulders to downshift, and now he splays his palm over Lance's thigh. Lance looks up at him and finds that Robbie is staring down at his own hand between the parted lapels of Lance's coat, his thumb grazing the fabric of Lance's jeans gently, like he's testing the thread-count.

"If you need to get back to Chicago, I'll drive you. Or I'll loan you the truck, if you want to go alone," he says, taking Lance by surprise.

A funny feeling turns in Lance's stomach. "That's what you're thinking about?" He tries to keep his tone light, like he's making a joke. "How to get rid of me?"

Robbie's eyes snap to his. "Of course not."

Lance smiles weakly.

Robbie sighs. "I just don't want you to feel like you're stuck here. Or stuck with me."

The funny feeling grows and twists. "I want to be stuck with you." *I love you*, he doesn't say, because he doesn't know if he can. It's too terrifying—which is ridiculous, because they both already know about Lance's love, and have for a long time.

Robbie's mouth pulls into a small smile, but it doesn't last.

"I hope you'll stay as long as you want to. But you have work, friends, a life. I know that."

Lance bites his lip, unsure what to say. He does need to go back to Chicago at some point, but it's the last thing on his mind right now—especially when he'd rather not dwell on Niall's parting threat. "My life has *been* there. But lives change," Lance points out.

Robbie smiles at him again, but there's a definite sadness in the expression. "We shouldn't sit out here in the cold. Come on."

They're both quiet as they walk up the steps to the hayloft. Robbie only takes off his boots and gloves before he goes into the kitchen. Lance pauses halfway through stripping off his own shoes. "Are you going back out?"

Robbie glances at him, his smile warmer now. "Well, I have a calf to feed." A complicated look crosses his face. "I kind of...stole her."

Lance is startled into a laugh. "What?"

Robbie tells the story, and Lance listens intently, fascinated and delighted. When Robbie finishes, his guilty look makes Lance laugh out loud again.

Robbie frowns. "It's not funny," he murmurs, filling the mixing bowl with warm water and reaching for the whisk he's been using to break up the powdered milk in the water. "It's a crime."

"As the hardened criminal here, I disagree," Lance assures him. "It isn't like you lied."

Robbie gives him a flat look.

Lance grins and shrugs. "Okay, so maybe I'm arguing a technicality." He frowns thoughtfully. "I'd say, at worst, it was some petty fraud. We'll have to ask Danny."

"*Fraud* sounds even worse," Robbie groans. "And we're never telling Danny."

The *"we"* and the suggestion of a future where they're

both talking to Danny—and by implication, each other, too—lights Lance up from the inside. He re-laces the boot he just untied. "Well, I'll be your accomplice."

"No," Robbie says, still seeming half-serious in his worry, to Lance's amusement. "I'll take responsibility for my own felony, thanks." He finishes mixing the bottle and screws on the lid while Lance chuckles. He notices Lance is still standing, dressed and in his coat, at the door. "You're coming?" Lance nods. "Okay, but change first. I don't want to get you dirty."

Lance buttons his wool coat. "I'll just watch, I promise."

In the end, though, he can't resist trailing after Robbie into the straw-strewn stall and petting the calf's warm, white fur while she nurses the bottle. She's standing with sturdy balance, and her eyes are bright. When the bottle is empty, she bawls in protest and butts her head so hard against Robbie's legs that he has to take a backward step.

"What a little fighter," Lance says, grinning. "It almost makes me want to change her name."

"What?" Robbie frowns. "No. Her name is Baby."

Lance, who hadn't realized Robbie had latched onto something already, groans. "No. She won't be a baby forever. Her name is Bubbles." When Robbie just stares, Lance rolls his eyes. "Because of the tub."

"I don't remember any bubbles."

"Come on, it's an adorable name."

"So is Baby."

"No."

Robbie rubs the calf's head, tipping his head toward the stall door to beckon Lance out while she's still distracted. Then, he quickly slips out after him, sliding the door shut before the calf can follow. She gives a low, disappointed moo, then licks the milk off her upper lip with that remarkably long black tongue.

A grin spreads over Lance's face. "I know what we should call her."

Robbie looks at him askance. "I told you, her name's—"

"Felony," Lance supplies, and to his delight, Robbie bursts out laughing.

————

Lance can't find the right segue back to the topic of the future. Hoping it will help him think, and figuring that it's definitely his turn to feed them, he insists on making dinner. He enjoys Robbie waiting on him, but he doesn't want to seem entirely useless.

Robbie, seeming to expect a show, settles on one of the stools across the counter to watch. Lance opens a drawer at random, and blinks at the unexpected sight of a Christmas card.

"Is this from Johnny?" Lance muses, holding it up. Sending an overly formal card with gilt edges seems like the kind of prank that Johnny would find amusing. But when Lance sees Robbie's grimace, his smile falls.

Robbie shakes his head. "No. My uncle. Go ahead, you can read it."

Lance hesitates, but Robbie seems sincere, so he unfolds the card and skims the message. There's a printed script that reads *Season's Greetings!*, and below that, in a cursive so elegant that it looks like calligraphy: *Best wishes to the honorable custodian of my ancestral home.*

He looks up at Robbie, brows raised. "Wow. That's not very subtle."

Robbie laughs mirthlessly and rubs his beard, leaning his elbows against the counter. "No, it's not, is it?"

"He sends these every year?"

Robbie nods.

"Damn. What a stone-cold douchebag. But why keep it?"

He shrugs. "I don't know. I kept them all. I had a whole stack in the house, and when this one came, I had that same...urge. I don't know, it seemed like I needed the reminder, I guess?"

Lance imagines a shoe box or something, full of years' worth of these poisonous little notes, and for the first time, he's almost glad of the fire. He doesn't realize he's muttered the sentiment out loud until Robbie laughs again.

"I can't really disagree. You know, losing the house was awful. But losing all of the stuff—that was more complicated. Some of it felt like weight around my neck. I don't know how to explain it." He shifts on the stool, frowning. "Sorry, I'm being—" He waves his hand in substitution for an actual word.

Lance looks at the card again. "Well, this deserves to be burned." Without asking permission, he walks over to the wood stove, carefully opens the door, and shoves the card into the embers with the poker.

Robbie is watching him with his brows raised, but he looks more pleased than distressed. Lance approaches him and Robbie twists the stool around so they're facing each other, parting his knees so that Lance can step between. He settles his hands on Lance's hips.

"I'm sorry you lost all that stuff," Lance murmurs, leaning into him and butting his head against his shoulder. "Especially all your parents' stuff. Your dad's things."

"There's really just one thing I strongly associated with him, honestly, and it actually made it out of the fire."

Lance leans back to see Robbie's face. "Yeah? What?"

Robbie smiles, but it's not exactly a happy expression. "He had a silk handkerchief. An old-fashioned one like cowboys wore around their necks in the movies. My mom got it for him before she realized that's not really a thing in modern-day Nebraska."

Lance's heart has taken on a panicked rhythm.

Robbie, apparently oblivious, strokes Lance's hips and goes on, looking a little lost in thought, smiling fondly at the memory. "I used to keep it with me all the time. It was a little too—I don't know, pretty? At least for me to wear. But I kept it in my shirt pocket. Sometimes, I liked to reach in and touch it there, or get it out and play with it."

"I remember," Lance manages, and Robbie's eyes rise to his, as though pleasantly surprised.

"Yeah?"

Lance swallows and nods.

"I lost it a few years ago. Before the fire, that is. I was really upset at the time, but...well, at least it didn't burn, you know? It probably fell out of my pocket or something. Maybe it's stuck in a tree or got carried out to the river." He shrugs and smiles lopsidedly. "Anyway. That's the only thing that always made me think of my dad."

There's a lump in Lance's throat that feels like the moon. He slips out of Robbie's loose embrace and walks over to the sleeping area, his heart pounding in his ears.

"Lance? Are you—sweetheart, are you okay?"

Lance closes his eyes at the endearment, feeling woefully unworthy. He opens his suitcase. The scarf is folded on top, where he tucked it right before carrying his luggage into the hayloft. He turns and holds it out all in one movement before he can lose his nerve.

Robbie has been walking after him, and is close enough that Lance's hand, and the handkerchief, are only inches from his chest. His eyes slowly lower, and he blinks several times in surprise.

When he looks up, Lance flinches. But there's only surprise on Robbie's face, and no ire—at least, not so far.

"I took it," Lance blurts. "The day I left."

He falls silent, unable to say more, as Robbie lifts a shaking hand and takes the dangling corner of the handkerchief between his thumb and forefinger. Then, unable to stand another second of silence, Lance babbles some more.

"It was something I always thought of as being with you. Like, this—this part of you, that I could have. It was so wrong, I already knew that, even before I knew it was your dad's. And now that I know *that*, I—"

Unfathomably, Robbie is smiling. He tugs the handkerchief out of Lance's weak grasp and steps forward, so that Lance's arm folds between them, trapped, and he can only clutch at Robbie's neck with his other hand, knees unsteady.

But Robbie's there, big hands a firm cradle on Lance's hip and thigh. He kisses him.

"My little magpie," he says, so very fondly. Lance stares up at him, dumbfounded. Robbie puts the cloth around Lance's neck and knots it. "My dad used to say wearing this scarf made me look like a real Chase." His smile turns softer, and so does his voice. "I like the look of it on you."

Lance can't speak, but when Robbie looks into his eyes, wide and stinging with tears, he seems to see in them what Lance can't bring himself to say.

"Will you stay here with me, at least for a while?" His forefinger is hooked between the silk scarf and Lance's neck.

Suddenly, Lance finds that words come easily. Or, one word does.

"Yes."

———

Thank you for reading *Long Winter*. If you enjoyed the book, please consider leaving a review at the retailer where you found it.

If you want more of Robbie and Lance, you can find the rest of their story in *Signs of Spring*.

AUTHOR'S NOTE

This story includes details about the Bureau of Land Management, or BLM. Some of those details are accurate, and some of them are skewed for the purposes of this story. It's true that private ranches across the United States are in business with the federal government to provide long-term care for wild horses born on and gathered from public lands throughout the west. The horses remain the property of the government throughout their lives, and the ranchers who house and manage them are paid a daily fee for their care.

Most of the ranches working with the BLM are much larger than Riverside, the Chases' ranch in this book. In 2020, the public solicitations for new ranches to participate in the program that I could find expected applicants to request at least two hundred horses.

ABOUT THE AUTHOR

Rachel Ember is a lover of the outdoors, animals, families both biological and found, and, of course, love stories. She lives in the midwest United States with her family, which includes two kids and several horses, most of them in varying stages of retirement.

The best way to keep up with Rachel's writing, new releases, books she's reading, and cute pictures of her pets, is by joining her mailing list from her website, www. rachelember.com.

ALSO BY RACHEL EMBER

WILD ONES SERIES

CONTEMPORARY ROMANCE

Long Winter
Robbie & Lance

Signs of Spring
Robbie & Lance

IN STEP SERIES

CONTEMPORARY ROMANCE

Jaywalking
Jay & Emile, a novella

Sleepwalker
Blake & Oliver, a short novel

Cakewalk (forthcoming, 2021)
Bria & Miles, a short novel

Printed in Great Britain
by Amazon